The Other Game

A Dean Carter Novel

by

J. Sterling

The Other Game

Edited & Formatted by:
Pam Berehulke
www.bulletproofediting.com

Cover Design by:
Michelle Preast
www.MichellePreast.com
www.facebook.com/IndieBookCovers

Print Edition

ISBN-13: 978-1517051150
ISBN-10: 1517051150

Please visit the author's website
www.j-sterling.com
to find out where additional versions may be purchased.

Dedication

This book is for everyone who fell in love with the Carter Brothers and always wanted more of them. I'm so happy that I could give this to you. I hope you love it.

Frat Party

I GLANCED DOWN at the red plastic cup in my hand, still filled with just as much beer as I'd started with when my brother and I first arrived at the frat party. Only now it was lukewarm instead of ice cold. I wasn't sure why I continued to clutch the cup like it was some sort of safety net. Or maybe it was—as long as I held it, no one bugged me and tried to get me to drink anything else.

Lord knows I had enough to deal with just being the brother of Jack Carter. It was my responsibility to make sure we got home all right. Not that Jack tended to drink all that much during baseball season, but still.

"Hey, Dean." A leggy blonde wove her way through the crowd in the fraternity house's front yard to reach me. I had no idea who she was.

"Hey," I said back, not wanting to be rude, but knowing from experience what would come next.

"Where's your brother?"

And there it was, the one thing that ninety-nine percent of the female population at Fullton State cared about—my older brother, Jack.

Without saying a word, I pointed in the direction of the driveway where he stood with a few of his teammates, watching another blond girl dancing.

"Wanna introduce me to him?" She batted what had to be fake eyelashes at me, and I blew out a long breath.

"Not really. He's not hard to talk to, I promise. Just go say hi."

I gave her a little shove, which was probably rude, but hell. Sometimes it was annoying being the younger brother of a future major league baseball player. That was part of the reason why everyone wanted a piece of him, especially the girls. They knew he was going places, and they wanted to hitch a ride.

Girls were weird, and I'd never understand them.

I looked back at my brother, realizing he held a short girl by her arm for half a second before letting go. The little pixie stood there, apparently annoyed, scowling up at him as she tapped her foot on the concrete. Jack leaned toward her, saying Lord knows what.

That was when I realized who she was.

Melissa.

Please, God, if you care about me at all, don't let Jack be interested in her. Or vice versa.

I had a class with Melissa, and often found myself staring at her tanned legs instead of paying attention to the teacher. I'd caught her staring back at me too, and on the few occasions she sat next to me, her leg would occasionally bump mine, or her shoulder brushed against me, and I'd get a whiff of the fruity scent of her shampoo.

We flirted, that much I knew. And she seemed interested, but so far I hadn't worked up the nerve to do anything more than ask for her name. I'd thought of those big blue eyes and silky brown hair more often than I cared to admit.

Hell, maybe I was more like Jack than I realized, I thought, but then gave myself a mental slap. *No, no way.* I didn't want to sleep with Melissa and then never do it again. That kind of shit wasn't in my DNA the way it was in my brother's.

Melissa passed by me in a huff as she stormed into the frat house, and I smiled to myself before chasing after her. Being pissed off suited her. Her blue eyes practically gave off sparks when she was mad, making her look like a pissed-off Tinker Bell.

"Melissa!" I shouted over the music, but she didn't seem to hear, so I shouted her name once more as I reached for her arm.

She instinctively yanked out of my grasp and whipped around to face me, her eyes narrowed and blazing, ready to do battle. But once she realized it was me, everything softened. Her expression, her body language, everything relaxed. Then her pretty face broke out into a big smile.

"Dean, hi!"

When she launched herself into my arms and gave me a big hug, I hugged her back and breathed her in, trying not to look like a douchebag. She smelled like summer and sunshine. After a beat, I reluctantly released her.

"Was my brother bothering you?" I nodded my head in

the direction of the front door.

"Your brother's an asshole."

Thank you, God, I thought, assuming that this meant Melissa was not, and never would be, interested in him. He could have all the other girls in Southern California, but not this one.

"He's not so bad," I said, defending him out of habit.

Melissa groaned. "I don't care. Apparently his latest conquest is my best friend, Cassie. I don't want to deal with that fallout."

"The blonde dancing in the driveway?"

"That's the one."

"She looks tougher than most," I said with a smile, hoping to calm her fears a little.

"I hope you're right," Melissa said, but she sounded unsure. "I have to go to the bathroom. I'll see you in a bit." She gave me another quick hug before she disappeared into the crowded hallway.

I walked back outside and saw the leggy blonde who'd wanted an introduction still hadn't moved. The girl's eyes stayed trained on my brother, and I wondered what on earth could be so interesting.

That was when I noticed what appeared to be a verbal battle. The girl who'd been dancing in the driveway wasn't leaning into my brother as he spoke to her like most girls did. No, Melissa's best friend—Cassie, I think Melissa said her name was—appeared annoyed, disinterested, and disgusted.

Suddenly she spun away from him, shaking her head.

"I like you," Jack shouted after her as Cassie stomped away.

"So you're dumb too," she shouted back at him over her shoulder. "I'll add it to the list of your many redeeming qualities."

Surprised, I let out a belly laugh. This chick was too much. I'd never seen any girl act that way toward my brother, and I got way too much pleasure from it.

Jack saw me laughing and headed toward me, a perplexed look on his face. "You think that's funny?"

"Hell, yes, I think it's hilarious. What was that?"

"I don't even know," he said, shaking his head. "But I liked it. She was hot as hell, and her sassy little mouth just turned me on."

"But, what happened? Was she actually not interested in you?"

Shocked, I glanced up at the sky, looking for pigs flying. All the girls at Fullton were interested in Jack. Well, apparently all except for Cassie and her best friend, Melissa.

Thank God.

"She's interested," Jack said smugly. "She just doesn't know she's interested. Lucky for me, I'm very persistent."

I'd forgotten all about the other blonde standing near us until she cleared her throat.

"Um, Jack," she said tentatively, and then bit at her bottom lip.

"What's up, sweetheart?"

"I'm interested."

"Of course you are," he said with a smile before grabbing the girl's ass and pulling her mouth to his.

I walked away from the two of them, shaking my head.

Welcome to being Jack Carter, I thought. It's a rough life.

Campus Life

I PRACTICALLY FREAKING skipped into class on Monday, knowing that I'd get to see Melissa. After I ran into her on Friday night, she'd plagued my thoughts all weekend.

Jack had even mentioned Cassie a few times in passing over the weekend, which surprised me, especially after he'd hooked up with that other chick after pissing Cassie off. I figured he'd forgotten all about Melissa's roommate, but apparently he hadn't. I wondered if Cassie had consumed his thoughts the way Melissa had haunted mine.

Scanning the small classroom, I didn't see her, so I took a seat in the middle of the room and hoped she'd show up. It would be the worst kind of torture for me if she skipped class today.

Within minutes, a pink bag was tossed in the seat next to mine, and my little pixie sat down. I closed my eyes for a second, taking a discreet whiff, and smiled. Today she smelled like strawberries.

"Hey, Dean." She pulled a pen from her bag and bit at the cap.

I stared at her mouth before getting a hold of myself.

"Hey. Did you have a good time Friday?"

Melissa narrowed her eyes. "Friday, Friday, what was on Friday?"

My heart sank a little before she laughed.

"Just kidding. It was all right. Typical frat party, you know. Dumb drunk guys. Even dumber drunk girls. And your stupid brother to round it all out."

I laughed at her assessment, thinking how right she was. "Yeah, pretty much. It was good to see you, though," I said, hoping I didn't sound stupid.

"It was good to see you too. I still don't understand how you're related to Jack, though. Are you sure they didn't mix up babies in the hospital?"

She smiled, but it seemed a little forced. Something was different. Her leg didn't accidentally touch mine, and her body language seemed closed off. I wasn't sure why she was being this way, but I knew I didn't like it.

Before I could answer, the professor cleared his throat, signaling the beginning of class.

Melissa nudged me with her shoulder, and when I glanced at her, she offered me a cute smile. God, she was truly adorable. How could I be expected to pay attention to the teacher when this pint-sized goddess was sitting next to me, smelling like summer.

Somehow I managed to get through the class. Not only did I pay attention, but I took notes as well. When the class ended, Melissa hopped out of her seat and told me good-bye before I could stop her.

Disappointed, I gathered my things. As I stepped out of my row and into the aisle, a hand on my shoulder made me pause. I turned around to see an unfamiliar pair of brown eyes looking back at me.

"Can I help you?" I asked, staring at the girl as other students filed out around us.

"You . . . you're Jack Carter's brother, right?"

I had to force myself to respond. "The one and only." I faked a yawn.

"Oh my gosh. Okay. Well, um." Seeming nervous, she twisted her hands together as she asked, "Do you know if he's seeing anyone right now? I mean, is he single?"

Confused, I studied her through narrowed eyes. "He's always single." If this girl was as big of a groupie as she appeared to be, she should know this already.

The poor girl actually blushed. "Oh, right. Of course he is. Well, I just think he's really hot and so good at baseball. I mean, he's so, so good. And it must be so cool being related to him."

Is this chick for real?

"The coolest," I said sarcastically, hoping she'd catch on.

Instead, she let loose a thrill-filled mini scream. Horrified, I looked around before realizing thankfully that the class was empty.

Her eyes bright, she said quickly, "Well, can you give him this for me, please? Just tell him it's from Tarah. We met at the party last weekend." She thrust out her hand to hand me a folded piece of purple note paper.

I looked at her face, trying to place her as the chick Jack had made out with after Cassie left, but this girl's hair was light brown, not blond, and she wasn't nearly as tall or leggy. It wasn't her. I would have sworn I'd never seen this girl in my life.

Not wanting to be rude, I took the note. "Okay. I've gotta go, though."

"Oh yeah, of course. Thanks. Thanks a lot." Tarah flashed me a grateful smile as she squeezed her binder against her chest, and then brushed past me and ran up the stairs.

Shaking my head, I trudged up the same stairs, wondering if I should trash the note or actually give it to Jack. It wouldn't be the first time I'd had to act like his personal assistant.

Curious, I unfolded the paper, which smelled like bubblegum for some reason, and saw a phone number written in black Sharpie. Underneath the number was her name surrounded by a bunch of red hearts and hand-drawn swirly things. I felt like I was looking at a note written by a twelve-year-old.

I belted out a laugh. Oh yeah, I was definitely delivering this to Jack.

I walked into the student union and headed down the stairs to the pizza joint. Once inside, I scanned the room, searching for my brother's table. It usually wasn't very hard to find considering he sat surrounded by a bunch of girls acting like fools.

They pawed at him, each trying to get a hand or two on some part of his body like he was a rock star. I would say it was the most ridiculous thing I'd ever seen, but since this had been a regular occurrence since we were in high school, I'd be lying.

"Make room for Dean," Jack demanded as I neared, and the girl closest to him begrudgingly moved her things out of the seat so I could sit down.

After tossing my backpack onto the floor, I sat, my stomach grumbling.

"Here, bro, eat." Jack shoved some pizza toward me before tossing his arm around my neck. "You'll never get big like me if you don't eat," he teased, and I wrapped my arm around his neck in return.

"I don't wanna be big like you. I wanna be little forever," I said, laughing since Jack and I were almost the same size and build.

"Shit, you're already as big as I am."

I grabbed a slice of pizza and had just taken a bite when I noticed Melissa and Cassie watching our table from a distance. Half tempted to wave at the girls, I stopped myself, not wanting Jack to notice them if he hadn't already.

My eyes locked with Melissa's just as I was about to look away. I sent a small smile her way before I focused on filling my stomach with food.

"Oh, I almost forgot. I have a present for you," I said as I reached into my pocket and pulled out the purple paper.

Jack took it out of my hand with a puzzled look on his face. "What's this?"

"Just open it," I mumbled, my mouth filled with food. I chewed as he carefully unfolded it, and tried to stifle a laugh.

He glanced at it and scowled. "Who the hell is Tarah?"

"Some chick in my class," I said as the laugh I'd been trying to hold in burst free. "I figured maybe you knew her."

"I don't," he said with a shrug. "Is she fourteen?"

"She might be."

I swallowed the last bite of the slice before remembering that Melissa and Cassie were seated just a few tables away. I glanced back at their table, but they were both gone.

Jack crumpled up the note before tossing it across the table at Brett, one of his teammates.

"What's this shit?" Brett asked as he unfolded it. "Is this for me or you, Carter?"

"You can have it," Jack said with a sly smile.

"I just might. What's she look like?"

I clenched my jaw. It was one thing to make fun of Tarah with my brother, but it was another to involve the damn baseball team. I knew firsthand how cruel their pranks could be, and didn't want the poor girl to get harassed by these assholes.

"Don't call her, Brett. Give it to me," I said with a tight-lipped smile, and held out my hand.

Brett didn't argue, which surprised me. I figured I'd have to battle him for the damn thing. Instead he balled up the note and chucked it at my chest.

After pulling it from my lap where it had landed, I stuffed it back into my pocket, determined to throw it out after lunch.

"Are you heading home after this?" Jack asked as I chewed my pizza.

"Yeah, why?" Where else would I go?

"Will you ask Gran to make lasagna tonight?" he said with a stupid grin, then added, "Please?"

"No way. You know how long that takes her. I can't ask her at four in the afternoon to whip up some homemade lasagna for dinner tonight."

Thank God for Gran and Gramps. They showed up when our parents abandoned us when we were little, and have been there for us ever since.

Our parents bailing on us the way they did affected Jack and me in different ways. I was on my best behavior from that moment on, hoping that somehow if I was extra good, maybe she'd know and come back home.

But Jack went the opposite route, determined to get into trouble whenever possible. He picked a lot of fights and kept everyone, except for the three of us, at a distance. He refused to let anyone in—not wanting to be vulnerable, I guessed—and started treating girls like crap pretty early on. Truth be told, the girls allowed it and almost encouraged it, so I wasn't sure if it was all our mom's fault.

Baseball was the only thing that saved my brother from completely going off the deep end. He wasn't allowed to fight on the field, and once he started pitching, he was like a whole other person on that mound. It was the only place he felt like he had any control, and he was always something to watch.

Jack used to confide in me that he was terrified one of our parents would come back around one day, wanting money or to be a part of our lives if he got drafted. When I asked him what we would do if that ever happened, he always said, *"Nothing. Just like they did for us."*

"Come on. Don't I deserve lasagna?" Jack turned toward one of the girls still pawing at his bicep. "You think I deserve lasagna, don't you?"

"I think you deserve whatever you want," the girl said, and then deliberately ran the tip of her tongue over her lips.

I wanted to ask what the hell was wrong with all these chicks, but stopped myself. There was no point. When it came to my brother, they simply didn't care what it took to get him, even if they knew it wouldn't last longer than one night.

When Jack cocked an eyebrow at me, I pointed at his cell phone on the table. "Then you ask Gran."

"She'll tell me no. But she won't say no to you, Dean. You're her favorite."

I choked out a laugh and raised my eyebrows, pretending to agree with him. "That's because I'm nicer than you are."

It wasn't true, though. Gran didn't have a favorite.

Jack frowned, considering. "Will you ask her to make it tomorrow then? For after my game?"

I huffed out a dramatic exhale. "Fine. That I can do. But if she says no, you're out of luck."

"Love you, little brother."

"Yeah, yeah. I love you too." I smiled as I snagged another slice.

THE NEXT AFTERNOON I entered the student union to find Jack with his harem of girls right at the entrance. He flexed his muscles for a couple of them, who screamed when they grabbed his bicep. "Hold on," he said as he lifted them into the air before putting them down again.

There were days I couldn't believe I was related to him. Maybe Melissa was right.

"Show us your pitching motion again, Jack!" one of the girls said with a squeal, and he showed off his moves in slow motion, much to the girls' pleasure.

I looked up and noticed Cassie and Melissa watching the spectacle with disgusted looks on their faces. Without a second thought, I walked over toward their table and leaned down close to Melissa.

"Hi, Melissa."

"Oh . . . hi, Dean."

"Would you mind if I sat with you?" I smiled at Melissa's soft and sweet response, and kept my eyes locked onto her beautiful baby blues.

"No. We're much better company than your brother's table, anyway," she teased as she poked me in the ribs.

Glancing in Jack's direction, I shook my head and placed my food on the table before I sat down. "It just gets old sometimes, you know?"

I stretched my hand across the table and reached for Cassie's since we hadn't been introduced yet. "Hi, I'm Dean."

"I'm Cassie. I'm Melissa's roommate." She took my hand and squeezed with a small smile. "It's nice to—"

"Dean! What are you doing over here?"

Jack's voice echoed throughout the student union, and I suddenly was sorry I'd come over here. Both of these girls seemed to hate Jack, and my presence only drew him over. When I mouthed *sorry* to Melissa, she just shrugged as if she'd been expecting it.

"Oh, Kitten. I see you've met my little brother." Jack winked at Cassie before placing his hand on my shoulder and squeezing.

"Thank God he seems nothing like you," she said. "I might actually be able to tolerate him."

Cassie tilted her head and smiled tightly before taking a bite of her sandwich, and I fought off the urge to laugh. I noticed Melissa and Jack sharing an amused glance, and I didn't like the idea of them having some sort of inside joke.

"You need me to work some of that aggression out of you?" Jack offered with his typical smile that usually worked on all the ladies. Must be the stupid dimples.

"I'd rather eat dirt," Cassie mumbled, her mouth filled with food.

This time I did laugh. The girl was funny as hell.

Jack chuckled. "I almost want to see that."

"You would. Go torture someone else," she said before looking away.

Not a bit fazed, he grinned and moved to sit in the empty seat next to her. "But I like torturing you."

"Uh, no!" she shouted before throwing her bag right where he was about to plop down.

Jack stopped short and stood back up. "Why so angry, Kitten?"

"Why so annoying, jackass?" she said, mimicking his tone, and I shot Melissa an amused smile.

Jack bent over to bring his face close to hers. "You'll come around; you'll see. You can't resist me forever."

Cassie inhaled before she choked a little, and swallowed hard as Jack walked away, smiling.

"Sorry about my brother." I forced a smile as I defended Jack. I liked Cassie, and could tell he liked her too. "He isn't really a jerk."

"He just plays one on TV?" Cassie said before coughing into a napkin.

"Something like that. Don't take him too seriously. He's just having fun with you."

She half smiled. "*I'm* not having fun."

"But you are. And he knows it," I added, knowing damn well that a girl like Cassie enjoyed the verbal jousting match she seemed to have with Jack every time they spoke.

Jack walked back over to our table and shoved a napkin into Cassie's hand without saying a word. I watched him walk back to his table, wondering what the hell he'd just given her when she crumpled it up and tossed it into her bag.

"What was that?" Melissa asked.

Cassie swallowed hard. "His phone number, I think. I didn't really look at it."

"H-he gave you his number?"

Shock rolled through me. My brother didn't give his

phone number to any girl. *Ever.*

"I think. Maybe I'm wrong. I'll look at it later." Cassie's cheeks turned pink, and I frowned.

Melissa turned to me, her brows drawn together. "What's with the face?"

"He doesn't give out his phone number. There's no point with him." I moved my gaze from Cassie to Jack's table as I tried to read his mind.

"He has a cell phone, right?" Melissa asked.

"Yeah?" I squinted at her, not seeing her point.

She rolled her eyes. "I'm just saying, caller ID."

I shook my head. "His number is private. It doesn't show up."

"Really? Who does that?"

"Someone who had to change his phone number fifteen times in high school because it never stopped ringing." When both girls looked at me with amazement, I added, "Or pinging with text messages."

I thought back to those high school years when girls posted his phone number on all the social media sites, or included him in group text messages so everyone else in the group could get his number. Whenever Jack's number got out, he not only got calls from the girls at our own school, his phone blew up from girls all over.

Jack had been the subject of more than one national article on baseball and its future rising stars. He wasn't only well known in our hometown; he was well known in the entire baseball community. And apparently the cleat chasers, aka baseball groupies, started early.

"*Fifteen times*?" Cassie said loudly, and everyone around our table turned to stare at us.

I shrugged. "It might have been more, but it was insane. Girls would post his number online, and his voice mail would fill up within a day. And then they'd all start calling my phone, looking for him when he didn't answer."

What I didn't tell them was that I had to eventually change my number as well for the same reason. Not that those girls wanted to talk to me, but when you were a freshman in high school, you tended to believe the things that girls said. I learned my lesson about being used pretty early when it came to girls lying to get what they wanted.

"Holy shit, that's bananas!"

Melissa broke out into laughter, but I didn't join in. This was the story of my life, and it really wasn't funny.

"That's why it's weird that he'd give you his number." I frowned at Cassie, wondering just what game my brother was playing. "He doesn't give anyone his number."

"Well, like I said, I could be wrong," she said quickly.

Melissa gestured toward her bag. "Then get it out and read it now."

"No. Not in the freaking student union while he's right over there. Later."

Cassie grabbed her things and pushed back from the table to walk toward the trash cans. Jack jogged over to her and they exchanged words, their body language resembling that night at the frat party.

"Come to my game tonight!" Jack shouted as she stomped away and opened the glass doors.

"I don't think so," she snapped back.

"Don't you want to see me pitch?" he asked, his voice cocky.

She paused, holding the door open with one arm. "I saw you pitching earlier. In slow motion, remember? I think I got the gist."

As Cassie left, I turned back to Melissa, who was frowning.

"Well, this oughta be fun," I said with a laugh, but she shook her head.

"Fun for you, maybe, but there's no way this is going to end well," she said sadly. "He's going to wear her down, and she knows it."

"I honestly think she likes him," I offered with a shrug before taking another bite of pizza.

Melissa watched as Jack stared after Cassie.

"I think so too," she said. "And that's what worries me."

Baseball Is Life

"GRAN, ARE YOU almost ready?" I yelled from the living room where I waited with Gramps.

"Don't you know better than to try to rush a woman, son?" Gramps looked at me over his glasses.

I glanced at my watch as I paced the small living room. "I don't want to be late for the game. And you don't either."

"No. That's why I let you yell for her, so I don't get in trouble." He shot me a devilish grin, and I rolled my eyes.

"I'm coming, I'm coming," Gran shouted from their bedroom.

The smell of lasagna filled the entire house, and my mouth watered at the thought of digging into it later. Jack knew Gran would make him whatever he wanted, but he always made me ask anyway.

"Dinner smells amazing, Gran," I told her when we finally headed outside.

She snorted. "It better. I spent all morning making it."

"No one does it better than you do," Gramps said with a smile as we piled into their car, an aging Honda that flipped over the odometer long ago.

Gran buckled up in the front seat and narrowed her eyes at us. "You two stop buttering me up. What do you want?"

"I don't want to be late," I said from the backseat.

"Then you'd better get going." She smacked Gramps's shoulder as he stepped on the gas and pulled away from the house.

Thankfully we didn't live too far from campus, so the drive there was quick. I hated missing a single pitch when Jack played. Watching him was one of the coolest things ever. He had a presence on the mound that you couldn't teach, and it filled me with pride every single game.

From the moment he stepped onto the field, Jack was all business. Screaming girls shouted his name from the stands, many of them wearing jerseys with his number on them, but none of it mattered. All he saw was the catcher's glove sixty feet away from him, and all he focused on was hitting the pitch that was called.

We'd spent too many nights to count talking about baseball and his love for it. It actually made me a little envious sometimes, and I wished I loved something as much as he did. I often reminded Jack how lucky he was to be great at the one thing he wanted to do for a living.

Many amateur athletes loved the sport they played and wished for a future in it—a career—but it would never happen for them. That was just how life worked. It wasn't enough to want something; it had to want you back.

And baseball wanted Jack. He not only excelled at the sport, he exemplified it.

Gran, Gramps, and I made our way to our regular seats above the dugout. I glanced to my right once I was comfortable and noticed Cassie and Melissa arguing before taking their seats.

The sight made me smile. Cassie *had* come to see him pitch after all. I made a mental note to let my brother know she had shown up. Jack never paid attention to anything or anyone in the stands during a game, so he wouldn't have a clue if she was here or not.

I smiled to myself, happy that she was here to watch him. He liked her; I knew that much already just by the way he acted around her. Cassie might be a challenge for him, which was always attractive, but his interest in her seemed to be something more than that.

Jack wasn't used to being told no by a girl, but it also wasn't in his nature to waste time on one. There had to be a reason he couldn't leave her alone whenever he saw her, why he chased her.

Gran leaned forward, scanning the stands. "There's a lot of people here to watch him tonight," she said, probably not even aware of her hands twining nervously in her lap.

The scouts were out in full force tonight. It was always a spectacle when Jack pitched, but each game drew more and more of them.

"I was just thinking the same thing," I told her. "His crowd seems to get bigger every time."

"I always get so nervous when he pitches," she said with a sigh before resting her head against Gramps's shoulder. He put his arm around her and kissed the top of her head.

I waved a hand as if the pressure were no big deal. "Don't be. Jack's not."

But I understood her anxiety. I felt it too each time he pitched. You couldn't help it when you cared about the person and knew their hopes, dreams, and fears. I wanted the best for my brother, and each time he took the mound, I wanted the same thing for him that he did—to get drafted this June. And to do that, he had to impress the scouts in the stands each and every time he pitched.

"Ladies and gentlemen, welcome to Fullton Field!" The announcer's voice filled the air as the screaming fans slowly lowered their volume. "Here to sing the national anthem is our very own Fullton State student, Laura Malloy!"

Cheers filled the stadium as Laura smiled nervously before closing her eyes and singing the opening words beautifully.

I glanced over at Melissa, but was distracted by the camera in front of Cassie's face instead. It looked complex and professional, and she actually seemed to know what she was doing. She leaned forward, adjusted the lens, and clicked the shutter multiple times before placing the camera back on her lap.

"We have a sold-out crowd tonight, folks, and we all know why! Taking the mound against our rivals from Florida is the one and only Jack Carter!"

The announcer spoke Jack's name like he did every Friday night when Jack pitched—reverently, as if Jack was all that mattered. Thankfully, Jack knew it took a team to win ball games, and he never let it go to his head, or acted like it was all about him. Off the field, he was a different beast altogether, a cocky campus stud, but on the field, he was the consummate professional.

I leaned over Gramps and poked my grandmother in the arm. "Hey, Gran, want to see something?"

"What?"

"See that blond girl over there with the giant camera?"

Gran squinted as she tried to find Cassie. "Oh yes, I see her."

"Well, your grandson harasses the living shit out of her every day at school," I said, finding pleasure in ratting out my brother.

"Dean! Language!" She scowled at me, and I bit back a smile. "And which grandson might that be?" She waggled her eyebrows at me as Gramps leaned over to check out Cassie too.

"The baseball-playing one," I said, then added, "I like her friend."

"Hmm," was all Gran said about my revelation before turning away to face the field.

Gramps elbowed me. "I'd date 'em both," he whispered before casting a quick glance at Gran to make sure she hadn't heard him.

"Now taking the field, *your* Fullton State Outlaws!" The announcer paused for a few seconds before continuing. "And now taking the mound, Jack Car-terrr!" He dragged out our last name, just like one of those wrestling announcers on TV.

The stadium erupted with enthusiastic noise. Every Friday night home game started out the same way with ear-piercing shouts, cheers, and screaming girls as Jack walked toward the strip of white rubber on the tall dirt mound. He kicked at the dirt in front of the pitching mound, adjusting it to his liking before he stood tall on top of it. After he warmed up with a handful of practice pitches to the catcher, the game officially started.

The first pitch flew by in a rush, and I sensed that he was *on* tonight. The sound of the ball hitting the catcher's mitt was so loud, it echoed against the backstop. The batter stepped out from the batter's box and looked nervously at his coach before stepping back in. Two more pitches screamed by, and that was out number one of the night.

"Strike three! You're out!" the umpire shouted, and the crowd cheered loudly.

Jack was in the zone.

The rest of the game played out much like the first inning. When it was all said and done, Jack had pitched the entire game, giving up only three hits and one run.

Afterward, Coach pulled Jack aside and escorted him over to the press area where he was besieged by reporters, scouts, and fans. This was the usual post-game wrap-up, and it could take up to an hour or longer.

Gran, Gramps, and I took our time leaving our seats, shuffling behind the rest of the crowd as they filed out. I looked over to where Melissa had been sitting, but her seat was empty.

My stomach growled, reminding me of Gran's lasagna waiting for us.

I tapped her on the shoulder and said, "Gran, we can start

eating before Jack gets home, right?"

She looked back at me like she wanted to smack me upside the head, and I was thankful when she didn't. After glancing at the delicate gold watch on her wrist, she said, "Only because it's already ten. And I'm starving."

WHEN JACK WALKED through the door an hour later, we all shouted our greetings at him from the kitchen table.

"Thank God for lasagna and you, Gran," he said as he came into the kitchen and planted a quick kiss on her cheek.

"Great game tonight, bro." I put my fist in the air, and he tapped it with his before grabbing a plate.

"Thanks. I felt really good." He shot me a quick smile.

"You looked better than good."

"You threw so well tonight, Jack. I'm really proud of you," Gran said with a smile before giving him a hug. "Now, eat."

"I'm starving." Jack dropped into his seat at the table and piled his plate with more lasagna than a normal person should be able to consume in one sitting.

Since the rest of us had already finished eating, Gran placed her hands on the table and slowly lifted from her chair. "I'm going to bed. You boys clean up, will you?" she asked as she headed toward their bedroom.

"Of course. Thanks again, Gran," Jack called out, and I knew damn well he'd make me clean up while he watched. Supervised, as he called it.

"I'd better go with her," Gramps said with a wicked grin, and then clamped a hand on Jack's shoulder before shuffling out behind her, and I tried not to think about them being an actual married couple who did married-couple things.

Shaking my head to rid myself of any gross thoughts about my grandparents, I swallowed another bite and waved a finger in the air toward Jack. "You know who was there tonight?" I asked, hoping to surprise him.

"I saw," he said with a smirk.

"You saw?" That shocked me. Jack never saw anyone. He never looked in the stands, never paid attention to anything or anyone when he was pitching.

"I saw," he repeated matter-of-factly.

"When the hell did you see? You never see," I whisper-shouted, not wanting to disturb Gran and Gramps, but still not believing what I was hearing.

"At the end of the game. I looked right at her."

"Shut the hell up."

"I know." He shrugged. "I never do that shit. But she makes me crazy."

I couldn't stop the smile that crept over my face. "I'm well aware. You turn into a complete idiot around her. But it's fun to watch."

Jack forked a pile of lasagna and threatened to toss it at me, but I shook my head in warning. "You wouldn't do that after all Gran's hard work, would you?"

He shoved the food into his mouth instead. "She wants me."

"Who, Gran? Gross, man."

"Not Gran, asshole. Melissa's best friend. She wants me."

"Melissa's best friend? Don't you know her name?"

"No. She's never told me. I keep calling her Kitten and it pisses her off, which I think is funny. I like getting a rise out of her."

He munched on a crunchy piece of garlic bread, sending crumbs all over the table that I knew I'd have to clean up later.

Frowning at him, I said, "I noticed. I think she secretly likes it. And her name's Cassie."

"No!" He threw the rest of his bread at me. "Why'd you tell me that? Now I'm going to have to pretend like I don't know her name so I can keep calling her Kitten and pissing her off. Damn it, Dean."

Realizing he'd lost his bread, he groaned. "Give me my bread back."

I chucked it at him. Jack caught it and shoved it in his mouth.

"Anyway, *Kitten* came to my game tonight. And she brought her camera. I saw her taking pictures of me."

My jaw dropped open slightly. "You really were paying attention to her tonight. I'm shocked."

"You and me both," he said with a shrug.

"So, what are you going to do about it?"

"Get her to go out with me, of course," he said as if it was the most obvious answer in the world.

"And what if she says no? She's pretty good at blowing you off."

"I won't let her."

"You won't let her say no? How the hell are you going to manage that?"

Jack pointed his empty fork at me. "Don't you worry, little brother. I've got this."

I had no idea what he meant, but I couldn't wait to watch and learn.

He Did It

I STARTED TO feel like I spent more time in the pizza restaurant at the student union than I did in my classes. But sitting at a table with Melissa made it all worth it.

The girl was beyond adorable, so petite and feisty with those stunning blue eyes that drove me wild. She was funny and sassy, and I liked being around her. Melissa made things fun. The fact that she never asked me about Jack, which I secretly loved more than I should, was an added bonus.

You know how when you meet a person who sparks something inside you? That was how I felt around Melissa. She made me feel more alive, and not for any other reason other than simply being herself.

"Did you have fun at the game last night?" I asked.

"How'd you know I was at the game?" Amusement danced in her eyes, replacing her initial surprise.

"I saw you. Nice seats," I teased, remembering how close they were to the dugout.

She laughed. "I did that on purpose to torture Cassie. I wanted to embarrass her."

"Did you?"

"Did I what?"

"Did you embarrass her?"

She clasped her hands together in front of her face and hid her adorable smile. "Oh my gosh, yes. She was mortified. It was awesome."

"Anyone ever told you that you're a crappy best friend?"

"Hey!" She slapped her hand on the table. "You take that back. I'm a great best friend. I wanted her to see that Jackass, the baseball player, was awesome. Nothing like Jackass, the stupid guy on campus."

I laughed again at the way she talked about my brother. Her clear-eyed impression of Jack was refreshing. "What did she think?"

"She was impressed. Although she'd never admit it."

Melissa glanced up, and I followed her line of sight to see Cassie heading our way. She tossed her bag on top of the table before sitting down.

"Hey, Dean." She smiled at me, and when I smiled back, she glanced over my shoulder and her smile died.

"Thought you weren't coming to my game?"

Jack surprised us all by sliding into the seat next to Cassie. I had to chuckle a little inside as she pretended not to enjoy that attention from him.

"My roommate threatened to set me on fire if I didn't." She tried to sound nonchalant as she scooted her chair away from Jack's.

"Well, at least now I know how to get you to go out with me."

"I'm not going out with you." Cassie frowned before shooting both Melissa and me a desperate look. *Save me*, it said.

"At least give me your number then," Jack said, as confident as ever.

"No thanks."

"Why not?"

"'Cause I don't want to."

"Aw, come on, Kitten," Jack said, and I almost lost it, thinking back to our conversation from last night.

"Stop calling me that!" She stood up from the table before abruptly grabbing her things. "I'll see you later," she announced, her gaze focused solely on Melissa. Then she bolted from the student union with my brother hot on her heels.

"Damn, I almost want to follow them," I admitted.

"Me too. But I'll make Cassie tell me everything later. I'm sure Jack will tell you too."

"Yeah, but it's not as fun as seeing it live and in person." I grinned, and Melissa nodded in agreement before shooting up from her chair.

"Where are you going?"

She grabbed my sleeve and pulled me up by it. "Come on. I have to see this."

She didn't let go of her grip on my arm until we were outside, but we saw no sign of either Cassie or Jack. It wasn't until I scanned the campus and noticed a small gathering in the distance.

I pointed. "That has to be them over there. See that little

crowd?"

Melissa looked up at me, hands on her hips. "Are you joking? You think I can see anything from down here?"

I squatted to her level and realized that she couldn't see shit. "Guess not. Want me to put you on my shoulders? Then you'll be the tallest person here." I was half joking, but if she wanted me to, I'd gladly hoist her up. She couldn't weigh more than a hundred pounds soaking wet.

"No thanks. I like missing everything." She laughed as she walked in the direction I'd pointed. "Does it ever annoy you the amount of attention he gets?"

"Only every day."

"Because he's a jerk?" she asked, her short but shapely legs working double-time to keep up with my regular pace as we headed in the direction of the crowd.

"No. He's not a jerk. It annoys me because he can do anything he wants and everyone eats it up. Girls, I mean. I just don't understand how instead of hating him, they all worship him. It's not like he's boyfriend material or anything."

Melissa nodded. "Exactly! That's what I don't get either, but I've stopped trying to figure it out because everything about Jack Fucking Carter gives me a headache. Except this stuff with Cassie. Because I've never seen him act like this before."

"Me either," I admitted as we caught up to the small group of people.

"Really?" She shot me a look.

"Swear."

"I enjoy my dates to be disease-free," Cassie shouted, drawing our attention.

"As do I," my brother shot back, giving a head nod to someone who walked by.

Cassie belted out a laugh. "Right. I've heard you're not really particular about who you date."

He took a step closer and said, "Well, you heard wrong then."

"Oh, that's right. Actually I heard you don't *date* at all. You just sleep with any girl who bats her fake eyelashes in your direction."

"Ooh," Melissa whispered at me, and squeezed my arm.

"I really need to meet your sources," my brother said with a grin.

Cassie mumbled something under her breath before turning her back to Jack and storming away. The second I thought it might be over, he took off after her, clearly intent on winning this battle.

I glanced at Melissa once they disappeared inside the building.

She grabbed my hand, pulling me along with her. "We've come this far," she said as she opened the doors and stepped inside.

I had no clue where Jack and Cassie had gone until I heard my brother's voice again coming from a nearby classroom.

"Don't make me beg, Kitten. Don't make me beg in front of all these people. It's embarrassing."

Melissa and I ran down the hallway and stood in the classroom's open doorway like we were watching a live play.

"I'll go out with you, Jack," some other girl shouted from her seat, and Melissa rolled her eyes at me.

"Typical," she whispered.

"Perfect! I'm sure you two will have a great time together." Cassie dropped into her seat and tried to bury her head.

Jack used the moment to his advantage and crouched next to her, whispering something none of us could hear.

"Ooh, he's good," Melissa cooed, and I wondered what exactly he was saying to Cassie.

"What are you doing? Get out of here," Cassie tried to whisper back, but the pitch of her voice carried.

Jack said something else to Cassie, and when we couldn't make it out, Melissa stomped a foot in irritation. "I want to hear, dang it."

"Promise you I'll think about going out with the school's biggest player?" Cassie said as Jack knelt next to her, his face so close to hers I thought she might hit him. "Oh, sure, I'll think about it."

"Promise me," he demanded, his insistence unrelenting.

Blinking rapidly, Cassie glanced around the room before looking at Jack. "Fine. I promise I'll think about it. Will you go away now?"

A wide grin appeared on Jack's face as he stood up without another word and walked out of the classroom.

"Told you," he said as he passed me, not slowing his pace.

"She said she'd think about it," I yelled as I caught up to him.

"She'll go, just watch. Won't she, Meli?" Jack said over his shoulder.

"Probably," Melissa said from behind us, hurrying to catch up.

We headed outside and followed Jack toward a cement bench, where he pulled his baseball hat even lower over his eyes. Then he sat down and looked up at us, his eyes all but hidden.

"What are you doing?" I asked, expecting him to get up and continue walking back to the student union with us.

"Waiting."

"For what?"

"Her class to end. I'm going to ask her out in front of everyone. She won't be able to say no then," Jack said with a big grin.

"Make sure you show those." Melissa pointed at the pair of dimples on his face, and his grin only widened.

"I knew you secretly liked me. But I know you like him more." Jack nodded toward me, and Melissa scowled.

"Don't listen to him." I threw my arm around her shoulder and steered her back toward the student union. "See you at home, brother."

"'Bye, you two lovebirds."

"You're so little." I looked down at Melissa and smiled, wishing for once that I'd been born with at least one dimple for her to admire.

She scowled again. "I'm not that little."

But she was. I was six feet tall, and she might hit five feet if she stood on tiptoe. I towered over her, and I loved the manly feeling it gave it me.

"Do you have any more classes today?" I asked.

"Nope. You?"

"Just one."

"Sucks."

"Only because it's not the class I have with you," I said with a smile, and she swatted my shoulder.

"Dean Carter, did you just feed me a line?"

I chuckled and stopped walking. "No. Did it sound like a line?"

"Yes." Melissa smiled, but kept walking.

I watched as her perfect little butt moved with each step she took, her entire body sashaying like it couldn't help it. She stopped and turned around to catch me staring.

"What are you looking at?"

Terrified that she might think I was some sort of pig like my brother, I practically stuttered. "Uh, nothing."

"Uh-huh." She waited as I hurried to catch up to her. "So, do you want to maybe study together sometime?"

I cheered inside my head, and had to stop myself from throwing my fist in the air and doing a victory dance.

"Definitely. I could use the help," I said, trying to keep my voice even. I knew damn well that I was doing perfectly fine in that class, but if she thought I needed help, she wouldn't bail on me.

"Okay, good. I always do better if I have a study partner."

My mind whirled at her words. How many study partners

had she had? How could I convince her to only study with me?

I could have sworn that before Jack's antics with her roommate that Melissa and I were on track toward something. I couldn't help but want us to get back on that road, wherever it was leading.

"Can I get your number?" I asked while I still had the nerve.

"Oh yeah, of course." She recited her phone number while I tapped it into my phone. "Send me a text so I have yours too."

I did as she asked.

DEAN: Hi. It's me. You know, Dean. The other Carter.

When her phone pinged and she read the text, she laughed. "Got it. I'll just put you in here as the Other Carter."

"Or the only Carter you like," I suggested with a smirk, and she smiled back.

"That'd work too."

"All right. I'll talk to you later. You know, to set up studying and stuff," I said, stumbling all over my damn words.

"'Bye, Dean." Melissa laughed as she sashayed away.

WHEN JACK WALKED through the front door that afternoon, I shot out of my room and walked into his, and plopped onto his bed to wait for him.

He walked in and tossed his bag on the floor. "What are

you doing in here?"

"I wanted to know if she said yes or not."

I didn't want to tell him that I'd been dying to hear what happened with Cassie after her class. Sure, I could have used it as an excuse to text Melissa and ask her, but I decided to wait for my brother to get home from practice and hear it from him.

"Of course she said yes."

When Jack smirked, I grabbed his mini basketball and shot it at the net attached to the back of his door. I missed.

"Did you really ask her out in front of everyone?"

"I had to. She's stubborn."

"What'd you say?"

I shot the ball again. *Damn.* Another miss.

"I told her she only had to go out with me one time and if she hated it, I'd leave her alone forever. Something like that."

He waved a hand at me like it was no big deal, but I knew the truth. Jack didn't date, and this was definitely a date. And without a doubt, it was a big deal.

"That honestly worked on her?"

"I think she just wanted me to shut up. But it worked, and I took the win." He shrugged. "Speaking of, when are you going to ask out that feisty little fun-sized roommate of hers?"

I swallowed hard. "Melissa?"

The ball rolled back to me, and I attempted another shot. Missed again.

"No, Matilda the Hun. Yes, Melissa." He shot me a knowing glance. "She likes you, you know."

"I don't know. She's flirty, but then she's not. I can't read her at all. But I got her number today, so we'll see."

"Good. Make sure you use it. Now get out of here so I can take a shower."

Jack picked up the little basketball and tossed it at my head.

He didn't miss.

Ball of Nerves

JACK YELLED FOR me, I stopped what I was doing to go see what he wanted. But when I stepped into his room, I didn't see him anywhere. Then his closet door popped open and he stepped out, buttoning up his shirt.

"I can't believe she said yes," he said as he finished getting dressed.

"Bullshit," I said, calling his bluff. "You said you weren't going to let her say no."

"I know," he said with a shrug, and averted his eyes. "But now that she's said yes, what if she hates me and never lets me see her again?"

I snorted. "She won't."

"How can you be so sure?"

"Because you're actually taking a girl out on a date, Jack. In public. At dinnertime. I haven't seen you do anything like that in years."

It was true. Jack hooked up with girls all the time, but this wasn't a hookup. This, whatever it was, wasn't his usual MO. Everything about this was different, not to mention the fact that he actually seemed nervous. Girls didn't make my brother nervous, but for some reason, this one did.

When he pulled a paper bag from his dresser and rolled it up to stuff it into his pocket, I squinted at him. "What the hell is that?"

He smiled. "Quarters."

"Quarters?"

"The first time I met her at that party, she told me it cost fifty cents every time I touched her."

"So?"

"So this right here"—he shook the paper bag at me, and it jingled—"is a shitload of quarters . . . for a shitload of touching."

I shook my head, both impressed with his resourcefulness and half shocked with his gal. "Nice."

"She'll love it, right?"

"Who wouldn't?"

Jack looked at himself in the mirror one last time before turning to me. "How do I look?"

"Hot," I said in a high-pitched voice, trying to hold a serious expression.

"You're no help. Keep your phone on in case something happens and I need you," he said as he stepped into the hallway.

"First of all, why would I turn it off? And second, why the hell would you possibly need me?"

He shrugged. "I have no idea, just tell me okay."

"Okay," I said, hoping to calm his jitters. "Have fun. And use your manners," I told him with a laugh, and he flipped me off. "That's not them!"

Once Jack left, I pulled out my phone to text Melissa. I figured since both of us would be alone tonight, we could be alone together.

DEAN: *Want to study tonight?*

MELISSA: *On one condition.*

DEAN: *?*

MELISSA: *You bring me a cherry Slurpee from 7-Eleven.*

DEAN: *Seriously?*

MELISSA: *Do I sound like I'm kidding?*

DEAN: *Why cherry?*

MELISSA: *Because I'm craving it and you're on your way here and it's on your way and pleeease? I'll make you brownies.*

DEAN: *Deal.*

MELISSA: *Sucker.*

I smiled at her last text as another one followed with her address.

Pumped up, I headed for the living room to ask if I could borrow the Honda. Gramps was there as usual in his favorite chair, watching TV.

When I asked, he said, "Of course. Where are you going?"

"Remember that girl I pointed out to you at the game the other day?"

"Isn't that who Jack is out with tonight?" His eyes narrowed as he peered at me over his glasses.

"Not the blonde, the other one. They're roommates," I explained.

He scratched his chin before nodding. "Okay."

"We have a class together, and we're going to study."

"Study, huh? Is that what they're calling it now?" He huffed out a laugh.

"Seriously. We're just studying."

Gramps gave me a small frown and turned back to the TV. "Sounds boring. Be safe."

"Thanks, Gramps. I will."

"Don't be late, Dean," Gran called out from the kitchen.

"I'll be home before Jack," I yelled back.

That was most likely the truth. The only way I'd be home after Jack was if he did something stupid and pissed Cassie off. For some reason, she didn't seem to have a high tolerance level for his shit.

WITH A GIANT cherry Slurpee in one hand and my notebook in the other, I kicked on Melissa's apartment door and waited for her to answer.

She threw it open and squealed when she saw me. Before I could get too excited at her enthusiastic welcome, she snatched the drink from my hand and began sucking it down like it was her savior.

Not me; the damn drink.

Her face scrunched up almost immediately and she stomped on the floor. "Brain freeze, brain freeze, brain freeze!"

I laughed, but when the smell of fresh-baked brownies assaulted my senses, I sympathized with her sudden craving.

"That freaking hurt!" she said, clearly recovered. "Come in."

I stepped through the door and leaned down to wrap her in a hug. She gripped my back tightly, her fingertips digging into my muscles, and I wished I had the balls to try to kiss her. It would have been out of nowhere, but being this close to Melissa made me want to do all sorts of things to her.

Our eyes met for a second before she looked away, releasing me from her embrace and breaking our connection completely.

"The brownies smell incredible," I said, practically drooling.

"Still have twenty more minutes to go, but they do smell good, huh? Thank you for my Slurpee."

"You're welcome. How was Jack when he got here?" I cut straight to the chase, wondering if my brother seemed nervous to her or not.

"Ha!" She laughed. "Good. Cocky as ever."

"Was Cassie excited?"

"I'm not sure that's the right word," Melissa said as she walked into her kitchen. "Can I grab you something to drink? I have water or soda."

"I'll take a soda. Do you think they'll be okay?"

She tossed me the unopened can, and I knocked on the top of it with my knuckle before opening it.

"I don't know, he's your stupid brother. Do you think he can act like a normal human being for one night?"

"Probably not," I said with a chuckle.

"Didn't think so. Here, sit."

She waved at the kitchen table, covered with a mess of papers and textbooks, and I added my notebook to the pile before I sat down. Other than the table, the apartment appeared spotless, which was impressive.

I couldn't even keep my room clean, let alone multiple rooms. Gran was always yelling at me and Jack to pick up our stuff, to wash our dishes and put them away. I wanted to be neater; I just didn't see the mess. When Gran looked around the kitchen, she saw every single glass and utensil out of place. Me? I only saw food. The other stuff never concerned me, but I promised Gran I'd try to do better, and had to repeat that promise every other week or so.

"How long have you and Cassie known each other?" I asked.

Aside from flirting with each other in class, I didn't know much about Melissa. Not to mention the fact that we didn't get much alone time, and the one time when we had been alone at the student union, it hadn't lasted more than five minutes.

"We've been friends since high school." She smiled. "I came here right after graduation, but Cass's parents forced her to go to a junior college instead. She's only been here since this year."

"Why'd they make her do that?"

Melissa looked me square in the eye. "Money."

I nodded slightly in complete understanding. "But your parents let you come right away?"

"Yeah. They don't have money issues," she said with a shrug.

"Are your parents still married?"

"They are. Are yours?"

The question rattled me. The fact that our parents had abandoned Jack and me wasn't something I told most people. And my sharing that with Melissa would mean she not only knew something extremely personal and private about me, but about Jack as well. So I thought better of it.

"No, they're not."

"I'm sorry. That sucks. But I guess it's rarer to have parents still be married than anything else, these days," she said, and I nodded.

"Do you get along with them?" I wondered what it was like for her, to have rich parents who were still together.

"Oh my gosh, yes. They're the greatest. We have the best relationship, honestly. My mom owns a PR firm in Hollywood, and I work for her every summer."

"Is that what you want to do? Work for her once you graduate?"

She nodded. "Yes and no. I want in the family business, for sure. But I want to start my own firm in a different location. I think it would be cool to expand, but I think it makes my mom nervous. It's okay, though." She waved her hand. "I still have time to convince her."

I loved seeing this side of Melissa, and hearing about her determination and ambition. It made her even more attractive in my eyes. Plus, I had to admit that the whole idea of Jack and me dating best friends was appealing. We used to joke when we were kids about how cool it would be if we ended up dating girls who were sisters. I think it was more me suggesting it than Jack, but he agreed that it would be fun. Two girls who were best friends seemed like the next best thing.

"What about you? I know you're only a freshman, but any idea what you want to do?" She cocked her head to the side.

"No. I wish I did, but I just don't know yet," I admitted, hating how indecisive I sounded.

"That's okay. I don't think most people know what they want to be when they're eighteen. Those of us who do probably aren't normal." She laughed.

"You're definitely not normal," I teased, and she narrowed her eyes at me.

"Ha-ha. You're hilarious."

I swallowed, thinking about her and Cassie again. "I bet it's cool to have your best friend with you at college."

"You would know." Her cheeks pulled in dramatically as she sucked on her Slurpee. "I mean, I just assumed that you and Jack were that close."

"We are."

Jack had always been my best friend, and while we both had other acquaintances or teammates, it wasn't the same as having a brother who shared your family history. We were bonded by blood, but stayed close friends by choice.

"But we still live at home, so it's not like we're out living on our own like you girls are."

"Yeah, it's pretty awesome to be living together, to be honest."

I leaned my elbows on the table. "So, I have a question for you."

"Another one?" She quirked an eyebrow.

"Yeah. How did I get lucky enough to have you in a freshman class with me?"

"Oh." She laughed. "I still had one general ed course to take, and so I picked that one."

"Lucky me." I was trying to be charming, which was really my best Jack impression.

"Are you flirting with me?"

"I'm damn well trying. I don't know if I'm very good at it, to be honest. I have a horrible teacher," I said, referring to Jack.

"The worst." She agreed quickly, but her cheeks turned pink. "But I like it," she said. "The flirting, I mean. Not your brother."

The buzzer went off in the kitchen, and I silently cursed it as Melissa hopped out of her chair and ran in the kitchen. I couldn't figure this girl out, and I was too nervous to come out and ask.

"The brownies are done. Yeah!"

"Anyone ever tell you that you're crazy?" I called out from the dining room as she buzzed around in the kitchen, moving from one side to the other like someone with wings.

"No." She stopped flying. "Why, did you hear something?" Then she doubled over, laughing at her own joke before she pulled the brownies from the oven and set them on top.

I waited patiently for her to come back to the table, but when I glanced back at the kitchen area, she was nowhere to be seen.

"Melissa?" I shouted.

"I'm in the bathroom. I'll be right out," she called out, her muffled voice coming from somewhere else in the apartment.

At the sight of the pan of brownies on top of the oven, I seriously contemplated cutting myself a large piece, but thought better of it when I imagined how pissed off she'd be. Melissa was cute, but feisty, and I imagined that she probably had the temper of Tinker Bell. Everyone always loved that fairy, but I seemed to be the only one who remembered that she was mean.

Why the hell am I thinking about a cartoon fairy right now? And why the hell do I know so much about Tinker Bell?

I smacked the side of my head as Melissa reappeared, bearing gifts.

"Beating yourself up while I've been gone? It can't be that bad."

"Ha-ha."

She placed a small plate in front of me with three perfectly cut brownie squares on top. "Be careful, they're still hot."

I didn't listen as I shoved one into my mouth. "Shit," I yelled around the molten lava now burning up the roof of my mouth, but too hot to chew or swallow.

"I told you they were hot," she shouted before pointing at an unopened can of soda she'd set on the table in front of me.

Frantic, I leaned my head back and opened my mouth wide while I breathed quickly in and out, hoping to cool the bite off. When I finally took a chance on chewing, I was relieved to find it no longer felt like I was trying to eat something straight out of a volcano.

Melissa was grinning from ear to ear. "Now I know what I must have looked like when I had brain freeze earlier. That was pretty entertaining."

We hunkered down for a while, going over notes for the test and quizzing each other. I tried to let her know that I was interested in her, but her reactions to me were always hit or miss. Sometimes she would reach over and touch me when she didn't have to, and other times she kept her distance when I was certain she'd come close. I tried not to read too much into it, but I couldn't help myself.

An hour and a half later, I said, "I'd better get going. Thanks for helping me." I pushed back from the table and stood up, stretching my arms out over my head.

"You didn't need my help. You just wanted to come over," she said playfully.

I leaned down and picked her up while I hugged her tight. When our heads pulled back slowly, our faces were so close that I could have kissed her if I'd had the nerve. She tensed slightly in my arms, and I allowed the moment to pass. The last thing I wanted was for her to be uncomfortable around me.

"I'll see you tomorrow," I said lightly, not wanting to push her.

"Okay. Thanks again for the Slurpee and for hanging out tonight. I had fun."

"Me too."

Frustrated, I pulled her apartment door closed behind me. That hadn't gone how I expected. Then again, I wasn't sure what I thought would happen.

As I pulled out of the parking lot, I noticed Jack and Cassie pulling in at the same time. Jack didn't see me from the driver's seat of his lifted vintage Bronco, and I headed home, hoping he wouldn't be much longer. I wanted to hear all about his date with Cassie.

WHEN I GOT home, I hung the keys to the Honda on the key organizer beside the front door and tiptoed to the bathroom. Gran and Gramps had already gone to bed, and I didn't want to wake them.

The front door opened and shut when I'd almost fallen asleep. A little drowsy, I rolled out of bed and shuffled down the hallway to meet Jack outside his room.

"You're still up?" he asked.

"I was waiting."

He snorted. "You're such a girl."

"I feel like one right now. I want to hear everything," I said, not caring what he thought about me.

"Let me grab some water, and then I'll come in your room."

I yawned and headed back to my bedroom, where I sat on my bed to wait for Jack. He came in carrying two glasses of water, and handed me one.

"Thanks." I placed the water on my nightstand. "So? How was it?"

"Epic." He plopped down onto the bed next to me.

"Epic? How? Why?"

"Shit. First of all, listen to this." He shook his head. "I got into a damn fight at the restaurant. That dickhead Jared came up and tried to start something. I was going to let it go, but then he started saying stuff to Cassie, and I lost it. I just wanted him to shut his fucking mouth."

"Jesus, Jack." I rubbed my hand across my forehead. "You sleep with a guy's girlfriend, and then you hit him?"

"Yeah, and I couldn't stop hitting him, but only because of what he said to Cassie. But before that, everything was great. And after that it was great too."

"Cassie wasn't pissed? She seems like the kind of girl to get pissed over something like that."

Jack nodded. "I think under normal circumstances she might have been. But this wasn't normal. He was a dick. She didn't say so, but I think she was happy I hit him."

"How's your hand?" I glanced at his left arm. His throwing arm.

"Hurts like hell. But I hit him with the right, so it's all good."

"I saw you guys come home," I said with a smile of my own, and he cocked his head to the side.

"What?" He gasped. "Were you with Melissa while I was out with Cassie?"

"Yeah, but nothing happened. I can't tell if she's into me or not," I said, hoping he'd have some insight.

"I can ask Cassie, but Melissa seems stubborn. Like she might be a tough nut to crack, little brother."

"You might be right. Good thing I'm a patient guy. Cassie's cool, though?"

Jack breathed out a long breath, and then smiled. "She's beyond cool. She's so normal. She doesn't care about the baseball aspect at all. I mean, she cares, but only because I do. She doesn't see me the way other girls do, you know? She's smart and opinionated and gorgeous. She has all these rules that she lives by, and I'm going to prove to her that I can live by them too."

"Wait, wait, wait." I put my hand up to stop his Cassie-filled love rant. "Rules? What kind of rules?"

"Oh, just these four like, I don't know, rules. Don't lie, don't cheat, don't say things you don't mean, and don't make promises you can't keep," he said, rattling them off as if he'd memorized them for a test.

I was lost. "And you're supposed to prove them all to her?"

"No. I mean, well, yeah. She has a fucked-up relationship with her dad, and so I think that's where they came from. Shouldn't be that hard; they're pretty normal requests for any person."

"You're right. I've just never met a girl who had rules before."

Jack shrugged and his face turned serious. "I told her about Mom and Dad."

My jaw fell open. "Wow. Really?"

We rarely ever told anyone about our parents, especially girls. Jack and I had worked hard to keep our personal life private, at least when it came to our childhood. What had happened to us in our past wasn't something we enjoyed sharing. Of course, people asked questions about why we lived with our grandparents, but we avoided those mostly, only offering bits and pieces of the truth.

"Yeah. I mean, I hadn't meant to, but the timing and the conversation just evolved and . . . I don't know." He pulled at his hair. "It just felt right. Are you upset that I told her? It involves you too."

"No, I'm not upset. I trust your judgment." And I did. If Jack wanted to confess to Cassie about how our parents ditched us when we were kids, who was I to stop him?

"Do you think it was a mistake to tell her?" he asked.

"Do you?"

"No," he answered without hesitating. "I wanted to. It felt good to talk about all that crap with her. I don't know why, but I felt relieved once she knew."

"I think you might really like this girl," I said, stating the obvious.

Jack met my eyes and nodded. "I think I might be in serious trouble when it comes to this girl. And I've never wanted to get into more trouble in my life."

"Did you kiss her?"

He laughed and slapped my knee before using it to push off my bed. "You know who I am, don't you?"

"So that's a yes?" He hadn't really answered my question.

"That's a yes, little brother. And it's more than you did with little Funsize tonight. I expect more from you."

"Challenge accepted."

As he walked out the door, I wondered how in the world I was going to get that beautiful little pixie to want me back.

Jack poked his head back in my doorway as I was getting settled underneath my covers. "Cassie tried to say that our kiss changed nothing, but I told her it changed everything."

"Did it?"

"Yeah." He nodded. "But she asked me to prove it."

"Because she doesn't believe you?" I shook my head, half-amazed at the things that came out of that girl's mouth. Even more surprising was that it didn't send my brother running for the hills.

"Exactly."

"How the hell are you supposed to do that?"

"I have a few ideas, but I might need your help," he said before disappearing without waiting for my answer.

He knew I'd do anything he needed.

Things Are Changing

THE PAST FOUR weeks had been fun to watch. Jack and I talked about the things he could do to prove to Cassie that she could trust him. Hell, I even wrote down a list of ideas, but he didn't need it. He'd already known what needed to be done when it came to her. It was weird, but he had these spot-on instincts about her.

The day after their first date, he stopped eating at his normal table. His legion of fangirls practically whined themselves to death when they noticed him not only eating at another table, but doing so with a girl. One girl.

I thought one of them might faint at the sight, but thankfully they all remained upright. That didn't stop the girls from throwing themselves at Jack every chance they got. He could barely walk through the student union without girls grabbing him, trying to pin him down with questions.

Jack used to tolerate the madness when he was single, but now that he was chasing Cassie, he had no patience for the fangirls. His body language completely changed, more closed off, and he got a little meaner.

He'd also started spending more time at Cassie's apartment, which meant that both Cassie and Melissa saw my brother more than I did. I wasn't too upset, though, because I saw how happy he was, and I'd never seen him like that before.

On campus, the four of us became pretty much inseparable. At lunchtime in the student union one day, I saw Jack putting an overfilled tray of food on the table that we shared, and I made my way over with my own lunch tray to join him, Cassie, and Melissa.

Before I could get there, a sorority girl named Andrea stopped me with a hand on my arm. "When is your brother going to dump that girl?"

I pulled away from her. "Hopefully never," I said with a smirk before walking away. I'd never understand these girls.

As I neared the table, Jack was saying, "Cass, I don't ever want to hurt you, but I can't promise you that I'll never screw up or make you mad."

"He's good at pissing people off. Isn't that right, big brother?" I smirked down at Jack, and he took a halfhearted swipe at me before I set my tray down next to him.

"That's the rumor." He nodded with a smile, but Cassie didn't look pleased.

"Plus, if he pushes you away, then you won't be the one who left him. He'll be the one who made you leave," I added a little too helpfully.

Jack glared at me before looking back at Cassie. My insight into his motivations clearly struck a nerve.

"I don't plan on going anywhere," Cassie said as she looked into his eyes. "So don't try to make me."

Melissa frowned at both of them. "Jesus, I've never met two people more scared to let someone love them than the two of you." Her gaze pinged between them, making her ponytail swing from side to side. "And don't even try to deny it. You're both all messed up from your stupid parents."

She lifted her hand in Cassie's direction. "Cassie here, with her dad's constant lies and inability to follow through on even the simplest, most mundane thing, has been disappointed and let down most of her life."

Then she pointed at my brother. "And you, with your mom up and leaving, telling you it was your fault because you were a *bad kid*. You're convinced that no one will ever stick around, that eventually they'll leave you too. And somewhere in your twisted, screwed-up psyche, you probably think you deserve it."

And me, I just sat there slack-jawed that Melissa had the guts to bring up something so private in such a public place, and then throw it in my brother's face. Apparently I wasn't the only one stunned into silence; no one else said a word.

Thank God this wasn't my fault. Jack told me that Melissa had dragged our story out of him late one night, and that he had felt okay with her knowing. I wondered if he was regretting that decision right about now.

Melissa took a quick breath and then delivered her final assessment. "You're both so screwed up alone, that together you're like the perfect mess."

I sat there absorbing her words, even though they weren't meant for me, and wondered how much of what she said might be true.

Will I behave the same as Jack when I give my heart away?

Cassie recovered first, but her feelings were clearly hurt. "That's an attractive analogy. Thanks for saying I'm screwed up," she snapped.

Jack reached for Cassie. "I'll be the perfect mess with you anytime."

She quickly swiped under her eye and leaned her head against his shoulder. A deep sigh escaped her. "Melissa just doesn't know anything about having messed-up parents. Hers are perfect. She can't relate."

"Hey! It's not my fault I won the parent lottery." Melissa eyed Cassie. "Plus, we both know I'm not strong enough to deal with the shit you've dealt with. I would've had a nervous breakdown by now. I could never handle everything your dad's put you through."

Cassie released a small laugh, but it was enough to ease the tension at the table. I was thankful for the reprieve.

"I don't know if it's because I'm strong or because I've gotten really good at turning off my emotions," she added in a low voice.

"It's definitely both," Melissa said before turning toward my brother again. "And, Jack, I've never seen anyone completely shut off the way this one can." She nodded in Cassie's direction. "If you push her too far, she'll flick off like a light switch. It's scary."

"Really? That's impressive," he teased, and I stayed quiet, taking it all in.

"You won't feel that way if she does it to you," Melissa said, her face the scary kind of serious. "Trust me."

"Well, I hope I never have to see it."

"If I didn't compartmentalize, I'd never be able to function," Cassie said hotly. "It's the only way I can survive without being a total basket case."

"I get it, Kitten. Still impressive."

Jack smiled at her with what looked like love in his eyes, and I found myself desperate to change the subject.

"So, when do you leave for Texas?" I asked Jack, then took a bite of my cheeseburger.

"We fly out Thursday morning. Why?"

"Just wondering," I mumbled around my bite.

Cassie straightened up and turned to Jack. "What do you do when you're there? Like, how does it work? Do you practice? Do parents go?"

I laughed at Cassie's intense curiosity. I'd seen her on more than one occasion ask Jack a million and one questions at a rapid-fire pace when she didn't understand something.

Jack snagged one of my fries and popped it into his mouth. "Well, we typically fly in the day before our games start. We check in at the hotel. We'll have practice and work out, and have dinner as a team. Some parents go, but not many."

"Does everyone get their own room?"

"No." Jack laughed. "We share rooms."

"Do you have like bed checks and stuff?"

Melissa leaned forward, clearly interested in this topic of

conversation, and I leaned toward her.

Jack nodded before taking a bite of his pizza. Once he'd swallowed, he said, "We do. Usually Coach comes by and makes sure everyone's in their rooms by ten."

Cassie breathed out in what looked like relief. "Any other rules?"

"No girls and no drinking." Jack raised his eyebrows and glanced at me as Cassie shoved against his shoulder, almost pushing him over.

"I'm sure those rules never get broken, huh?"

"Nope. We're all complete angels when we're on the road." Jack's gaze darted between Melissa and Cassie, before stopping on me in some sort of silent dare.

I burst out laughing. "Angels, my ass."

"No, wait wait wait!" Cassie's voice broke through the chorus of laughter. "Do you guys sneak girls in your rooms? Like random strangers?"

Her gaze was focused solely on Jack. She wouldn't settle for any less than the truth, and I glanced at him, wondering how he would handle this.

"Yeah."

She rolled her eyes.

"Kitten. The eyes."

Cassie rolled her eyes a lot, and Jack had taken to giving her shit about it each time she did it. It didn't make her stop, though, and I believed he secretly enjoyed that side of her.

"You're such a pig." She shook her head.

"This isn't news! But I'm a changed man, Kitten. I swear

it."

I had to suppress a smile at the sight of my brother pleading with his girlfriend, who was clearly disgusted at the news of his old road-trip behavior.

"We'll see about that." She stared back at him, her tone cautious.

"Care to make a wager?" Jack offered.

She narrowed her eyes at him. "Please, tell me you don't need a bet to stay faithful. I swear to God, Jack."

"He doesn't need a bet to stay faithful, Cassie," I said, trying to help my brother out of the hole he'd apparently dug himself into. Although being faithful and in a relationship was completely new to him, even I had to admit that he'd been doing a damn fine job so far.

"It sounds like it to me," Melissa chimed in, but to me, neither of our opinions was helping.

I glanced at Melissa. "Maybe we should leave them alone."

"I have to get to class, anyway."

She picked up her things, and my heart sank. That wasn't what I had in mind. Not at all. I watched as she walked away, my eyes focused on her ass again.

"You *love* her," Jack said in a singsong voice, and I socked him in the shoulder.

"Shut up." I cast Cassie a sideways glance, and she laughed.

"I think it's cute," she said, her mood suddenly lighter now that the focus wasn't on her and Jack.

"I don't know what either of you are talking about," I lied.

Jack shook his head and let out a snort. "I see the way you two look at each other. I don't know what you two are waiting for."

"It's not me. She knows I like her. She just doesn't like me back."

Cassie's face twisted into a frown. "It's not that. I don't know what it is. She hasn't said anything to me, but I think she's scared."

"Of me?"

"I don't know, Dean. She's weird when it comes to boys sometimes."

"But Dean's not just any boy. He's a Carter. And my little brother. She should want to go out with him," Jack said, talking me up, and I sat up a little straighter at his praise.

"I agree," Cassie said. "But she's stubborn. More stubborn than I am."

Frustrated, I grabbed my bag and hiked it over my shoulder. "If we're done discussing my lack of a love life, I'm gonna take off."

Before they could say another word, I left.

When the Team's Away

JACK MIGHT BE leaving school in the morning, but the rest of us still had tests and homework to do while he was gone.

Me, I had a love/hate relationship with his traveling, hating it because I didn't get to see him pitch. Knowing he was out there throwing and I wasn't able to watch was a special kind of torture for me. My entire childhood was filled with memories of Jack playing baseball, pitching better than anyone else we knew, and being able to hit the ball as well.

When he excelled, I couldn't help but feel proud. Especially after he'd gotten into so many fights, prompting some people to say he wasn't going to amount to anything, and that he was a loser. Jack being able to pitch the way he did was like a giant middle finger to all the doubters who never believed in him. And it was as much a middle finger from me as it was from him.

On the flip side, I loved Jack's road trips because I thought they were cool. The whole idea of getting to travel someplace new to play baseball seemed like the best of both worlds. Plus, Jack always had the best stories when he came back. If he went somewhere that was known for something famous, he made sure to always bring something home for our grandparents and me. That thrilled us all because Jack was the only one in our family who ever left town. It was sad, but true.

"I'm gonna stay at Cassie's tonight," Jack told me as I sat at my desk, highlighting an upcoming chapter in my history textbook.

"And you're telling me this, because?" I asked, not even bothering to look up from my work.

"Because I'm going to have her take me to the bus tomorrow morning."

I placed my pen on the desk and looked up to see him standing in my doorway, his duffel bag slung over his shoulder. "Are you leaving the Bronco with her?"

"That's what I'm trying to tell you. Although she calls it the deathmobile," he said with a laugh, and dropped his bag to the floor.

I gaped at him. "She doesn't like your truck?"

What wasn't there to like about Jack's Bronco? Sure, it was covered with dents and scratches, and the paint had chipped in places, but the thing was a classic. And it looked badass.

Jack shrugged. "I think it scares her. Anyway, she doesn't have a car here, so I thought I would leave it with her. But only if you don't need it, and you're cool with that."

I thought about it for a moment. For the last two years, I'd driven Jack to the bus for every road trip, and then he'd left his truck with me. As much as I loved driving it while he was gone, I knew I didn't really need it.

"I don't need it," I said, and picked up my pen again to highlight more passages.

"Are you sure? I know you usually take me and then you get the truck, but I figured if you didn't mind—"

"Seriously, it's cool. She should take you, and I don't need it. Plus, I'd sorta love to see Cassie driving that thing," I said with a laugh. I couldn't picture her in the driver's seat, and that sight alone might be worth it. "I don't have any plans this weekend, and I can always borrow Gran's car if I need to."

Jack grinned at me. "I promise I'll buy you a car when I get my signing bonus, you hear me? You and Gran both. New cars." I waved him off, not wanting to hear any more. I honestly didn't care about any of that. When Jack got drafted, that would be enough for me to know that he'd accomplished his dream, reached his number-one goal. I didn't need a stupid car out of the deal.

"Go, already. Take your deathmobile to your girlfriend's house and—" A thought struck me. "Wait! This is the first time you're staying over there, isn't it?"

He cleared his throat. "Uh-huh."

"You, uh, have everything you need?" I waggled my eyebrows as I reached into my back pocket to pull out my wallet. I peered inside. "Shit, I don't even have one. I think it got old, and I threw it out."

"I'm good, but thanks for your concern."

"So you're protected then? Of course you are. You're Jack Carter, king of condoms and getting laid."

"I'm actually all out, but I don't plan on sleeping with her tonight."

I almost choked. "What? Why?"

He shrugged, not meeting my eyes. "I don't know. Maybe because I'm fucking in love with her. I'm so in love with her, I can't imagine not being in love with her. And it doesn't seem like the right time. I can't have sex with her and then leave the next morning for four days. Something about that seems fucked up."

"You really are in love with her." I smiled, wondering when I would get used to hearing him talk this way about someone.

"That's what I've been trying to tell you."

"Well, go tell her. She's probably the one that needs to hear it." I threw my highlighter at him, hitting him square in the chest.

Jack grabbed his bag and smirked at me. "I'm trying to leave, but my little brother keeps trying to give me old condoms from his wallet."

"You suck!" I yelled at his retreating back.

"No, you do," he shouted back. "So blow me!"

Laughing, I bent over to pick up my highlighter from the floor.

WHEN THE BASEBALL team was out of town, it seemed like the entire campus shut down. Not really shut down, per se, but it was a hell of a lot quieter and not nearly as interesting as when the guys were here.

There were fewer females hanging around, and the normally crowded student union wasn't even halfway filled. The lack of obnoxious fangirls was actually a relief, but I did miss my brother. It felt odd being here when he wasn't.

The day after the team left, I sat at our usual lunch table, waiting for either Melissa or Cassie to show up. Frowning, I forked at my plate filled with meatballs. The crappy sauce they served here tasted nothing like Gran's.

Melissa slammed her bag down with a bang before plopping down next to me.

"Shit. I didn't even see you come in," I said nonchalantly, trying to act like she hadn't just scared the shit out of me.

"I noticed. You were too busy having a love affair with your balls to notice me." She batted her eyelashes and poked out her bottom lip in a pout.

Damn, I want to suck on that lip. Or at least kiss it.

I thought I'd get over my crush on Melissa the more time we spent together, but it only seemed to intensify, which frustrated me. I didn't know what to do about it.

The best-case scenario would have been for Melissa's feelings for me to grow as well, but they didn't seem to. I enjoyed the times when she flirted easily with me, and rolled with it, but the second I even hinted at crossing the friendship line, she pulled back and pretended nothing was going on between us.

I was still too much of a wimp to confront her about it. I told myself it was because I didn't want to put her on the spot or make her uneasy, but the truth was because I was terrified of her response. What if I scared her off altogether and she stopped wanting to hang out with me? Avoiding the awkward conversation meant that I got to hang around with her, so I ignored it and hoped that one day I'd get her to change her mind. Or maybe she'd attack me with her mouth.

I was about to say something witty to Melissa about my balls, but the sound of laughter caught my attention. Not a funny-ha-ha type of laughing, but the mean kind girls did when the joke was on someone else.

A girl had stopped Cassie and was showing her something on her cell phone while her friends waited nearby, laughing as they watched. Cassie seemed unfazed as she sauntered away from the girl, but once she met my eyes, hers changed completely. If looks could kill, Cassie would have incinerated me.

"What was that?" I asked when she got to our table.

She was practically vibrating with emotion when she dropped into one the chair across from her. "That was a picture of some chick walking into Jack's hotel room." She swallowed bravely before swiping at her eyes. "And then another one of him closing the door behind her. Did I mention the smile plastered all over his face?"

"No way." I shook my head, not believing for a second that my brother would cheat on Cassie.

"Yes, way. Fuck. I'm such an idiot."

I put my hands on top of Cassie's and squeezed. "Maybe they're old?"

"What are you talking about?" she asked as she yanked her hands away.

"There are a lot of pictures of Jack and other girls out there, Cass. Maybe they're old?" I shrugged, offering the only explanation I could think of in the moment.

There had always been pictures of Jack circulating around campus, so it made sense to me that maybe these pictures weren't recent. Maybe the girls were just trying to get a rise out of Cassie, jealous that Jack liked her and not them.

"Jack wouldn't do that to you," Melissa said to reassure Cassie, and I nodded in complete agreement.

"I wouldn't go that far," she choked out, her tone ice cold.

Melissa frowned. "Why would you say that?"

"Because Cassie knows my brother." I glanced at Melissa before looking back at Cassie. "And she's waiting for him to screw up because he keeps telling her he's bound to."

"Well, for the record, I want it noted that I don't believe it," Melissa said with confidence. "Not for one second."

I wanted to hug her, but settled for giving her a small smile. "I don't either."

"Well, it was definitely Jack in those pictures," Cassie said, her voice tight. "And the shirt he was wearing was packed in his bag. I saw it the other night."

She tried to fight the tears threatening to fall, but lost. When one dropped to her cheek, she jumped up from the table and sprinted away.

Melissa stood up just as quickly. "I'd better go see if she's okay."

"I don't think he'd do anything, Meli. Honestly."

"I don't either." She rested her hand on my shoulder before jogging off to the ladies' room after Cassie.

I waited for the girls to come back to our table, too upset to finish my lunch. A few people gave me curious glances as they walked past while I pushed the meatballs around, watching them get cold.

Melissa came back a few minutes later. Alone.

"No Cassie?" I asked as she sat down next to me.

"I pissed her off. She thinks I'm taking Jack's side, but I just don't think he'd do that to her. I saw them together before he left, Dean. He's crazy about her."

"He's in love with her."

"See? And Jack Fucking Carter doesn't just fall in love all willy-nilly," she said as if trying to convince me.

I sighed. "My brother doesn't fall in love at all. Sure, he's been an idiot in the past, we all know that, but he's trying his damnedest to be good enough for her."

Her concerned blue eyes bore into mine. "So, what are we going to do?"

"I don't know," I said with a shrug. "She's your best friend. Go fix her."

Drama, Party of One

LATER THAT AFTERNOON, my laptop was propped up on my bed as I lay next to it. Jack's baseball game was scheduled to stream live through a website I'd found, and I was checking the connection, making sure I could get it to work before his game started. I was psyched to be able to follow his game while he was away, and I knew Gramps would be too.

My cell phone beeped.

JACK: Is Cassie okay?

DEAN: Why? What's up?

I'd responded right back but was noncommittal, not wanting to tell him about all the drama that had ensued while he was away. The last thing Jack needed was for his focus to be divided. If he knew Cassie was upset, he'd do whatever he had to in order to make it right.

But he needed to concentrate on baseball, and his game later tonight, and it was my job to protect him from this other shit until the time was right.

And the time was definitely not right.

JACK: She won't answer my calls, or return any of my texts. I'm starting to freak the fuck out.

DEAN: *I don't know what to tell you.*

JACK: *Tell me what the fuck's going on, Dean. How about that?*

I started to type a response, but apparently took too long trying to formulate an answer that would settle him. My phone rang in my hand, and it was Jack.

"What's up?" I said, trying to keep my voice light.

"Dean. What the fuck is going on there? I've called Cassie and sent her a dozen texts. She hasn't responded to any of them, or picked up my calls. What the hell is happening over there?"

I bit the inside of my cheek as I attempted to lie. "I don't know. Maybe she's just busy?"

"Too busy to answer a single text? No, I don't buy it. Did you see her today?"

"Yeah, I saw her."

"Was she okay?"

"She seemed fine," I lied. "We had lunch, and she was good."

"Something's wrong," he said, his voice tight with emotion. "I have to pitch later, but all I can think about is the fact that my girl is ignoring me. It's making me crazy because I know something's wrong. I can fucking sense it."

When I said nothing, he shouted, "I can't pitch with my head all fucked up, Dean! Why won't she talk to me? I told her I loved her and now she's ignoring me? I feel like a damn lunatic right now, little brother. You gotta help me."

"I'll fix it," I said quickly, and hung up.

I scrolled through my contacts for Melissa's number. Calling Cassie would be pointless, but Melissa answered right away.

"I wondered when you'd call," she answered without saying hello.

"Put her on the phone. I need to talk to her now."

"Jack's been calling and texting her, and she refuses to respond to him."

"I'm more than aware. Put her on, Melis!" I shouted, my irritation reaching an all-time high.

"Hold on." She pulled the phone away from her mouth and yelled, "Cassie, get out here!"

I waited on the other end of the line, my heart pounding in my chest when I heard Cassie ask, "Who is it?"

"It's Dean. Get on the phone," Melissa snapped at her.

I was proud of Melissa for standing up for my brother. I half wondered even if she realized that was exactly what she was doing. She'd never been Jack's biggest fan, but she seemed to have warmed to him.

"Hello," Cassie said, her tone bitchier than I'd ever heard it.

"Cassie, Jesus Christ, what the hell is going on? Jack's calling me acting like a lunatic. He's flipping out. Says you won't answer any of his phone calls or texts."

"So what."

So what? I let out an irritated huff. This girl was going to be the death of me and my brother.

"You gotta talk to him, Cass. You can't ignore him like

this when he's on a road trip. It's not fair."

"Yes, I can!" she shouted into the phone, and I pulled it away from my ear. "He's the one who had a fucking girl up in his hotel room, not me. So don't tell me I have to talk to him, Dean. And don't talk to me about what's fair."

I blew out another exasperated breath. "You're so damned stubborn! He's going ape-shit, and you're just going to let him?"

"I just can't call him, okay? I can't talk to him right now."

Cassie sounded exhausted, and I felt bad for a second as I put myself in her shoes. But I hated how easily she believed what she saw, without even giving Jack a chance.

"Just tell him I'm busy with a project for school or something," she went on. "He'll believe that."

I breathed heavily into the phone as my heart rate started to slow down. "Fine. I'll tell him. But, Cassie, he's not stupid. He'll figure out something's wrong, and then I don't know what he'll do."

"What does that mean?"

"It just means that I've never heard him sound as crazy as he was tonight. He was literally flipping out because he couldn't get a hold of you."

"I guess he should have thought about that before he invited some whore up to his hotel room," she snapped.

"You're completely unreasonable, you know that?" I asked.

"How am I unreasonable?" she shrieked.

"Because you'd rather ignore this entire situation instead of put an end to it," I snapped.

It would be so easy for them to fix this with just a single conversation. At least, I hoped that would be the case. While I was 99.9% percent sure that Jack didn't cheat on Cassie, I couldn't put it past him entirely.

"I'm not ignoring it. I simply refuse to discuss it over the phone. So what?"

"See? Unreasonable and selfish."

"Now I'm selfish too?" she shouted.

"Sort of. You're only thinking about yourself and your feelings. You're not thinking about Jack at all. This isn't just a game to him. This is his future, his career. He can't screw it up. Don't you care about that?" I said, my heart hurting for my brother.

"None of that matters if he cheated on me," she said matter-of-factly, and I felt like she'd slapped me across the face with her words.

"But you don't even know what happened! You don't know who that girl was. She could be an old friend of his, but you have no clue because you won't ask."

I dropped my head in my hand in frustration. Talking to Cassie was like talking to a brick wall.

"Nope, I won't. Not until he gets home. And don't you dare say a thing to him either, Dean. I don't want you tipping him off so he has an entire weekend to think up the perfect response."

Jesus, this girl was relentless.

"I'm not saying a word to him. But can you please at least send him a text?" I begged. "Just give him something so he can focus on the game. Please do that for him."

The line fell silent between us, so silent that I pulled the phone away to glance at the screen to see if we were still connected. We were.

"Fine," she finally blurted. "I'll text him as soon as you let me get off the phone."

I released a small laugh. "Talk to you later then."

"Wait! Dean?"

"Yeah?"

"You know I'm not picking him up on Sunday."

Damn it. I sighed, and said, "I'll come get his car."

"Thanks. 'Bye."

When she hung up, my thoughts pinged from wondering if Cassie was going to text Jack, to worrying how I was going to pick up his Bronco from her place. I didn't want to involve Gran and Gramps in any of the drama, and while the girls' apartment wasn't far, it was too far to walk.

A text message pinged, and when I saw my brother's name on the screen, I hesitated.

JACK: Any news?

DEAN: She said she's busy with a photography project that's due.

JACK: Thanks, man. Sorry I flipped out. I think I'm losing my mind.

DEAN: I told you she was fine. See you Sunday, bro. Good luck.

I pushed my laptop aside and fell back on my bed before I called Melissa again.

"What now?" she said.

"I need a favor."

She huffed out an exasperated breath. "Another one?"

"Cassie said she's not picking Jack up on Sunday. Can you come get me and take me back to your place so I can pick up his truck? I know it's a lot to ask," I said, and then waited for her to respond. It seemed like I was always waiting for this girl.

"No biggie. I'll come get you. Now?"

"Now works. Thanks."

I reached for my shoes and slipped them on before lacing them up, and then dug through the small drawer in my nightstand. When I found the bottle I was looking for, I pulled out three aspirin for the headache I felt coming on. After downing them with a sip of water, I walked into the living room where Gran and Gramps were sitting in their recliners, watching TV.

"Melissa's coming to get me so I can go get the Bronco. I'll be right back, though."

Gran narrowed her eyes on me, instantly suspicious. I could never get anything past that woman.

"Why are you getting Jack's truck?" she asked, then glanced at Gramps. "I thought Cassie was looking after it?"

"She was, but she hates driving it. She calls it his deathmobile." I tried to smile and hoped they bought my lame excuse. "So instead of having it sit there all weekend, I'm going to get it."

"Okay," she said slowly, thinking it over. "Then who's picking him up on Sunday?"

Shit. I'd forgotten about that part. "I am. Cassie has some big photography project she's working on all weekend."

"All right. Drive safe," Gran said, then added under her breath, "It is sort of a deathmobile."

"I like that car. Truck. Whatever it is," Gramps muttered as he lifted the remote to change the channel.

When Melissa's car pulled up out front a few minutes later, I shouted good-bye and jogged outside.

"Hey," she said with a smile, and I wished like hell that friends were allowed to make out. Her short shorts crept up on her thighs as she pressed down on the gas, and I wanted to rest my hand there more than anything else in this moment.

I tore my eyes away from her legs and looked at the road. "Thanks again for doing this. I really appreciate it."

"I wasn't doing anything anyway. And Cassie's being unreasonable and annoying right now, so I was happy to get away."

"Any idea why she's being extra difficult?" I couldn't help but be curious since I didn't know much about Cassie's personal history, other than the bits and pieces I'd overheard.

Melissa sighed. "I think she's comparing Jack to her dad, and her dad's basically a giant liar. I don't think she realizes that she's making Jack pay for her dad's sins, but that seems to be what she's doing. Or maybe it's somehow wrapped up in it."

I completely understood. Jack and I were both well versed in Fucked Up by Your Parents 101.

Nodding, I asked, "Did you try to tell her that?"

Melissa frowned at me before looking back at the road. "Of course I tried to tell her that, but she won't listen. She has to come to that conclusion on her own. It can't come from me," she said grimly.

"You know he's going to flip out when he gets home Sunday and she's not there to pick him up." Usually I looked forward to picking Jack up after his trips, but thanks to all the drama, this time I was dreading it.

"I know. I'll be prepared for all hell to break loose at some point on Sunday." She ran her fingers through her hair before tossing it over her shoulder. "You know, you could do me a solid and send me a text when you pick him up. That way I can mentally prepare myself for his arrival."

I huffed out a small laugh. "How are you so sure he'll come there?"

"Are you kidding?" She shot me a look that said I'd lost my mind. "Of course he'll come there. He'll come straight there. Don't tell me I know your brother better than you do," she said before making a right into the complex.

I glanced around, looking for Jack's truck as she pulled into her covered spot and cut the engine. "No, you're right. He'll come right over. And he won't be happy."

"His truck's over there." She pointed somewhere behind us and off to the right, and I scanned the area before seeing it. "And his keys are in here." She popped open her glove compartment before pulling them out and placing them in my palm.

"Thanks again for the ride."

I got out of her car and started to wave good-bye but was stunned when she walked over and wrapped her arms around my waist. Her head pressed against my chest, and I instinctively weaved my fingers through her hair.

"You're welcome," she said before letting me go. "Don't forget about that text."

"I won't," I promised.

Melissa walked a few steps away but paused and turned around to look at me, conflict in her eyes. Then her eyes hardened, and she spun around to head toward her apartment.

Just when I started to think we might be having a moment, it ended before it began.

Damage Control

I SAT IN Jack's truck, drumming my fingers on the steering wheel as I waited for the team bus to arrive. To be honest, I wasn't excited about the conversation that lay ahead of us. Jack wasn't going to be happy to see me in his truck instead of Cassie. Hell, I knew he'd be confused more than anything.

The bus pulled into the parking lot, huffing out black smoke, and my nerves surged. I got out of the truck as the brakes squealed loudly and the bus came to a stop. A moment later, the team started piling out one after the other at a sluggish pace.

I saw Jack before he saw me, his face expectant as he scanned the parking lot for his vehicle. When he noticed me leaning against it, his expression fell, and he gave me a small nod of acknowledgment.

He retrieved his bag and slung over his shoulder, and headed toward me at a slow pace. Jack looked tired, which wouldn't be good for his mood. I knew that from experience.

"What's up, bro?" he asked. "Where's my girl?" He peered inside the truck like she might be hiding there.

"I'll tell you in a second." I motioned toward the Bronco,

not wanting to have this conversation in the middle of the school parking lot. It wasn't going to be pretty.

He chucked his bag into the backseat before pausing at the driver's door. "Tell me now. Something was wrong, huh?"

"Just start the truck," I said as I tossed him the keys.

His jaw clenched tightly, he slid into the driver's seat and started the truck, and then turned to face me. "I started it."

"Smartass."

"Tell me what the fuck is going on, Dean. Where's Cassie?"

I exhaled slowly, hating to be the bearer of this news.

"Okay, just listen first. Some chick grabbed Cassie at school and showed her a bunch of pictures of you letting some girl into your hotel room in Texas. I didn't see the pictures, so I only know what I heard. But Cassie is really messed up over it. She thinks you cheated on her."

"What the fuck?" He slammed his hands on the steering wheel before revving the engine and pulling out of the space we were parked in. "Did anyone tell her I didn't fucking cheat on her?"

"Melissa and I tried, but hell, we didn't really know." I gripped the oh-shit handle as he made the turn a little too quick. "Dude, slow down. You trying to kill us both?" I yelled over the sound of the wind whipping through the truck.

"I need to get to her place. I have to talk to her," he yelled back.

"Well, you're not going to get us anywhere if you don't calm down."

He nodded and eased off the gas, apparently listening to me for once. Giving me a quick glance, he said, "What else? What else happened? Tell me everything, hurry."

"I don't know. She saw those pictures and took off for the bathroom. I think she was crying. Melissa went in after her."

He stayed silent for a minute, maybe two, and I wasn't sure exactly what was going through his head, but I knew it couldn't be good.

Jack's expression darkened as he made the turn into the girls' apartment complex. The tires squealed as he pulled us into a visitor space and came to a screeching halt. He turned off the truck, and the truck's engine ticked for a moment as it cooled.

"What else do I need to know?"

"I told you everything," I insisted, thankful I no longer needed to shout to be heard.

"Why the fuck didn't you tell me this when I called you? She was already upset by then, wasn't she?"

"Yeah, but I didn't want you to have to deal with that kind of drama when you had to pitch. I know how important every game is for your future. I was only looking out for you."

Jack practically growled at me. "Next time, tell me the fucking truth so I don't come home to this kind of ambush. A little warning would've been nice."

He hopped out of the truck before pointing a finger at me.

"Stay put," he insisted before sprinting toward Cassie's place.

I should have run after him, but I didn't. I pulled out my

phone, thinking about texting Melissa like I'd promised, but I didn't do that either. Jack seemed pissed at me, and it made me feel like shit.

A few moments later, a door slamming echoed in the distance, and I instinctively knew it was Jack. I glanced up to see him stalking toward me, looking more pissed off than happy.

When he jumped back into the truck, I asked, "What the hell happened?"

"She doesn't trust me."

He started the engine and pulled out of the parking lot, turning the truck toward home. When he glanced at me a few blocks later, his eyes were a little wild.

"We had sex before I left. I told her I loved her, and she doesn't fucking trust me. At all. She never even considered that I was innocent." He clenched his jaw, looking straight ahead as his fingers tightened around the steering wheel. "I can't do anything right by this girl. She knows how different she is to me, and she never even gave me a shot. She tried and convicted me before even asking my side."

The words flowed from my brother's mouth like I'd never heard before, full of emotion. His pain was evident, and my heart hurt for him. My mind spun as I tried to come up with something to say that might make it better.

"Put yourself in her shoes," I suggested, surprising myself.

"Whose side are you on?" he asked bitterly as we cruised through the side streets, avoiding the freeway. Jack usually did that when he needed time to think, and I knew he needed that now.

"Yours. But I'm just saying."

Jack's phone blared, and he glanced down at it before pressing IGNORE.

"Was that her?"

"Yeah," he said, fuming. "I can't talk to her while I'm driving. Or right now. I'm too pissed off."

"What are you going to do?"

He didn't say anything for a moment, and I wondered if this would be the end of him and Cassie. The thought made me sad, which surprised me. Jack and Cassie weren't perfect, by any means, but they were a good match. They both had issues, but I'd never thought those issues were bigger than the two of them together.

"I need to talk to Gran," he blurted, interrupting my thoughts.

Good idea. I smiled to myself. Gran had a way of seeing things clearly when we couldn't. She lived for this kind of stuff.

Jack parked his truck at the curb in front of our house and practically jogged inside. I grabbed his bag and had to hustle to keep up.

"Gran!" he called out as he burst through the front door.

"Jack! How was Texas?" Gran beamed at him as she came out of the kitchen. "We watched your game on Dean's computer. That was fun." She gave him a tight squeeze and a kiss on the cheek before really looking at him, then sobered. "What's the matter?"

Jack started pacing back and forth in the living room. "It's

Cassie. She—" He paused, seemingly unsure of where to start.

"Come on," Gran said calmly, and shook her head at Gramps as he shuffled in with a big smile on his face, ready to welcome Jack home. "Let me get you some lemonade. I just made it this morning."

Hanging his head, Jack followed her into the kitchen before sitting down at the table. Gramps and I were right on their heels, not wanting to miss this conversation.

Gran poured us each a glass and sat down at the kitchen table with the rest of us before looking at Jack. "Now, tell me what's going on."

"Kitten thinks that I cheated on her!" Jack shouted.

Gramps laughed, apparently at the nickname, and when we shot him a concerned look, he straightened up and said, "Who's Kitten?"

Jack frowned. "Sorry, Gramps. Cassie. I call her Kitten and she hates it, so I keep doing it."

Gramps shot me a conspiratorial grin and I held back a smile, knowing what would come next. Gran kicked him under the table.

"Anyway," Jack said, "apparently she saw some pictures of me from Texas letting this chick into my hotel room."

Gran raised a hand in the air to stop him. "And why were you letting a girl into your room?"

"She was there for Brett. But Cass saw these pictures and just assumed the worst of me without even giving me a chance to explain. She's so damn stubborn." Jack shook his head before taking a sip of his lemonade.

"Sounds like someone else I know." Gran raised an eyebrow at Gramps before looking back at Jack. "I understand why you're upset, and you have every right to be. But you also need to look at this from her point of view as well. I'm sure she's heard all about the Jack Carter that existed before she came along. And I'm trying to think of how I would feel if I had seen something like that. My heart wouldn't have wanted to believe it, but sometimes it's hard to argue with what you see with your eyes."

"But what she saw was wrong," I added, wanting to contribute to the conversation.

"She didn't know that," Gran said. "She only knew what she saw. Or what she thought she was seeing. It wasn't right of her to mistrust you so easily, and I'm sure that had to hurt." She reached out for Jack and rested her hand on top of his.

"That's why I'm so pissed," he said hotly. "She didn't even ask me what happened. She just shut me out without even giving me a chance. And I haven't done anything to deserve that."

I sat at the table and couldn't believe what I was seeing. Witnessing my brother spill his heart like this was eye opening, to say the least. I always knew he had a heart, but I'd never seen him use it before.

Gran patted his hand. "You need to talk to her, Jack. Instead of sitting here with us, you need to be over there with her. Let her explain her side, but stand up for yourself as well. Be understanding and compassionate, but still be firm. Relationships aren't easy," she said, pinning him with a stern gaze, "but the right ones are worth the work."

Her words resonated with me, reminding me of my situation with Melissa. Was she the girl for me? I thought so, but convincing her that I was right for her seemed to be an uphill battle.

But about the rest of what Gran said, was she right? Was Melissa worth the work?

I pictured in my mind the blue-eyed girl that dominated my thoughts, and the answer was a big fat *yes*.

"You're right," Jack said, pulling me from my thoughts. "Thanks, Gran. Love you guys." Jack bolted from the table and ran to his room.

He must have changed clothes, because a minute later he yelled, "Be back later," before the screen door slammed and his truck started.

I stood up and leaned over to give my grandmother a hug. "How'd you get so smart, Gran?"

Letting out a little huff, she pushed up from the table. "Years of practice," she said with a pointed glance at Gramps before grabbing Jack's glass and walking it to the sink.

Meeting the Grandparents

I ASSUMED JACK and Cassie worked out all their issues since he came home that night wearing a huge smile. So when Gran insisted that he bring Cassie over one night the next week so she could finally meet the family, he was all too agreeable.

"You think they'll like her?" he asked me before leaving to pick her up Wednesday night.

I curled my lip in mock disgust. "No, of course they won't."

"Dick."

"Don't be stupid. What's not to like? She's great. I love her. If you ever break up with her, I'm going for it," I teased, not meaning it at all, but the look on his face made it worth it.

"Back off." Jack practically growled at me, and his reaction only made me want to mess with him more.

"Just go get her already," I said, shoving him in the shoulder.

When he finally left, I realized that Jack had never brought a girl home before. Ever. And our entire family buzzed with the anticipation.

"Am I going to like her," Gran whispered to me, although I had no idea why she was whispering.

I nodded. "You're going to love her."

"How about me? Will I love Kitten?" Gramps said with a laugh.

"Is there any girl you don't love?" I rolled my eyes at him and he shrugged, playing with the unlit pipe in his mouth.

"I better get back in the kitchen," Gran said. "I have a pie in the oven."

A little while later, I yelled, "They're here," like a kid on freaking Christmas morning. Why I was so damned excited, I didn't really know.

Before they could reach the door, I pulled it open and greeted them with a smile.

"It's about time." I winked at Jack before pulling Cassie into a bear hug.

"I will hurt you. Get off her," Jack said as he playfully shoved me away.

Cassie laughed before lifting her chin and sniffing at the air. "It smells incredible in here."

"It's Gran's homemade sauce," I told her.

"Welcome home." Jack smiled down at her, his adoration obvious.

Watching his face light up like that, I realized I'd probably pay good money to see him like this. Jack had pushed people away for far too long. It was about time he let someone in.

"I'll see you two in the kitchen," I said before walking away, but neither of them paid me any attention.

I'd just settled at the kitchen table as they walked through the entryway. Gran immediately leaned over the stove, stirring her sauce over the heat even though it didn't need it. Gramps pretended to read the newspaper while I sat watching the two lovebirds.

"Oh, Ma, they're here!" Gramps folded the paper and stood up, extending his arms as he headed straight for Cassie. "You must be Cassie. It's so nice to finally meet you." He squeezed her hard, and her smile only grew.

When Gramps released her, Jack reached for her hand and pulled her toward the stove. "Gran, this is my girl, Cassie."

Gran wiped her hands on her apron as Cassie turned to her. "It's so nice to meet you, Cassie. We've heard so much about you."

"It's wonderful to meet you both. Thanks for having me," Cassie replied with a warm smile, and then asked, "Can I help?"

I almost choked. Gran never let anyone help with the cooking. The cleaning, you bet your ass, but not the actual cooking part. Her kitchen was her domain, and she never let us forget it.

"Oh heavens no, dear. I'm almost finished. Go sit down and make yourself comfortable. Jack, you get her whatever she needs, you hear me?" Gran's voice took on the tone she only used with me and Jack.

"Yes, Gran, of course," he said a little too sweetly before kissing her on the cheek. "Do you need anything, Kitten?"

"I'm fine, thanks."

Gramps pulled out the empty chair next to him and patted it. "Come sit down next to me, Cassie. Or do I get to call you Kitten too?"

When he winked at Cassie as I took a sip from my glass, I almost shot water out of my nose. *Gramps just winked at Jack's girlfriend.*

I couldn't stop laughing. "I think we should all start calling her Kitten."

Jack shot me a murderous glare. "Only I get to call her Kitten. You'd be wise to remember that."

"Jack, stop threatening your brother," Gran said while waving the steam away from her face.

"Yes, Gran," he said nicely before kicking me under the table.

I moved my foot to kick him back and missed.

Gramps leaned on his elbow and studied Cassie. "So, Cassie, Jack tells us you're a photographer."

She nodded. "That's what I'm studying right now. I'd like to start my own business as soon as I graduate."

Gramps slapped his hand against the table. "Well, that's just great! Isn't that great, dear?"

Cassie answered all my grandparents' questions about her photography and her hopes for the future. Whenever we could get a word in edgewise, Jack and I both sang her praises.

The girl had a natural talent. She was a gifted photographer, and I'd never seen anyone photograph things from the angles she did. Jack seemed truly impressed not only by her passion, but by her talent as well. I had to admit that it was pretty awesome seeing them support each other's passions.

"If it doesn't work out, you can always go into sports photography and follow your boyfriend around the country," Jack said with a laugh.

Everyone laughed with him, but I knew he wasn't joking. He meant it.

"So, I'd just wake up and take pictures of you all day?" Cassie asked with a teasing smile.

"Sounds like a dream job to me."

"Oh Lord." Gran sighed. "Forgive me, Cassie. I did the best I could with him."

She laughed. "It's okay, Gran. He's perfect just the way he is."

I wanted to stick my finger down my throat and make a gagging sound, but knew that both Jack and Gran would murder me later for being rude, so I stayed quiet.

"Jack, Dean, come help me serve, will you?" Gran asked.

We jumped up from the table and returned carrying steaming dishes filled with homemade Italian food. It smelled fantastic. I couldn't even eat at Italian restaurants after having Gran's meals. She'd ruined me.

"Dig in, please. Cassie first," Gramps said, which was his way of giving us guys a reminder to be hospitable and not attack the food like ravenous wolves.

Cassie reached for the bowl of spaghetti and dished out a huge helping before grabbing two slices of garlic bread and dropping them onto her plate. As she was dishing out some salad onto her plate, her eyes grew wide and she froze, as if she'd only realized how much food she'd piled on.

"Get enough, Kitten?" Jack teased.

"I think I got excited in my serving sizes," she admitted as her cheeks pinked.

"Don't worry about it. Just eat what you can."

"This all looks incredible, Gran," she said, her apology in her eyes. "Thank you so much."

"You're welcome, dear. We're so glad you came."

"Jack, we need to talk about the draft," Gramps mentioned between bites.

"What about it?"

The conversation continued about the upcoming major league draft and Jack's role in it. We'd been told that he'd most likely be picked up by a team in the first round, which was a big deal that included a significant signing bonus.

Cassie apparently didn't know a thing about it, so we all tried to fill her in on how it worked, including the fact that there would be cameramen at the house filming Jack's reaction to whoever drafted him.

When Jack mentioned his two agents, she got even more confused, not understand how he could have agents already when he was still playing in college. After explaining the technicalities to that as well, she seemed to take it all in stride until it finally hit her that Jack getting drafted meant that he was leaving.

"When is it, anyway?" she asked, referring to the draft.

"The first Monday in June," I answered before anyone else could.

"And then when do you leave?" Her eyes were firmly focused on Jack as if the rest of us were no longer a part of the conversation.

"I don't know for sure, but I think right after," he said.

She looked as if she was about to cry. "Like that day?"

"No. But within a week, I think."

Cassie was obviously upset. Tears were going to start falling any second. How had Jack not discussed this with her at all?

I kicked him under the table and this time I didn't miss, wanting to be sure he knew what an insensitive idiot he was.

The mood sobered a bit with Cassie's continued questions and Jack's nonstop answers that did nothing to soothe her. I felt bad enough until Gran asked what they planned on doing about their relationship once Jack left. Then I felt horrible for them.

The look on their faces said it all—they hadn't talked about shit.

I mentioned something about long-distance relationships being awful, and that sent Gran and Gramps into a lecture about how beautiful and wonderful they could be. I had zero experience with it, but it sounded like a crap idea. Then again, if the only other option was to not be together, then I would try it too if I were them.

"Well, that's enough of that talk for one night. I'm sure the kids don't want to think about all this stuff right now." Gran waved a hand in front of her face before rising from the table, followed by Gramps.

"No, it was really nice to hear. Thank you." Cassie smiled, and I wondered if it was just for show.

"We'll get the dishes, Gran. Go lie down," my brother suggested with a smarmy smile.

"Thank you, Jack. We'll just be in the other room," she said before slowly making her way into the living room.

When it was just the three of us, I addressed the elephant in the room. "You two *are* gonna stay together, right?"

Jack turned toward Cassie, who was already staring right at him. "She'll probably be sick of me by then."

"Most likely," she said in response.

I hoped they were kidding, assumed they were kidding, because I couldn't believe the topic had never come up.

Leaning back in my chair, I said, "You guys seriously haven't talked about any of this?"

"Not yet."

"Dude, June isn't that far away. And you'll leave right after the draft. You two are hopeless."

I stifled a shout as Jack rammed his foot into my shin full force.

"Why don't you shut the fuck up, Dean, and worry about your own love life? Or lack thereof."

I shoved out of my chair, sliding it across the kitchen floor with a loud squeak.

"Ow, Jack! Jesus! I was just saying you two should probably get your shit together and actually start doing that whole communicating thing Gran was talking about. 'Cause the last time I checked, you sort of sucked at it."

Jack stood up and pushed his face inches from mine, breathing hard. I tensed and braced myself, worried for a moment that my own brother was going to hit me.

"You're being a real asshole, Dean, you know that?" A muscle jumped in his jaw, telling me I'd struck a nerve.

"Jack! Sit! Down!" Cassie yelled as she tugged at the hem of Jack's shirt.

"Let's go," he gritted out, and Cassie scowled at him.

"What? No. We haven't even done the dishes and—"

"We're leaving. I'll do the dishes when I get back," he shot back, acting like a little bitch.

Cassie sighed and gave me an embarrassed smile. "'Night, Dean."

"'Night, Cass. Sorry." I shrugged, feeling a little bad about the conversation and hoping she didn't hate me, but her smile told me she didn't.

After they left, I looked around at the mess in the kitchen. As my way of apologizing without saying sorry, I rinsed all the dishes off before putting them in the dishwasher. At least when Jack got home, he'd know I wasn't intentionally trying to start a war with him. I'd truly been surprised to hear that they hadn't talked about any of those things.

June was right around the corner, and then what?

I'd already started to feel like Cass was a sister to me. I didn't want to lose her either.

Take It to the Head

EVEN THOUGH I swore I wasn't going to apologize to my brother, I still did. I hated the idea of anything being off between us. Aside from Gran and Gramps, he was all I had in this world, and I needed him on my side.

Jack forgave me easily, telling me that I only pissed him off because I was right and he hadn't wanted to hear it. I told him that I hoped him and Cassie talked about everything before it happened from now on. He told me to stop being such a know-it-all when I didn't know shit about being in a relationship. I wanted to argue with him, but he was right.

On Friday afternoon a couple of days later, Jack poked his head into my doorway, his keys in his hand. "Tonight, we're going to Matt's place to hang out before the softball game. You in?"

Since the baseball team only had practice this week and no games, Jack had been asked to throw out the first pitch for the school's softball team. It was good PR, or so he said, so he'd agreed to it.

"Yeah. Should I just meet you there?"

He nodded. "Yeah. I'm going over to Cassie's now, and

then we'll probably head there together later. I'm trying to convince her to come straight to the game with me, but she keeps telling me no."

"Sounds like your girlfriend," I said with a grin. "What time?"

"About six. And that's good because if she doesn't come with me, then I want her to be with you, Dean. You understand what I'm saying?" He leaned against my door frame.

"Not really. You want me to babysit your girlfriend?"

"No. I want you to make sure you don't leave her alone on the walk there. I want to know that if she isn't with me, she's with the only other person in the world I trust. Okay?"

I grinned back, happy that he needed me. "Okay. You got it."

"Good."

As he turned to go, I asked, "Do you think Melissa will come?"

He shrugged. "I don't know. You should invite her. I'm out," he said, jangling his keys on his way out the door.

I pulled out my phone and sent Melissa a text.

DEAN: Come out with us tonight. Please?

MELISSA: Can't. I'm heading home for the weekend. Next time?

DEAN: I'm holding you to that.

MELISSA: I dare you. :)

That girl. She turned me into a sap with a three-word text message. She knew what she did to me, and she toyed with me at every turn.

Damn it, I wished she was going to be in town.

AT MATT'S FRONT door, I could hear the rowdy shouts from inside, so I didn't bother knocking. I just opened the door and stepped inside Jack's teammate's apartment.

"Dean!" the group of five baseball players all shouted at me in unison.

"Dude, where's your brother?" Matt looked up from the kitchen table where they were playing some sort of drinking game that involved cards.

"Probably with his girlfriend," I said with a shrug.

"It's so fucking weird that Jack has a girlfriend. You know that, right?" he asked before downing a shot, his face contorting into a grimace as he gulped it down.

"It was at first," I said, but it actually wasn't weird at all anymore. What would be weird would be them not being together. I hated the idea.

"Come play with us," Ryan insisted as he stared at the cards in his hands.

I moved to a small space at the table as Matt's girlfriend, Jamie, brought me an extra chair. "Thanks," I said before she wandered back into the kitchen area.

The guys taught me the basics of the drinking game, mostly telling me that I needed to play to really learn it. I was half terrified I'd be a drunken mess by the time I got the hang of it. As they dealt the next hand, I glanced at my phone and wondered where the hell my brother was.

"President!" Cole slurred from across the table as he slammed down a card.

I had no idea what he was talking about, but I pretended to play along. I wasn't sure how much time passed before the front door opened and Jack finally walked through it.

"Carter! What's up, buddy! Hey, Cass," Matt yelled, his eyes trained on the game.

"Hey, Jack. Hey, Cassie," Ryan said without looking up from his hand.

"Finally! Where have you two been?" I asked, wondering what had taken them so long.

"Not sure I'll ever get used to you holding some girl's hand," Brett added, his gaze locked on their joined hands.

"Get used to it, BT, she's not just some girl." Jack planted a kiss on Cassie's cheek, and we collectively groaned at them to get a room, and tossed other good-natured insults their way.

Jack asked to be dealt in and the banter continued, the usual guys being guys and teammates giving each other shit because they could. He was lucky to get along with his teammates. I knew quite a few guys who had left the state to play ball and couldn't stand half of their team. Jack never had that problem. Ever since freshman year, his teammates had welcomed him, and now they were some of his closest friends.

We played a few more hands, and every time I had to drink, I barely sipped my shot. No one else noticed, thank God, otherwise I'd have been too plastered to walk anywhere later, let alone make sure Cassie stayed safe. I had no idea how half these guys still had their eyes open.

When it was time for him to leave, Jack stood up from the table and headed for Cass. What followed was a ridiculous display of affection, including things I wished I could un-see and un-hear.

Once they'd said good-bye, Jack headed for the front door but stopped to address the group. "Make sure she doesn't walk alone to the game."

"I don't need a babysitter," Cassie said, echoing what I'd said earlier.

Jack frowned and shot a look my way. "Dean?"

"I got her, J. I promise we'll all go together. She won't be alone." I smiled at him and Cassie, hoping to ease his worries.

"See you guys at the game."

When Jack closed the door behind him, we all turned toward Cassie like vultures.

"What? Don't look at me, I'm not the crazy one!" she yelled.

"Just so you know, I've never seen him act this way about anyone other than Gran," I told her, hoping she knew that he was just looking out for her. Jack was protective of those he loved and wanted to make sure she stayed safe.

WE WRAPPED UP our drinking game a little while later and left for the softball game. Cassie had her camera with her, something I hadn't noticed earlier when she first came in.

"Are you taking pictures of Jack tonight?"

"I plan on it," she said with a smile.

"Cool."

Matt and Jamie held hands as the seven of us walked in a group toward the far end of campus where the softball field was located. Even though I had no idea what Jack was so concerned about, I wanted to keep my word, so I walked close to Cassie or kept her in view at all times. But then Brett started messing around with me, tapping my shoulder as he ran by, trying to get me to chase him, which I did.

When I realized that Cassie wasn't next to me anymore, I stopped and turned to see her squatting and removing her lens cap. She waved me ahead, signaling that she wanted to shoot pictures of us, so I rejoined the group and let her go to work. I knew she'd yell at me if I tried to stop her. Photography was as important to her as baseball was to Jack.

Figuring I'd give her something to shoot, I knocked Brett's hat off his head and he chased me, trying to punch me in the arm as I ducked and weaved around everyone else to avoid his fist. I glanced back to make sure Cassie was getting all of this when I noticed a man standing way too close to her. Cassie's eyes were huge and she was frozen in place, clutching her camera to her chest.

Shit.

I was too far away to hear what was being said so I walked toward her, wondering what the hell was going on, when I saw her head snap to one side and her hair whip around.

Stunned, I halted in my tracks, unable to believe what I'd

just seen.

"That guy just hit Cassie! Hey!" I shouted at Jack's teammates and started running, not knowing who else was following me, but hoping they all were.

Rushing toward Cassie, I watched helplessly from a distance as the stranger struck her again and she stumbled, knocked off-balance from the force of the punch. My mind spun, not able to comprehend exactly what the hell was happening, but one thing was certain. Jack was going to kill me for letting Cassie get hurt. And I was going to kill this guy for hurting her.

I started sprinting at full speed when the man tore away from her and gunned for me. I came to an abrupt stop, expecting the two of us to collide, but he stopped as well, dangerously close to me. I looked past his shoulder to see Cassie holding her cheek, and furious, I shoved him, wanting to get to her.

"You wanna die?" He was holding something in one hand as he pointed to his hip with the other, which was covered by an oversized shirt. A bulge underneath it looked like it could have been a pistol.

It only took a second of my taking my eyes off him for him to catch me completely off guard. The sound of glass breaking followed by excruciating pain in my head took my breath away. My head snapped back as beer spilled into my eyes, blurring my vision, and my knees buckled. I tried to scream for Cassie to run, but I couldn't formulate the words as the rest of the world went black.

Blink. Pain.

Blink. Pain.

Blink. Pain.

Dazed, I had the feeling of being dragged along, my feet scraping against the concrete like they no longer worked. It almost felt like I was floating, but the pain that followed felt nothing like floating. It felt like hell.

When I opened my eyes, I realized that I was in someone's arms. I glanced to my left, my head feeling like it weighed a thousand pounds, to find Brett practically carrying me across campus, his arm looped underneath mine.

I recognized where we were. "Hey," I croaked out, and he slowed down.

"Thank God. Are you okay?" He glanced at me, his eyes wide and worried.

"My head hurts like hell." I reached up and pulled my hand away, surprised to see blood wetting my fingertips.

"It was worse before. It's actually almost stopped," he said, and I assumed he was referring to the blood.

It was then when I noticed his shirt was stained red down the front. I pointed at it.

"Mine?"

"Yours." He nodded, pulling the fabric away from his body before letting it go.

"What the hell did he hit me with, anyway?"

"A forty-ounce bottle of beer," he answered, shaking his head at the memory.

No wonder my head hurts so damn bad.

"Where are we going?"

"To the campus police station," he said, and it all came back to me in a rush of pain and fury.

"Where's Cassie? Is she okay? What the fuck, Brett? Where is she? Where's Cassie?"

I tried to pull out of his grip, desperate to find Jack's girl, but I was too unsteady. My vision was still a little blurry, and my head pounded with each beat of my heart.

"I don't know," he said with a shrug.

That answer couldn't have been more wrong. I shoved at him, trying to push him off me.

"You don't know? We have to go back!" I shouted. "We have to fucking go back and get her!"

"Dean?"

I thought I heard Jack's voice coming from somewhere so I called his name out, although not very loudly in case I was hearing things.

"Dean!"

A figure in the distance sprinted toward us. When he got closer, I could see Jack's face looked horrified and confused.

"What happened?" he demanded. "Why are you so bloody? Are you okay?"

Jack reached for me, patting me over to see where I'd gotten hurt as he looked around, frantic. Then he froze and said, "Wait. Where's Cassie?"

I looked into his eyes, terrified that I'd let him down and he'd never forgive me.

"Where's Cassie, Dean?

"I don't know," I admitted. "But you've gotta go find her, Jack."

"What do you mean, you don't know where she is?" he growled, but more at Brett than at me.

"Dean was unconscious, man. What was I supposed to do?" Brett said, trying to explain.

"Where are you two going?" Jack looked at the two of us as if suddenly realizing that we were walking into campus instead of out of it.

"To the police station," Brett said before I could.

I grabbed my brother's arm. "Jack, please go find Cassie. I'll be fine. Some guy hit her."

His face turned cold with rage. "What do you mean, some guy hit her?"

"Just go. Ask questions later," I begged him.

Jack sucked in a sharp breath to calm himself and looked me in the eye, his expression filled with pain. "Are you sure you're okay?"

"Yes." *But I'll never forgive myself if Cassie isn't.* "Go find her. I'll be fine," I said, and he didn't hesitate for a second before he took off running.

Brett propped me up as we headed toward the campus police office in the distance, its blue light illuminating the small building. We walked in silence, neither of us knowing what to say.

When we reached the door, Brett pulled it open and shouted, "We need some help out here."

An older guy came around from behind a door and almost

dropped his mug of coffee when he saw us. "Shit. Are you okay? What happened?" He placed the mug on top of the counter and moved around the desk that separated us.

"I think it looks worse than it is," I said with a smile before wincing from the pain. Even the light in the room hurt; it was too bright, too glaring.

"Sergio, get out here," the first cop yelled, and another guy appeared, his mouth half-filled with food.

"What the—"

"You boys want to tell us what happened to you tonight? I'm Officer Candalle, by the way, and this is my partner, Officer Santos."

"I'm Dean, and this is Brett."

"And you're both students here at Fullton State?"

"Yes. Mind if I sit?" I motioned toward the uncomfortable-looking metal chair in the corner.

"No, of course. Do you need some ice?" Officer Candalle asked.

I shrugged. "I don't know." I honestly had no idea what I needed. All I knew was that my head hurt like a bitch and probably needed stitches. "Maybe some ibuprofen or something for the pain?"

Officer Santos frowned. "We're not allowed to give you medication. Sorry. Maybe we should get you to the hospital. We can ask you questions from there," he suggested, but I shook my head.

"Yeah, man, maybe we should get you looked at," Brett said. I'd almost forgotten he was still there.

"Not yet. I need you guys to catch the piece of shit who hurt my sister," I blurted without thinking.

Calling Cassie my sister had seemed like the smart thing to do. I knew from watching TV shows that if you weren't related, people didn't give you information. She was important to Jack, which meant she was important to me, so I needed to know everything there was to know about her situation.

Santos sat down across from me before giving his partner an order. "Lance, go grab the camera, please."

"You're going to record this?" I asked, assuming he was going to film my statement.

"Photograph. It's standard procedure. We need evidence of all your injuries." He glanced at Brett. "Do you have any injuries, or is that blood all his?"

Brett shook his head. "It's all his."

"We'll still photograph your shirt," he said as Officer Candalle came back carrying a digital camera similar to Cassie's.

"Can you point out your injuries?" he asked, and when I pointed to the top of my head, he snapped a few photos.

He studied me, his eyes narrowed slightly. "Does your face hurt at all anywhere?"

"No, why?" I looked at Brett, wondering why he was asking.

Candalle shook his head. "Nothing major. Just a few superficial cuts. Can you tell us what happened while we take the rest of the pictures?"

He snapped away, taking pictures of my head, my face, and Brett's shirt, while Santos typed quickly on his laptop.

"We were walking toward campus," I said, "on our way to the softball fields, when some guy came out of nowhere and attacked my sister. She was behind us, so no one noticed at first."

I felt light-headed, so I put my head between my legs for a moment. The room was quiet, and the officers waited patiently until I could continue.

"When I turned around, I saw her head fly to the side. He'd hit her. We all started running back for her at that point, but he hit her again. Then the next thing I remember was the guy telling me he had a gun, asking me if I wanted to die, and then I woke up with Brett carrying me across campus. But I'm sure more happened after I passed out. You have to ask my sister."

"Can you describe the assailant?" Santos asked, still typing.

"He was about five foot eleven, but skinny. Looked like he weighed maybe a buck fifty, not muscular in build, but quick. He was damn fast on his feet," I said, searching my mind for other details. "Oh, he had dark blond hair that went to his shoulders. It was stringy, and looked dirty. That's all I remember."

Candalle nodded and set aside the camera. "That's great, really helpful. Anything else you can think of? Did he have any distinguishing marks that you can remember? Any tattoos? Scars?"

"Not that I recall," I said, feeling like a failure.

"What about you, Brett. Did you get a good look at him?"

Brett shifted on his feet. "I didn't, actually. I just saw Dean fall to the ground, and I knew I needed to get him out of the situation."

Santos rose to his feet and came over to where I sat. "I'm not a doctor, but I did have some medical training. Do you want me to look at your head?"

"Please," I said, and relaxed a little with relief.

He dug around in his desk and found a pair of latex gloves. Once he'd snapped them on, he leaned forward and gently moved sections of my hair aside to check my scalp. As he did, small shards of brown glass fell to the floor.

"It looks nasty, but it's already stopped bleeding for the most part. I don't think you need stitches, but keep an eye on it. I'm not a doctor, so I'd advise you to stop by the ER or urgent care and get it checked out."

"Understood. Thank you, though," I said.

As he pulled off his gloves and tossed them into the trash can, I closed my eyes for a second, wishing I had something for the pain. My head hurt like a bitch.

"You mentioned your sister. Where is she now?" Candalle asked, and I shifted in my seat.

"I don't know. I hope she's home by now, but I don't know."

"Can you find out? And what's your full name and hers?"

I nodded, reaching for the cell phone in my pocket. "Dean Carter and Cassie Andrews," I said as I called my brother's number and held the phone away from my ear as it rang.

"Dean," Jack said, sounding relieved when he answered the phone.

"Hey. Do you have her? Is she okay?" I asked, trying not to sound as frantic as I felt.

Candalle leaned closer to listen.

"We're at her apartment. I was going to help her clean up her face," Jack started to say, and Candalle overheard and lifted a hand in the air.

"Don't let him clean off her injuries," he said in a hushed tone. "We need to photograph them too and get a statement."

I nodded and told Jack what the office had said.

"Okay. Are they coming now?"

I looked up at the officers and they both nodded. "Yeah, they're on their way."

Ending the call, I closed my eyes, willing the pain to subside, but knowing it never would on its own.

Brett stood up and said to the officers, "Do you think you could give us a ride to my car and then I'll take Dean home?"

Santos nodded. "Of course, no problem. Dean, can you give us your phone number so we can get in touch with you if we have any more questions?"

I rattled off my number before pushing up from the chair. Much to my annoyance, I was still a bit wobbly on my feet.

"I got you." Brett came over and reached out to brace me once more.

"Can you give us the address where your sister is?"

"Shit," I said before pulling out my phone again and texting Jack. He responded within seconds, and I gave the cops the information as we made our way to the back of the small station house.

Buckled into the backseat of the police car, I remembered that Melissa was out of town and would have no idea what had happened. I didn't know why she popped into my head when she did, but I fired off a text message to give her the CliffsNotes version of what happened tonight, and suggested that she check on her best friend.

My phone immediately rang and Melissa's name flashed on the screen.

"Dean? Are you okay? What happened exactly? Where's Cassie? And Jack?"

Her voice was shrill, the pitch so high I couldn't handle it at the moment. "I can't talk right now, I'm sorry. My head hurts."

"Okay, okay, I understand. I wish I was there."

"I'm glad you weren't," I admitted, thankful that she hadn't been around tonight because she might have gotten hurt as well. The very thought made me sick.

"I'm going to check on Cassie. I'll see you soon. Call me if you need anything, okay?"

I promised her that I would, and put my phone in my pocket. My head continued to pound. The officers dropped us off in front of Matt's apartment, and Brett and I climbed out of the car.

After we thanked the officers for the ride, they assured me that they'd be in touch.

Brett motioned toward the stairs. "Do you want to come up first? I'm sure Matt has some aspirin or something for your head."

"Yeah. Do you think they're even here?" I hadn't thought about anyone other than Cassie for what felt like hours, but was more like a handful of minutes.

"They're here," he said with a grimace. "They've been blowing up my phone."

We walked slowly, Brett still helping me keep my balance as we navigated the stairs. When he raised his hand to knock on Matt's door, I reached for my head.

"Please don't."

"Shit. Sorry," he said before turning the knob and pushing the door open.

Matt and Jamie jumped to their feet and rushed toward us. "Fuck, man," Matt said, "we've been so worried."

I tried to wave them off, but they took me out of Brett's care, each holding one of my arms.

"Seeing you collapse like that was some scary shit, man," Matt said, which made me think about what it must have looked like from their perspective. "Are you okay?" he asked as they helped me toward their couch.

"My head is killing me. It feels like it's murdering me with every breath I take. Please tell me you have some ibuprofen or something for this pain."

Jamie headed for the kitchen and called over her shoulder, "I'll go get you some. Anything else?"

"Just the ibuprofen. And water. Please."

I leaned my head back against the couch and closed my eyes, begging for a reprieve from the pain, but all I saw was a different kind of pain. Cassie getting hit, and me running toward her. My eyes shot open to stop seeing the image of her like that, and Jamie was there, holding an Advil bottle and a water.

"Your hair." She studied me and sucked in a breath through clenched teeth.

"That bad?" I had no idea what I looked like, and wasn't looking forward to getting in front of a mirror.

"It's pretty matted," she said, frowning. "Is Cassie okay? Have you talked to her?"

"I talked to Jack. He's with her now."

"Oh, good. I bet he's pissed, though," she said before looking at Matt and Brett.

Matt winced. "I'm sure we'll get an earful the next time we see him."

"Speaking of, I need to call him before we leave."

I pulled out my phone and glanced at Brett, who stood next to the couch, refusing to sit down in case the blood transferred from his shirt and stained the furniture. I hadn't been as thoughtful.

"Where are you?" Jack said instead of saying hello.

"At Matt's. Are you staying at Cassie's tonight?" I asked, already assuming the answer.

"Yeah."

"Can I stay there too?"

"Hold on." He covered the phone, muting his voice for a moment. "She says it's fine."

"Okay, cool. Do you guys need anything?"

"I don't think so. Hold on, I'll double-check." He covered

the phone once more before saying, “She says no.”

“Do you think Cassie will care if I stay there all weekend?”

The last thing I wanted was to give Gran and Gramps something extra to worry about. If I looked as bad as Jamie seemed to think I did, I could only imagine how Gran would react when she saw me.

No, it was best to lay low for a couple of days until I could pass muster.

“She won’t care,” Jack said. “But make sure Gran knows we’re both staying here before you leave.”

“I’ll talk to her.”

“Okay. See you soon.”

I put away my phone and moved to stand up. “I’m ready,” I said to Brett, and then looked at Jamie. “Thanks so much for the aspirin and water.”

“Of course. Feel better, and tell Cassie to call me, okay?” she said before giving me a cautious hug.

“I will. See you later, Matt. Sorry about the couch.” I glanced at it and grimaced at the small dots of blood I’d left behind.

“Don’t worry about it,” he said, waving me off. “Drive safe.”

Playing House

AFTER SOME DISAGREEMENT because he was worried about my driving, Brett finally agreed to follow me as I slowly drove Gran's car home. It was late and I was tired and felt like shit, but I couldn't leave her and Gramps without a car for the weekend. Thank goodness she had an extra set of keys, so I just left the car in the driveway and didn't have to go inside and risk her seeing me like this.

Afterward Brett dropped me off in front of Cassie's apartment, and I told him it would be better if he didn't help me inside. I had no idea what seeing him would do to Jack, and didn't want to risk some sort of showdown just as my head had started to ease up its incessant throbbing. I thanked him for the ride, assured him I could get upstairs on my own, and sent him on his way.

Only once I was standing outside Cassie's apartment in the dark did I realize that I hadn't called Gran. It was late enough that I knew she'd already be in bed, but I had to get this over with. Otherwise she'd send out an APB tomorrow morning when she realized that neither of us were in our beds.

The phone rang, still too loud for my liking, and Gran answered, her voice thin and sleepy.

"Hi, Gran. I'm sorry to wake you."

"It's okay, dear." There was a rustle in the background, and her voice sharpened. "What's going on? Is everything okay?"

I sucked in a quick breath, preparing myself for the lie I was about to tell, and hating it. I never lied to Gran. But if I told her the truth, she'd worry herself sick and make me come home so she could take care of me herself.

"Everything's fine. I just wanted you to know that Jack and I are going to stay at Cassie's this weekend, if that's okay with you. Melissa went home, and Cassie's all alone and doesn't like staying by herself. It makes her nervous, I guess."

I willed myself to shut up and stop my babbling. Too many details, and Gran would know I was lying. I held my breath, praying I hadn't overdone it.

"I guess that's okay," she said slowly, "since you'll both be there. But no funny business. Tell Jack that goes for him, as well. I guess I'll see you boys on Sunday then?"

"Yep. Thanks, Gran. Call if you need anything."

"I will. I love you."

"Love you too. And sorry for waking you up."

She huffed into the phone. "It's okay. I'd rather you wake me up than me wake up and be worried because you aren't here."

"That's what I figured. Okay, good night, Gran."

"Good night, honey."

I blew out a relieved breath after ending the call. I'd always been a horrible liar, and was surprised and thankful that I'd gotten away with it this once. There was no way Gran would have let me stay here with Cassie if she knew what had really happened tonight. Not that I could keep it from her forever; I just wasn't ready to go home yet. I felt like I needed to be with someone who'd experienced what I did.

I knocked on the door softly before opening it a few inches to peek inside.

"Kitten, Dean's here," Jack called out to her from the living room. Then he walked over to me and gave me a bear hug. "I'm glad you're okay, little brother."

"Me too. How's she?" I pointed toward the bedroom just as Cassie emerged from it, her face bruised and swollen.

"Dean, are you okay?" She ran straight to me and squeezed me tightly, locking her arms around me for a moment before releasing me.

"I'm fine. How are you? Are you okay?" I'd be okay, I was pretty sure, so now I was more concerned with her injuries.

She nodded. "You have no idea how scary it was to see you hurt like that." She shuddered, and I thought about how many times I'd heard that exact sentiment already tonight.

"And you have no idea how horrible it was to see some guy hitting you," I said, unable to hide the anger that welled inside me as I replayed the events in my head.

"Can we not talk about that right now?" Jack's voice was tight, his expression murderous.

"I'm just happy you're okay," Cassie said as she reached out to touch strands of my hair. "Does your head hurt?"

"Like a bitch," I muttered.

"Before I forget, Melis said you could stay in her room."

"Yeah? Well, I was going to stay in there even if she said I couldn't," I said as a manic laugh escaped. "It's okay if I take a shower, right?"

I felt gross, and needed to get the glass and dried blood out of my hair. Plus, I ached all over, and the thought of twenty minutes under the hot spray sounded like heaven right now.

"Of course." Cassie patted me on the shoulder and pushed me in the right direction. "There's a shower in her room. Extra towels are under the sink."

Jack reached for her hand and pulled her toward the living room couch. "We'll be out here when you're done," he said before sitting down and pulling her onto his lap.

I didn't need any more images of the two of them burned into my brain, so I walked into Melissa's room and shut the door behind me. Scanning it quickly, I took it all in—the collage of pictures on the walls, the framed and signed movie posters, perfume bottles on her dresser, necklaces scattered over every free inch of space.

And her bed. Jesus, I'd never seen so many pillows in my life. Who needed that many, and how did my tiny pixie not get swallowed alive by all of them?

The room smelled like her, like lemons and sunshine. *Hell, I might move right in and never leave.*

Thankful that girls were a lot cleaner than guys, I turned on the shower and adjusted the nozzle. When it was the perfect lukewarm temperature, I stripped off my clothes and cautiously stepped inside.

The water hit my head, reminding me just how injured I was, and I stifled a shout and winced before moving out of its path. Frustrated, I stood there for a second, not entirely sure how to do this on my own. I couldn't see where the blood or glass was, and every time I tried to run my fingers through my hair to check, I wanted to scream out in pain.

Finally, I decided to turn the water down so the pressure wasn't so strong. When it was barely flowing from the showerhead, I backed into it and allowed it to drip on top of my head. It still hurt, and I found myself wishing that Melissa were here so she could help me.

Once I felt certain there was no glass in my hair, I scanned the edges of her tub and reached for a bottle of pink shampoo. It was either that or something purple, so my options were limited. After squeezing a small amount into my hand, I sniffed at it. *Watermelon.* No wonder she always smelled like fruity scents and summer.

Rubbing the soap into a lather on my head was almost torturous. The soap stung my open wound, and the blood had caked on so thick, I wasn't sure it would ever rinse out. I stared down at my feet, almost in a daze as I watched the water swirl around them in a mixture of pink bubbles and red.

I wasn't sure how long I stood there; I just kept my head in the streaming water until it started flowing clear around my feet. All I knew was that I was shriveled up like a prune, and it felt like I'd spent an hour under the spray. When I determined that I'd done the best I could with my head, I turned off the water and stepped out, dripping as I searched for a towel under the sink.

After wrapping a blue-and-white striped beach towel around my waist, I walked back into the living room where Jack and Cassie still sat wrapped up in each other. Jack was running a finger down Cassie's cheek and looking at her like she was the most beautiful girl in the world.

I cleared my throat. "Remind me that it's going to fucking hurt next time I try to wash my hair."

"I'm really tired," Cassie said. "I'm gonna go to bed, okay?" She pushed off Jack's lap and walked toward me. "Love you both." She gave me another hug before whispering, "I'm so glad you're okay."

"So much for our weekend alone, huh?" Jack said with a frown.

I wanted to smack my brother for making me feel unwanted, but then Cassie looked at me, and our eyes locked for a moment.

"It's okay. This is better, anyway," she said, and I stuck my tongue out at Jack as she walked into her bedroom and closed the door behind her.

I yawned. "I'm think I'm gonna get some sleep too, bro. Sorry if I ruined your romantic weekend."

Jack stood up and wrapped me in a manly hug. "You didn't ruin anything. I'm glad you're here. And I'm really glad you're okay. I don't know what I would do if anything ever happened to you. Or her." He nodded toward the bedroom door.

"I know. Same here."

"Let me look at your head." He tried to see the top of my head, but we were basically the same height these days, much to Jack's annoyance.

"Bend down a little," he said, and I did as he asked. His fingers tugged at my hair, parting the strands so he could see my scalp, and I winced before pulling away.

"That hurts. What are you doing?"

"Sorry. There's still some glass in there. I'll stop. Let me see the cut." He searched through my hair again, trying to be gentle, but he was a guy with big hands and lacked the ability, even though he tried. "Found it."

"How's it look?"

"It's pretty swollen and a little mangled, but the cut itself looks good. It's not bleeding at all anymore." He stood up straight. "Hey, before I forget, did you talk to Gran?"

"I lied to her," I admitted, feeling guilty and trying to ease my conscience.

He laughed. "You," he pointed a finger at me, "lied to Gran? Sweet little old Gran?"

"Shut up, man. I feel bad enough, but I had to."

"What'd you tell her?"

I blew out a breath. "I just said that Cassie was all alone for the weekend and it made her uncomfortable. So I said that she wanted us to stay with her."

A loud hoot of laughter came from Jack. "And she believed that? Shit, she would have never believed that coming from me." He stood there, shaking his head and grinning at me.

"That's because coming from you, it would have been a lie."

"But it was a lie! So," he said, jabbing me in the chest with his damn hard finger, "you lied to Gran. How does it feel? Are you going to cry yourself to sleep tonight?"

I turned to walk away but stopped at the door to Melissa's bedroom. "You're an ass. It's not like I could tell her the truth. She would have made the three of us stay there all weekend and put us on lockdown until school started Monday morning."

Jack nodded, sobering. "No, you're right. You'd better hope she doesn't find out what happened, or she's going to flip."

"It's okay. If she hears anything," I said with a smirk, "I'll just blame you. She'll believe this was all your idea."

"I'm impressed. Now go to bed. Love you." He gave my shoulder a squeeze.

I smiled. "Love you too."

"Cass already put some Advil on the nightstand in the room for you. There's a couple water bottles in there too."

"Tell her thanks for me."

I had just lay down in Melissa's bed as my phone beeped.

> MELISSA: *I'm sick over everything that happened. I just wanted you to know that I was thinking about you, and I wish I was there to take care of you.*

Damn. I wish she was here to take care of me too.

MY EYES OPENED as soon as I realized I wasn't in my firm bed at home. Instead I was lying on something that felt like a cloud, surrounded by fluffy pillows that hugged my head and body. I blinked a few times before the room came into focus, and the memory of last night came crashing back to me.

I was in Melissa's room. Melissa wasn't here. And some guy broke a forty over my head and punched Cassie in the face.

When I sat up too quickly, my head spun and I felt woozy, so I lay back down, allowing Melissa's pillows to cradle me in a fluffy hug.

My head ached; my brain beat like a bongo drum inside it each time my heart beat. When I could no longer stand it, I grabbed the bottle of pain reliever and poured a few into my palm before tossing them into my mouth, and washed them down with some of the water Cassie had left on the nightstand. *Please, let them work quickly.*

Jack and Cassie's voices filtered through my closed door, and I was thankful they were already awake.

I moved slowly, not wanting to encourage the pain in my head as I padded toward the bathroom. Looking around at the floor, I realized that I didn't have anything to wear other than what I'd showed up in last night, so I reached for my shorts but left my bloody T-shirt in a heap on the floor.

When I stepped out into the living area, the scent of bacon assaulted my senses, triggering some major drool. I followed my nose into the kitchen.

"Mmm, bacon."

Jack turned from the stove and raised his eyebrows at me. "Dude. Shirt?"

"It's all bloody. I don't have anything else to wear."

Cassie hopped up from the bar stool at the snack bar. "Jack has some shirts here. I'll go get you one."

The bruises on her face had deepened in color, and I found it hard to look at her without getting upset.

"I can't believe you're cooking," I said to Jack.

"He won't let me do a thing, Dean!" Cassie came back to the kitchen to hand me a plain black tee, and I nodded a silent thank-you. "He's been babying me all night and morning."

"It's called taking care of you," Jack said. "And I'm trying really hard, but you're being a pain in the ass about it." He pointed at her with a greasy spatula before turning his attention back to the sizzling bacon.

"Just let him help you, Cass," I said as I pulled the shirt over my head. "He's never done it before, and I want to watch." I raised my eyebrows to waggle them at her, but cringed at the discomfort as I slid onto the bar stool next to her.

"Are you all right?" she asked.

"Yeah, it's just that facial expressions tend to hurt a little."

"Tell me about it. I had no idea how much my jaw moved until it hurt every time I moved it." She placed her hand against the side of her face.

Jack set a plate with a pile of bacon in front of us and then started cracking eggs into the same pan. "Eat," he demanded.

"Gladly." I reached for a slice of bacon and bit down, and the grease and flavor exploded in my mouth like heaven. "So good. Why is bacon so good?"

Cassie moaned as she took a bite as well, and when Jack turned around, his eyes firmly focused on her mouth.

"Kitten. Don't make those sounds during breakfast. We have company." He nodded in my direction, and she rolled her eyes.

"Dean's not company. He's family," she said, and I couldn't stop my smile.

"Thanks, sis." I nudged her shoulder with mine.

"I heard you told the cops I was your sister," she said, still chewing on her first piece while I'd already moved on to my fourth.

I shrugged. "It just came out. You're not mad, right?"

She pulled her head back in surprise. "Why would I ever be mad at that?"

"I don't know."

Jack joined us at the bar, carrying one plate filled with eggs and another piled high with toast. He set them down between us and I tried to stifle my shock.

"Wow. Jack, I've never—"

"Just say thanks and shut up."

"Thanks. Shut up," I said as I stabbed my fork at the pile of eggs.

Cassie leaned over and planted a kiss on his cheek. "This was really sweet. Thank you."

"Anything for you," he said.

I started to fake gag like I normally would to tease Jack, but stopped myself. The truth was that it was nice seeing my brother so happy, so I decided to take the high road this time.

"I talked to the cops this morning while you were in the shower," Jack said. "Still no word on the guy or your camera."

I choked, pounding on my chest with my fist. "What? What happened to your camera?"

Cassie turned to face me, her expression sad. "You don't know? I guess you wouldn't, huh? He stole my camera. That's what started the whole thing."

I dropped my fork and it fell to my plate with a clang. Stunned, I just sat there, shaking my head. "I didn't know that. I'm so sorry, Cassie."

"I'm going to find it," Jack said with conviction. "A guy like that doesn't steal a camera just to keep it. He's going to try to sell it somewhere and when he does, I'm going to find it. And if I don't, I'm going to buy her a new one."

Cassie smiled, but it didn't reach her eyes. Her camera represented her future, and I could only imagine what having that taken away must feel like.

We spent the rest of the meal in silence, each of us lost in our own thoughts. When I finished eating, I stood up and set my dish into the sink.

Jack's tired eyes met mine. "Leave it. I'll get it."

"I can clean up. You cooked," I said, but he shook his head.

"No. I got it. Go sit down. Rest that hard-ass head of

yours."

"You're worse than Gran." I sighed, and he tossed a piece of toast at my back as I headed for the couch.

Cassie stood up and started gathering the other dishes. "You don't have to clean up, Jack. I can help."

"I know I don't have to. I want to," he said as he took the dishes from her hands. "Let me do this, Kitten, please. I wasn't there last night, and it kills me, okay? I feel fucking helpless. And don't get me started on the bruises and cuts on your beautiful face. Just let me do this for you. It makes me feel better."

I watched him trying to convince her, knowing it wasn't the whole truth. Nothing he did for Cassie would make him feel better unless it was catching the guy who did this to her. When she relented and headed to her bedroom for a nap, Jack and I talked about how to do exactly that.

"I want you to show me where everything happened," Jack insisted. "And tell me what he looked like, anything you can remember."

"No problem. What are you going to do?"

"I'm going to drive there every fucking day until we find this guy. He wasn't there for no reason. He has to live close by or hang out there. He's going to show back up, and I'm going to be there to greet him."

I couldn't argue with him because I felt the same way he did. Jack wanted to find the asshole that hurt his family, and so did I.

"I'll look for him too," I offered, but he snapped at me.

"No. I don't want you anywhere near this asshole again. You can help me try to find her camera."

"Okay." I nodded. That sounded reasonable. "How do we do that?"

"We'll look online. Craigslist, eBay, anywhere they sell used goods. But I'm betting this guy probably doesn't have a computer, so that might be pointless, but we should search anyway," he said as he paced Cassie's living room. "And I'll go to the local pawn shops, tell them to be on the lookout for it. I don't know. Whatever else you can think of that might help."

"Is she all right? I can't believe he stole her camera."

Jack stopped his pacing and hung his head, wrapping his hands behind his neck in frustration. "She's really sad. She worked hard to save for it and now it's gone. But I'm going to buy her a new one, a better one. She'll probably hate it and won't want to accept it, but I'm doing it anyway. She's too good at it, and her future is too important."

I studied Jack for a moment. "I never thought I'd ever hear myself say this, but you're a really good boyfriend."

"Damn right I am," he said, giving me a mock snarl before heading into the kitchen to clean up.

"You're a good brother too," I added, and his lips curled up into a smile.

MELISSA WAS SUPPOSED to stay at her parents' house until Monday morning, but she came back early, bursting through the front door Saturday afternoon when we least expected her. Her jaw dropped open when she saw me and Cassie sitting on the couch, and she ran over to us, wrapping us both in a hug.

"Oh, Cassie, your face," she said with a concerned whine.

"I know." Cassie sighed.

"And Dean. How's your head?" Melissa touched the side of my face, and I lost myself in her eyes.

"Still hurts," I said with a small smile. "I thought you weren't coming back until Monday."

"It didn't feel right to stay away from you guys. I know I can't do anything, but I just wanted to be here. Where's Jack?"

Cassie pointed toward her bedroom. "Napping."

"I could use one of those, actually." I stretched and looked at Melissa. "But now that you're here, should I go home?" I pushed off the couch and hoped like hell I could still stay. I really hadn't planned on leaving anytime soon.

"No, no. Of course not. You can still stay in my room," Melissa said, and I breathed out in relief.

"Thank God. I wasn't ready to see Gran and Gramps yet," I admitted.

"Come on." She looped her arm around my waist and walked with me to her bedroom as if I was too injured to do it myself.

"I like Nurse Melissa."

She urged me toward her bed and watched as I lay down on top of the covers. Smiling, she reached for an extra blanket and pulled it over me.

"Do you need anything?" She ran her finger across my

head lightly, inspecting the wound. "Dean, that looks really awful."

"I know."

I'd checked it out in the mirror earlier this morning. The wound was puffy and pink, its edges dark with dried blood. I guess if I'd gotten stitches like the cop recommended, it wouldn't have pulled open again.

"Can I get you some more aspirin or water?"

Sensing that she wanted to be helpful, I let her. "Sure. Both would be great."

Melissa left for only a moment before she returned to place the aspirin in my palm and the glass of water in my other hand. After I swallowed the pills, she reached for the glass and set it on her nightstand. Then to my surprise, the bed dipped as she crawled in next to me, and rubbed my back as I closed my eyes. It was a small gesture, kind and comforting.

I fell asleep to the feel of her fingertips drawing loops on my shoulder blades.

Blood, Sweat, and Tears

EVEN THOUGH I'D promised Jack I wouldn't drive around and look for the guy, I still did. It had been three weeks since the assault, and I couldn't sit there and do nothing when I knew that I was the only one who would recognize the jerk the moment I laid eyes on him. I imagined seeing him on the street and wondered what I'd do, not having the faintest idea.

Which was exactly why Jack was better at being bad than I was. He knew exactly what he'd do, and he'd do it without hesitation.

He scoured the Internet every night, searching all the resale websites, and visited every pawn shop in the area personally, describing the camera and asking them to keep an eye out. I'd also looked online, checking out Craigslist for not only our county, but the next two counties over, just in case the guy was smarter than we'd given him credit for.

I'd avoided telling Gran what happened that night and she never asked, but I had a sneaking suspicion that she somehow knew anyway. She was psychic like that.

After that weekend, I'd convinced Jack to stop only hanging out at Cassie's place and to bring her by the house more.

Not that I didn't want to go over there and see Melissa, but I'd asked him more for our grandparents' sake, knowing that they missed him and would never ask him themselves.

He'd done as I asked, which thrilled Gran and Gramps. They loved it when we were all at home, and adding Cassie to the mix was icing on the cake. Gran said it was too quiet when we were gone, and I wondered how lonely she'd be once Jack got drafted. Granted, I'd still be living there, but it wouldn't be the same. Jack had always been the louder one.

My cell phone rang as I sat reading a textbook on my bed. I didn't recognize the number. "Hello?"

"Is this Dean Carter?"

I stopped reading and placed the book to my side. "Yes?"

"This is Officer Santos from the Fullton State Police Department," he said, as if I wouldn't remember who he was.

"I remember you. Did you get him?"

"We got him," he said with a smile in his voice. "He was trying to pawn the camera he'd stolen. He's at the downtown station. Do you think you could come here and ID him?"

I sat up immediately and hopped to my feet. "I'll be right there."

"Great. Thanks."

I grabbed my keys and jumped into Gran's car. Once I arrived at the station, I dialed Jack's phone before I left the car, knowing that he'd be in the middle of his new after-practice ritual of driving the streets, looking for the guy.

His breathing was heavy when he answered. "What's up?"

"They got him," I said, cutting straight to the chase.

"The guy?"

"They caught him trying to pawn Cassie's camera. He's in jail. I have to head down there to identify him." I hoped he could hear the relief in my voice.

"Can I get her camera for her?" Before I could answer, he asked, "Do you want me to come with you? I should probably come with you." His tone turned defensive, and I knew he wanted to see the guy for himself.

"I'll find out about the camera when I get there, but I think it's evidence now, so she probably can't have it back yet," I told him. "I'm in the police parking lot now, so I'll just head in and identify him. You should go tell Cassie they got him."

"I will. Thanks, and be careful," he said.

"It's fine. I'll call you after."

I shoved the phone in my pocket and sucked in a breath as I walked through the station's glass doors. A woman sat behind a reception desk in the waiting room, finishing up a call as I headed toward her.

"Can I help you?" she asked when she put down the phone.

"I'm Dean Carter. Officer Santos asked me to come down to identify a suspect."

"Have a seat, please." She pointed toward the row of chairs. "I'll be right back."

I sat down and tapped my feet, my nerves stretched taut as I waited for her to return. I definitely wasn't looking forward to seeing this guy again. Just being here brought back unpleasant memories.

The glass doors swung open, and I was surprised when Brett walked in.

"What are you doing here?" I asked.

He gave me a friendly slap on the back before sitting next to me. "Jack told me they got the guy. Thought I could help identify him."

"Cool. Thanks. How was Jack?"

Brett blew out a breath. "Mixed. He seemed relieved, but I think he wanted to catch the guy before the cops did."

"That wouldn't have been a good thing."

He nodded. "I know. We all tried to tell him that, but he's unreasonable when it comes to Cassie."

"Nah, he's just in love. And Jack's protective of people he cares about," I said, used to defending my brother's level of intensity.

The receptionist seemed surprised to see Brett when she came back to the waiting room. "Oh, now there's two of you? I'll let Officer Santos know. He should be right out."

Brett and I made small talk as we waited for Santos. I wondered what the hell was taking so long; it wasn't as if the station was busy. No sooner had the thought entered my mind than the doors to my right swung open.

Officer Santos stepped toward us, his hand extended, "Dean. Brett. Good to see you again. You're looking much better than the last time I saw you," he said to me with a nod.

"Thanks."

"Follow me," Santos said, and we trailed behind.

He led us down a long corridor and into a viewing room.

A large pane of glass that I hoped was a one-way mirror was inset in one of the walls, and five guys stood on the other side of it, looking like they'd rather be anywhere else than here.

Officer Santos explained how things would work. "You can see them, but they can't see you. They know you're in here, though. Just let me know if you recognize—"

"Three," Brett and I both blurted at the same time.

Officer Santos nodded before pressing a button on the wall. "You can send them back, thanks." He turned toward us and shook his head with a grin. "You didn't even let me do the fun part."

"What part was that?" I asked.

"Asking them to step forward, turn to the left, then to the right. It's the only part that makes them really nervous."

"Sorry. I'd rather just get this all over with," I admitted, although the idea of torturing the prick sounded fun in a sadistic, vengeful way.

"I understand. Thank you both for coming in."

Officer Santos walked us out the door and when I asked about Cassie's camera, told me that it was state's evidence now and it had to stay with them until after the trial, which could be months.

Cassie would hate hearing that, but I felt a little better knowing that Jack was going to buy her a new one, even if she claimed to not want one.

As Brett and I pushed through the doors and walked into the warm night, I said, "I'm so glad that's behind us."

Brett laughed. "You and me both."

"Thanks for coming down, man."

"Anytime. See ya at school."

We gave each other a knuckled fist bump before heading in opposite directions.

Personally, I was just thankful the piece of shit was behind bars and couldn't hurt anyone anymore. I was also glad the cops had found him before Jack did.

Draft Day

WITH DRAFT DAY for the major league right around the corner, our household had been far more tense than usual. Hell, our household wasn't normally ever tense, to be honest.

We all seemed to walk on eggshells around Jack, worried about the level of pressure he must be under. His two agents, who couldn't officially be his agents until he got drafted, called him almost daily with updates about the things they heard about him—what team was interested, what they were might offer, that sort of thing. Every phone call he got either gave him new information or contradicted what he'd been told the day before.

I knew they were only trying to keep Jack in the loop, but it seemed frustrating as hell on his end. But if he felt anything other than excitement and anticipation, he hid it well.

Gran and Gramps had been extra attentive toward him, following him around the house, asking if he needed anything. He endured their smothering in silence until he finally snapped one afternoon.

"I love you both, but you're driving me fucking nuts right

now. Just be normal!"

"Jack! Language!" was all Gran said before turning to finish cleaning the sink.

"Dean, come with me," Jack called out as he grabbed his keys from the key organizer and pushed open the front door.

I ran to catch up to him. "Where are we going?"

"Shopping," he shot back before hopping in his truck. He pulled out his phone, typed an address into a GPS app, and allowed it to guide us. "Do me a favor and call Melissa."

I shot him a questioning look. "Why?"

"Just do it, damn it. I can't talk while I'm driving. Just call her for me, please."

Without asking again, I dialed her number.

"Hi!" she answered, her voice chipper.

"Hey. Jack asked me to call you, so . . ." I glanced at my brother, waiting for some direction.

"Ask her what kind of camera Cassie had," he said, and understanding hit me.

"He wants to know what kind of camera Cassie had. Do you know?"

"Oh, hold on," she said before I heard a door slam. "Sorry, she's here in the apartment. Yeah, she had a Canon Rebel something or other."

I laughed. "That's helpful."

"It is helpful. You'll see when you get to the camera store."

"Okay, I think that's it." I turned toward Jack, who stared straight ahead as he gave me a nod. "I'll talk to you later."

"'Bye, Dean."

Jack pulled into the shopping center parking lot we'd been directed to and stopped for a moment to look around. Once he spotted the store he was looking for, he made a beeline toward a parking space in front of it. I hadn't realized that specialty camera stores even existed anymore. It seemed like everyone bought their digital cameras from megastores or online.

He hopped out of the truck without saying anything, and I knew better than to stay put. Jack was on a mission, and I was his partner in crime. I walked inside the overly air-conditioned store and was amazed at all the camera equipment that surrounded me. There were cameras of all types, tripods, cases, and lenses of all sizes. A store like this was probably something Cassie dreamed about nightly.

"How can I help you gentlemen today?" An older man stood behind the counter, his pants held up by striped suspenders.

"I need to get a camera for my girlfriend. Hers got stolen."

"Oh, that's too bad," the man said.

"Yeah, well, she had a . . ." He paused.

When Jack looked at me for help, I said, "Canon Rebel?"

The man stood up a little straighter, his eyes lighting up with recognition. "We have that in the newest model if you'd like to see," he said with a smile, but Jack shook his head.

"No. What's the next best thing? If you wanted to be a professional photographer and you were really, really good at it. What kind of camera would you want that would be good enough for now and for your future?"

Jack had clearly thought this out, and I was impressed. Cassie was going to blow a gasket.

"Most people upgrade from the Rebel to the Mark III. It's a significantly better camera that gives you more options."

"Perfect. I'll take it."

"Do you need just the body, or would you like a kit?" he asked Jack, and I stood there staring at him like he'd just spoken a foreign language.

"What's the difference?" Jack asked, unfazed.

The man chuckled. "Oh. Sorry. The body is just the camera, but no lens. And the kit would include a lens."

Jack shifted his weight. "Considering both her camera body and her lens got stolen, I guess I need the kit," he said with a nod.

I laughed as the man disappeared into a back room. "Cassie's gonna flip." I patted him on the back, proud of what he was doing for her.

"I hope she likes it." He suddenly looked nervous as the man returned, holding a large box.

"All right." The man punched some numbers into his computer and read Jack the total, and I braced against the counter for support.

"Wow." I let out a little whistle of surprise but Jack ignored me, handing over his credit card without hesitation.

"She's worth it," he said to me in a low voice. "And she deserves it. That money's nothing in the grand scheme of things, okay?"

He was referring to his signing bonus. Granted, he hadn't

gotten it yet, but it would definitely be a hell of a lot more than three thousand dollars.

"I had no idea they could be that expensive, was all," I said, trying to backpedal a little.

"It's like buying a computer," the man said as he handed Jack the receipt. "And the return you can make on this investment is well worth it."

"Yeah, Dean. It's well worth it," Jack said to me with a little attitude before taking the box off the counter.

"Thanks for the business," the man called out as we exited the store.

When we walked outside, it was like leaving an icebox and stepping into a sauna. The heat hit us and I groaned, not knowing which temperature I preferred.

"She'll love it, right?" Jack asked, seeming suddenly unsure of his grand purchase.

"What's not to love? It's amazing, Jack. Really thoughtful."

"Text Melissa and make sure."

"Since when did you and Melissa become best friends?" I asked, my jealous bone tingling.

"Stop being a baby. She's helpful. And it's not my fault you can't seal the deal with her," he said before socking me in the arm.

Was he right? Was it my fault that we weren't dating? I certainly didn't think so. Melissa had been running hot and cold ever since Jack and Cassie had gotten together. I wanted to believe that she flirted with me because she was interested, but I honestly couldn't tell.

At least she wasn't dating anyone else. I wasn't sure I could handle that.

"Where'd you two run off to?" Gramps asked when we walked through the front door.

"Jack bought Cassie a camera," I announced before remembering that they didn't know hers had been stolen.

"That was awful nice of you, Jack. What's wrong with Cassie's other camera?" Gramps asked, and I mouthed *sorry* to my brother as he glared at me.

"Nothing. This one's just better, and I wanted her to have the best," he answered easily with a smile.

Gran emerged from the kitchen, wiping her hands on a towel. "That's really sweet of you. She'll love it. When are you going to give it to her?"

"I think I'll give it to her the morning of the draft. That way we'll both be one step closer to our dream careers."

Gramps let out a little whoop. "This is so exciting. I get to see Kitten in action."

I chuckled. Hearing Gramps call Cassie "Kitten" made me laugh every time.

BY THE TIME draft day rolled around, the excitement level in our house had reached a fever pitch.

Early that morning, I woke up to the sound of Jack's alarm blaring from his room, which was pretty damn loud in my room too since we shared a wall. Glancing at my nightstand, I noted my alarm clock read 6:42 a.m. Why the hell was Jack waking up so early?

I had rolled over and covered my head, tossing and turning, willing my brain to shut off so I could go back to sleep, when Jack walked into my room.

"Morning, little brother." The mattress dipped deeply as he sat down on my bed, making me roll toward him.

"Ugh." I opened one bleary eye. "Why are you awake already?"

"Big day," he said, running his hand through his hair.

"Are you nervous?"

He smirked. "Nah. Not really. I'm more excited than anything else."

"You gonna give Cassie her present today?"

The smirk widened into a full-on smile. "Yeah. I can't wait for that either."

"Great," I grumbled. "Now, go away so I can sleep."

LATER THAT MORNING at a more decent hour, Gran walked into my room, looking more dressed up than I'd seen her in a long time. The last time I remembered seeing her in a dress like this one was at my high school graduation.

"You look really pretty, Gran."

She smiled. "Thank you. I wanted to make sure you put on something nice as well."

"What's Gramps wearing?" I asked, assuming that he'd be

in his typical ratty blue jeans and bowling shirt, which wasn't exactly dressy.

"He's wearing slacks and a button-down shirt. Dress nice, Dean."

"Can't I wear shorts? I have lots of nice shorts." I was actually half serious. I wanted to be comfortable, and I hated dressing up for no reason.

"No shorts," she said, giving me a pointed look before leaving me alone.

What the hell was wrong with shorts? I groaned before searching through my closet for something decent to wear.

Eventually the three of us gathered in the kitchen as we waited for Jack and Cassie to arrive.

"He'd better get here before everyone else does, or that will be awkward," I said, and then noticed both Gran and Gramps were both uncharacteristically quiet. "Are you two okay?"

"I'm just nervous is all," Gran said, tugging at the waistline of her dress.

Gramps gave me a wink. "I just want it to be over with so the cameras will leave and we can really celebrate."

I gave him the side eye. "The cameras aren't even here yet."

"But they will be. And they'll make us uncomfortable," he insisted.

To be honest, I hadn't given the cameras a second thought, assuming they'd be solely focused on Jack and not really on us. Was I being naive?

"I'll be right back." I hopped up from my chair and jogged

to my room to look myself over one last time.

If the cameras ended up on me at all today, I wanted to look good. Looking in the mirror, I realized that I looked tired. *Damn Jack and his stupid alarm clock.* I was splashing water on my face when I heard Jack come home.

"Gran? Gramps? We're here!"

Loud cheers and congratulations filled the house as I entered the kitchen. I walked in just as Gramps said, "That's great, dear. Oh, that's just great news."

Cassie was beaming, and Jack was smiling at her as if he couldn't be more proud.

"You got the internship, sis?" I guessed before glancing at both my brother and his girlfriend.

She looked beautiful, but my eyes widened a little when I saw she was wearing shorts. I opened my mouth to ask Gran if I could go change, but I stopped myself when I caught her casting a *don't even think about it* look my way. I'd swear that woman could read minds.

"I just found out. I wasn't going to take it, but now I can." She looked at Jack before I lifted her off her feet in a giant bear hug.

"Congratulations. That's awesome."

A quick rap at the front door pulled us out of our mini celebration. The laughter died and I glanced at Jack, anticipation stretching my nerves taut.

Unfazed, Jack pulled the curtain back and peered toward the porch. "It's just Marc and Ryan."

Jack left to greet his agents, and I followed. The men came

in all smiles, loaded down with stacks of paperwork, a bottle of champagne, and a box filled with baseballs.

"How you feeling, champ?" Marc asked.

"Good, thanks," Jack said before relieving him of the box of balls.

"Hey, Dean. How you doing?"

I smiled as Marc playfully punched at me, but I ducked and weaved, pretending to be some awesome boxer as I jabbed at him in response. We stopped after he almost dropped the champagne.

The two men introduced themselves to Cassie, who had followed us into the living room, and she handled herself like a champ, very friendly and not seeming nervous at all.

"Jack, you held back on how good-looking your girl is." Ryan winked at my brother with a chuckle and I tensed, knowing how jealous Jack could be when it came to Cass.

"Settle down. I haven't signed any agreements with you two yet." He smirked before wrapping his arm possessively around her waist.

Gran called us all back into the kitchen, the spot in the house where she felt the most comfortable and in control. "This whole thing is nerve-racking," she declared. "Why aren't you nervous?" she asked Jack, but he only smiled.

"Because there's nothing more I can do. I've worked my ass off and left it all out on that field every day for years." He shrugged. "It's out of my hands at this point."

"How'd you get so smart?" She cupped his face with both hands and planted a kiss on each cheek.

"I learned it from you. Now come sit with us and relax." He led her by the hand toward the table when the chime of the doorbell stopped them. "You sit, Gran. I'll let them in." Jack handed her off to me, and I urged Gran to sit.

Jack walked back in followed by two cameramen, a reporter, and a producer. They discussed how things would work—that we would basically be filmed waiting for the phone to ring and for Jack to get his offer. They would film his reaction and ours when the call came, and then interview Jack afterward. The producer kept reminding us not to look at the cameras and to act natural, as if it was completely normal to have two cameramen shoving lights and equipment in your face while you sat at your dinner table.

The draft had already technically begun, and when the sound of a reporter talking on the television in the other room filtered into the kitchen, I had to fight the urge to go watch the TV instead of sitting at the table.

I watched as Marc and Ryan kept busy texting on their phones, and realized in that instant that what they did for a living not only intrigued me, but excited me. I loved baseball, and if I couldn't play it like Jack did, maybe I could still pursue it as a career in a different way.

Our landline phone rang and Jack walked toward it, suddenly looking a little unsure. It was literally his moment of truth, and I held my breath as he answered. We all knew that Jack didn't care who drafted him. He simply wanted to play ball, and which team he played for was a minor detail at this point.

"Hello?" His gaze was drawn to the table, connecting with us as he talked. "Speaking." He paused only for a second before smiling. "Thank you so much. Yes, sir. I'll be in touch. Thank you."

He slammed down the phone before shouting, "Arizona!" and the room broke out into cheers and congratulations. "I'm a Diamondback!"

Jack gave me a hug, and I was surprised to find my eyes burning with tears. Not like a baby or anything, but tears of pride and joy blurred my vision, and I had to blink rapidly to force them back. I was overwhelmed, filled with genuine happiness for my big brother and everything he'd worked so hard to achieve. It almost felt like my win as much as his.

"Carter, come on," Ryan said. "Do we have to call these guys back and negotiate or what?"

The business of the draft was just getting started. These guys had a job to do, and getting an offer was only the first step.

"They said five," Jack said, and I wasn't sure what he was talking about. I must have missed something as I was lost in my thoughts.

"Yeah? Did they say five?" Ryan's eyes widened.

"That's what they said."

"Well, all right! How do you feel? Should we push?" Marc scribbled notes furiously onto his pad, and I realized they must be referring to his signing bonus.

"I think five is more than fair. I'm happy with it," Jack said, and I wasn't sure if he meant five hundred thousand or five million.

"I know it sounds like a lot of money right now, Jack, but you'll lose half in taxes and we take our cut. You won't be making much for the next few years in the minor leagues. We could probably get them to budge some," Marc suggested, still scribbling like a madman.

"I'm happy with it," Jack said with confidence. "I just want to play ball."

Marc stopped writing. "All right then. We'll accept the deal as is. Congrats!"

"Five million isn't a bad signing bonus, right?" Jack asked Cassie, and she choked on her surprise.

"That's what it is? Five *million* dollars?"

"What did you think?" He laughed as he pulled her in for a hug.

The reporter tossed Jack a Diamondback hat and a jersey with his name already on the back, and he immediately put them on.

"How do I look?" he asked with a grin, modeling the dark red jersey with D*BACKS emblazoned on it.

Gramps lifted his hand for a high-five. "Like a million bucks."

I grinned. "More like five."

"Can I get my camera?" Cassie asked. "Are we allowed to take pictures?"

The producer turned to her. "As soon as we stop rolling. Otherwise your camera's shutter clicking will filter into the sound bites."

They pulled Jack into the living room, where there was more natural light, and interviewed him as we all waited for him in the kitchen, talking in hushed tones amongst ourselves about the team and the bonus.

Before we knew it, the camera crew and agents had cleared out, gone as quick as they'd come, and it was just the Carter family again. And Cassie, of course, but she felt like family to more than just me at this point. I could tell that Gran and Gramps really cared about her.

"I'd really love to take some family pictures of you all, if you don't mind," Cassie asked, and Gran's face lit up. We'd never had them done before, and even I admitted that it was a great idea.

Cassie posed us out back under one of our big trees, smiling as she clicked away on her new camera. She organized us so she could take pictures of us alone, all together, and then separated us into groups like just me and Jack, and just Gran and Jack. I would have hated all the posing if it were anyone else asking us to do it, but Cassie made it bearable.

Gramps asked if he could take a photo of Jack and Cassie. I laughed, assuming it would come out blurry, or only Cassie's head would be in it. But apparently, after some instruction from Cassie, he did pretty well.

"Can we get one more with Dean?" Cassie asked before waving me over. "I don't have any pictures of the three of us. I really want one. Or twelve," she called out to Gramps.

My heart warmed inside my chest. The way Cassie always tried to include me was exactly why I couldn't help but think of her as family already. I was so thankful Jack had found her, and that she tolerated him.

"Thanks for including me, sis," I said as we ended the shoot, dying to get out of these pants and into some shorts.

"You know I love you," she said with a smile, and Jack glared at me.

"Back off, little brother. I might be gone in a few weeks, but I can still kick your ass," he said with a playful snarl.

"Yeah? You and what army?" I said before he broke away from Cassie and chased me into the house.

Carter Brothers on the Road

JACK SPENT HIS last few days split between Cassie's apartment and our house. As excited as he was to begin this chapter of his life, I sensed that a part of him hated leaving. Not only Cassie, but Gran and Gramps too. This house was all we'd known, and we'd never left. Neither of us even considered moving out when we got accepted at Fullton State, so for Jack, this would be his first time living away from home.

I sat on his bed while he packed a duffel bag full of clothes. "You all right?"

"It's weird to be leaving."

"I was just thinking that," I admitted.

He stopped folding a shirt to glance up at me. "Yeah?"

"Yeah. I mean, we've never lived away from home before."

He sighed. "I know. You've gotta look out for Gran and Gramps, okay? They're getting older, and I worry about them."

I waved my hand. "Stop it. They're not ninety. They're fine, but I'm not going anywhere."

"Except up north with me."

"What?"

"I want you to drive up with me. I mean, if you want. The house looks awesome, and I want you with me when I move in and meet the guys."

"You don't want Cassie to take you?" I asked, assuming that he and Cassie had already planned to go up together. Even though Jack got drafted for the Arizona Diamondbacks, he was heading to their Single-A baseball team up in Northern California first. Before you got to the major leagues, you had to work your way through the farm system.

"No. I mean, of course I'd like her to take me, but she has her internship. Besides, I really think we need a brothers' road trip before I leave."

"You taking the Bronco?" Internally I shuddered at the thought of what a nightmare that vehicle would be for long distances.

"Yep." When I groaned, he said, "Oh, come on. I want a car while I'm there. And how else am I going to take all my shit with me?"

Shaking my head with a chuckle, I said, "When do we leave?" and Jack grinned back. He knew I'd never turn down the opportunity to spend more time with him.

"Tomorrow morning. Go pack." He waved a hand to shoo me off, but I hesitated.

"How am I getting back home?"

"I'll buy you a plane ticket. Hell, I'll buy you a plane. Just go pack."

I practically ran into my room, excited at the prospect of spending some one-on-one time with my brother. I had no idea when I'd see him again after he left, so I would take any time he wanted to give me.

No matter how big of a jerk Jack could be to girls, to me he was a really great brother. Which was why I hated hearing people talk shit about him. They didn't know the real him, the great guy underneath the cocky attitude and big-shot bravado.

I tore my room apart, searching for my own duffel bag in my closet and under my bed, but it was nowhere to be found. Frustrated, I walked back into Jack's room.

"I can't find my—" I stopped short at the sight of my duffel bag on his bed, already halfway filled with shoes. "Bro, you have my bag."

Jack gave me a grin and a shrug. "Sorry. I'm bringing most of my shit. Ask Gramps to borrow his. I'm sure he has one."

Without another word, I found Gramps in the living room and asked him for a bag. Gran told him to stay in his chair and she'd bring it to me.

Gran was the best, always taking care of her three guys. What would she do when there were only two left?

JACK WOKE ME up at seven, insisting we both shower, eat, and get on the road by eight at the latest. I heard him on the phone and assumed he was talking to Cassie.

Gran and Gramps were both in the kitchen, wearing matching robes. Gramps sipped at his first cup of coffee of the day and read the newspaper while Gran fussed over the stove.

"New robes?" I looked at them, unsure what to think.

Gramps grinned at me. "Ma bought 'em. Said they were cute."

"They are cute." Gran twirled, and the blue-and-white checked pattern spun with her, nearly making me dizzy.

"Can't argue. Plus it's better to just do what she asks." Gramps smiled as he went back to his newspaper.

Jack entered the kitchen and put his cell phone in his pocket before looking at me. "You ready to hit the road?"

"I haven't even eaten yet. You said I had to eat."

"Well, now you can eat on the road," he started to say, but Gran clucked her tongue at him.

"I'm making eggs and toast. You can spend ten minutes with us before you go."

Jack looked at me, his eyes begging for help, but I sat down at the table instead. I knew who was boss here.

He scowled before looking curiously at Gramps, and then to Gran, and then back at Gramps. "What the—"

Gran held her spatula in the air. "Don't even say it, Jack!"

"I was just going to say what great robes you two are wearing. Did you buy some for me and Dean?"

I shot him a warning look and wished I had something to toss at his head.

"No. But there's always Christmas," she teased.

Five minutes later, Gran had breakfast ready. The four of us sat around the table in the kitchen, eating in silence. The mood was somber, as if this was our last meal together, and no one seemed to want to address the simple fact that nothing would ever be the same.

I refused to be sad about it because I was too damn happy for Jack. But still, it sucked to know he'd be gone until September.

Jack rushed through his food, shoveling it into his mouth like he was desperate to escape. I had only finished half my plate when he rose to his feet and told me that we needed to beat the morning commute.

Gran's eyes started to tear a little as she hugged him. "I'm so proud of you. Go show 'em what you're made of, honey."

"Thanks, Gran."

Jack's eyes got misty, and I realized that if my big brother cried right now, I was going to lose it too.

When it was Gramps's turn, he reached out like he was only going to shake Jack's hand rather than hug him. Jack's eyebrows shot up.

"It's been an honor," Gramps said before laughing. "Just kidding. Get over here, son." He grabbed Jack and hugged him hard. "We couldn't be more proud of everything you've accomplished. You deserve it. Now, go pitch your heart out, and we'll take care of your girl."

"Drive safe," Gran said before giving me a quick hug and a shove.

"Jeez. You don't have to push me out of the house, Gran," I grumbled as I grabbed my borrowed duffel bag and slung it over my shoulder.

Once outside, Jack loaded up his truck, which thankfully had the hard top on. It must have killed him to put it on, but I didn't even want to imagine what a long road trip would have been like without it.

"Why were you in such a rush to leave?" I asked as he took my bag from me.

"I just—" He shook his head. "I didn't want to cry, okay?" When I just stood there for a moment, not knowing what to say, he growled, "Get in the damn truck," and then hopped in.

"Thanks for putting the top on," I said as I pulled the door closed.

Jack turned the key in the ignition and the radio almost blasted me out of my seat. He reached for the volume and turned it down.

"Shit, sorry," he said with a sheepish glance my way.

We both looked toward the house where Gran and Gramps stood on the front porch in their matching robes, waving at us. Gramps held on to Gran as she wiped away the tears on her cheeks. Jack and I leaned out the windows to wave back at them.

Jack shot me a glance before he put the truck in gear. "Besides, I figured that seven hours was too long of a drive to attempt without the shell. We'd both be sunburnt and blown to hell by the time we got there."

"Not to mention the fact that our throats would have been sore," I said, and we both laughed at the memory.

We'd driven to San Diego once in high school for a concert, and Jack had left the top off. For the whole drive, we couldn't hear each other speak, and we had to shout over the sound of the wind ripping through the car. By the time we got back home, we barely had voices and our throats were killing us.

Jack pulled onto the freeway and I settled back in my seat, intent on getting comfortable for the long ride. "You already have a place, right?"

"Yeah. Marc and Ryan helped hook me up with a player who was already renting a house and had two extra rooms. I guess the other guys living there got moved up."

"Nice. How's Cassie?"

He inhaled a quick breath. "Good. She cried on the phone this morning, but that's only because she didn't know when we were going to see each other again. But fuck if it didn't kill me to hear her crying like that."

"I bet. So what'd you tell her?"

"I told her I'd fly her up as soon as I got settled. Hell, I'd ask the girl to move in with me and live with me forever, but she never would."

I smiled. "You mean that, don't you?"

He looked at me for only a second before looking back at the road. "When I think about the future, all I see is her and baseball. And when there's no more baseball, I still see her. You know? I've never felt this way about anyone. Never knew I could."

"That's huge coming from you." Actually, his revelation blew my mind. Jack had never given his heart to anyone before he'd met Cassie, not even a small piece of it.

"Well, we can't all be like you, Dean."

Frowning at him, I asked, "What's that supposed to

mean?"

He glanced at me and reached out to punch my arm. "You know. Perfect." Refocusing on the road, he said, "Nah, I just mean that you're willing to take a chance on love. You find a girl and you get attached." He coughed and said under his breath, "Funsize."

"I'm not attached. There's nothing to be attached to."

I looked out the window as the city flashed by, but was lost in my thoughts, not really seeing anything.

"You like her," Jack said. "She likes you too. I see the way she looks at you."

Frustrated, I waved my hand and said, "I don't want to talk about it."

When it came to girls, he and I couldn't have been more different. Everything about the opposite sex came so easily to Jack, but I always had to make sure any girl I was interested in genuinely liked me for myself, and wasn't just using me.

Back in high school, I had my heart handed to me when I fell for a girl who was only using me to get close to my brother. When the truth came out, I felt like such an idiot for thinking that someone like her could be interested in me, but I didn't know any better.

Despite all that, I was still far too trusting, especially considering how fucked up both Jack and I were over our mom abandoning us. I tended to believe the things girls said to me, and for that, Jack would call me a sucker. I probably was.

"Fine," Jack said. "But you're hung up on her is my point. You refuse to date anyone else because there's a possibility that

Melissa might like you back, and you don't want to miss out on that."

I stared at my brother in shock, wondering when he'd gotten so damn good at reading people.

"Am I wrong?" he asked.

I shook my head reluctantly. "You're not wrong."

"Then I think you should date someone else. See if it pisses her off. Try to get a rise out of the girl."

"Seriously? Make her jealous? That's your big plan?"

"Maybe it'll knock some sense into her for once," he said with a laugh.

I stared out the window and couldn't believe I was actually considering it. Maybe it would work. If Melissa had expressed even an iota of jealousy, then I would know for sure that she was interested, no matter what she tried to say.

"It might backfire," I said, my attention focused on the mountain range in the distance.

"Backfire how?"

"Maybe she'd date someone else then too. And I'd be pissed."

"Well, maybe that's what you both need."

I shook my head, not wanting to hear any more.

"I have a question that actually matters," I said, changing the subject and trying to pretend that I couldn't care less about Melissa. We both knew that wasn't true, but Jack humored me.

"Shoot."

"I was thinking about asking Marc and Ryan if I could intern for them, but only if you're okay with it. What do you think?"

I really hoped Jack wouldn't think me being around his agents was weird, but I wasn't sure. We were family, but sometimes people didn't want to mix family with business, and this was definitely Jack's business. If he told me no, I'd have to respect that.

Jack glanced at me, his eyebrows raised underneath his cap. "You think you want to be a sports agent?"

"I don't know for sure, but I'd like to find out."

Hell, I had no idea what I wanted to do with my life when I finally grew up, but I figured it couldn't hurt to try new things. Maybe it would be nothing like I thought and I'd end up hating it, but I'd never know if I didn't try.

After thinking it over for a few seconds, Jack nodded. "I think it's a good idea. You care about people, and that's important. I wouldn't have signed with Marc and Ryan if I didn't think they cared about me and my future, you know? If I was just another paycheck to them. I didn't want people like that in my corner. I could find assholes like that on the street."

He reached for the glove box to pull out a pack of cinnamon gum and put a piece in his mouth before offering me one.

I took it begrudgingly. Who loved cinnamon-flavored gum besides my brother? I didn't hate it, but the flavor lasted all of ten seconds before disappearing and leaving you with that weird metallic aftertaste. But for him, I chewed the damn thing anyway.

"Do you want me to call them and put in a good word?"

Jack offered as he snapped his gum.

"No, I got it. Thanks, though."

Reaching out to them was something I needed to do. If I wanted to work for them, I had to be man enough to ask.

We drove along the deserted freeway, the sound of the music from the radio and the wind the only sound for a while. That was how it was with Jack and me; we never needed to fill the silence. If it was quiet, we were content with it being so.

We could also talk to each other about anything, and there wasn't any big decision I'd made in my life that I didn't discuss with him, not that there had been many yet. He wasn't just my brother; he was my best friend.

Jack reached for the volume button on the radio and turned it down a notch. "You gotta watch out for Cassie while I'm gone, okay?"

Déjà vu hit me, making me ask, "Watch out for her how?"

"Just make sure she's okay and stuff. Check in with her. Don't fucking let her walk anywhere alone at night," he added, his voice turning bitter.

"Jack, I'm not her bodyguard."

He shot me a murderous glare. "I know. She keeps telling me I'm crazy, but I'll never fucking forget what that guy did to her. Or to you. I can't stomach something like that happening again."

"It won't," I said, trying to reassure him, but that particular topic was a lost cause.

"It can't."

"Don't worry. Just because you're gone doesn't mean that

I'm never going to talk to Cassie again. Hell, she's the only person I do want to talk to."

"The only person?" Jack's anger bled out as quickly as it had come, and amusement glinted in his eyes when he cut them at me.

"Well, her and Melissa, okay? We hung out with them all semester. Why would that change?"

"I don't know," he admitted. "I'm just saying don't go crazy or anything, but make sure you make time for Cassie. She loves you. And I'd feel much better if I knew you were around."

I scoffed. "Of course I'll be around. I'll be so around they'll think I moved in," I said, hoping to get a rise out of him.

"Watch it, little brother. I'll still find someone to kick your ass if I can't do it myself," he shot back, but I didn't believe him.

Not one bit.

New Digs

JACK FOLLOWED THE GPS's directions, and a few hours later pulled the Bronco to a stop in front of a two-story house. It looked brand-new, and a hell of a lot nicer than our house back home. Not that Gran and Gramps's place wasn't nice, it was, but it was just a lot older and smaller than this one.

"This the place?" I asked through my shock. I had wrongly assumed that he'd be staying in some shithole with his teammates, and this was anything but.

"Apparently," Jack said with a shrug before cutting the engine.

I gathered the mountain of empty fast-food wrappers we'd accumulated during the drive in my arms and walked them to the trash cans on the side of the garage.

"Looks really nice," I said as I walked back toward the truck.

Jack scratched his head. "It does."

The front door opened and three bare-chested muscular guys in baseball caps walked out, each holding a beer.

"Hey! You must be Jack," the tallest one shouted, and Jack

dropped his duffel to the ground before walking up the pathway to meet them.

"Yep," he said, reaching out to shake hands. "This is my brother, Dean." He indicated me with a nod.

"I'm Tyler, and this is Nick and Spencer. We're glad you're here, man. We've heard a lot about you," Tyler said before walking over to me and extending his hand, and I gripped it tightly. "Nice to meet you, Dean."

"Yeah, you too." I smiled. He seemed pretty cool. "What position do you play?"

"I catch. Nick here's our first baseman, and Spencer's a pitcher."

"Nice," I said with a nod.

"I'll show you to your room," Tyler said. "After you get settled in, come meet us out back by the pool."

"You have a pool?"

I couldn't help but be a little jealous. I'd always wanted a pool growing up, but Gran said there wasn't enough room. As a little kid, I believed whatever she told me, not knowing any better. I knew now, though, that there was plenty of room in the backyard for a pool, but they most likely couldn't afford the upkeep and maintenance, let alone the cost of putting one in.

Gran always hated telling us that they couldn't afford to buy us things, so she made up creative reasons as to why we couldn't have them. I loved her and Gramps for it, and for all the sacrifices they made in order to raise us. It had never hit me until this moment just how much they'd had to give up when Jack and I moved in. They never went away on vacations together, and the only ones who got new things in the house were me and Jack.

Jack slapped a hand on my shoulder. "You okay? You look weird all of a sudden."

"I'm fine," I said, ducking out of his grasp. "Just thinking, is all."

"Come on. Grab your shit," he said before following Tyler up the cobblestone walkway.

I pulled my duffel from the Bronco before hustling to catch up. When we walked through the front door, I was awed by the house's features—vaulted ceilings, wide crown molding, and hardwood floors. No four guys should be living in a house this nice.

"This house is ridiculous," I said, and Tyler laughed.

"No shit. We got super lucky. Jack, your room's upstairs, first door on the right. I'm gonna hit the pool. Come down when you're ready. There's beer in the fridge."

Jack took the stairs two at a time, and I unconsciously mimicked him the way I used to when we were little kids. He pushed open the door to a simple guest room with a pair of twin beds, a dresser, and a nightstand.

"You're so lucky you didn't have to furnish this." I couldn't imagine what a pain in the ass that would have been, moving every single thing he owned. Then I shuddered at the thought of his room at home being empty.

"I know." He tossed his bags on the bed closest to him and unzipped one to pull out two framed photos that I recognized from his room. One was of Gran, Gramps, Jack, and me under the big oak tree, and the other was of Jack and Cassie that Gramps had taken.

He placed the two pictures on his nightstand and turned to me. "I can unpack the rest later. Want to go out back and look around?"

"Definitely." I dropped my bag on the other bed and followed him down the stairs to the kitchen, which looked like it should have been featured in a magazine.

Jack opened the fridge, pulled out two beers, and handed me one. "After a long hot car ride, we deserve this," he said before twisting off the top and clanking his bottle against mine.

We stepped outside into the yard and were hit with giant nonstop streams of water to our chests without warning. I looked down at my now soaked shirt as Spencer sat floating on a green alligator raft, clutching a Super Soaker while he laughed hysterically.

Jack and I glanced at each other with a silent promise that we'd get him back, and then continued our self-guided tour. The yard was ridiculous. Expensive stonework and lush vegetation lined the pool area. Everything was perfectly manicured and super nice, much like the rest of the house.

Even though it felt like a thousand degrees outside, we found Tyler sitting alone in the hot tub.

"Are you cold or something?" I asked, wondering what the hell he was doing.

He downed the rest of his beer before opening up the one

sitting next to it. "My muscles are sore as hell. The heat helps."

I nodded in understanding, remembering that Tyler was the catcher on the team. In the same way that pitching could be hard on your shoulder and arm, catching was hard on your knees and legs.

I took a swig of my ice-cold beer. Damn, it tasted good. A yell yanked my attention back toward the pool, where I assumed that I was about to get shot with the damn water gun again. Instead, Nick came flying down backward on the built-in slide that I hadn't noticed before. This pool was freaking insane, and I was definitely jealous.

"Can I move in? Just for the summer," I asked Jack, and he laughed. "I'm not kidding. I want to live here. In this backyard."

"I don't care." Jack clapped my shoulder. "But then who will keep an eye on my girl? And who will make sure Funsize doesn't have a summer fling if you're not there to stop her?"

I practically growled, torn between my dream summer and my dream girl. "Fine. But can I come visit?"

He grinned. "As much as you want."

"Are you guys coming in or what?" Spencer asked, still holding on to the water gun and his alligator raft. His head looked hilarious pressed next to the giant painted eye of the gator.

"Hell yes!" I shouted like a five-year-old before running upstairs to change.

Jack came upstairs a few seconds later, and pulled out his phone to type a quick text.

"Cassie?" I asked.

"Gran. I wanted to let her know we're here. And Cassie, because I fucking miss her."

"Does Gran actually text you back?" I asked with a laugh.

"Not usually. But I know she reads the ones I send her. That's all that matters," he said before tossing his phone on the bed and pulling off his wet shirt.

"How are we going to get Spencer back?" I asked with a sly smile, reminding Jack of our ambush as we walked outdoors earlier.

"I was just thinking about that." Jack smiled back. "He's already in the pool, so getting him wet seems counterproductive at the moment."

"We could steal his alligator. Make him swim without his little floatie?" I suggested as Jack's phone beeped from the bed and he dove to grab it.

As he read the text, his face formed a love-struck smile with those trademark dimples that all the girls loved. "Goddamn, I love that girl," he said as he typed something quickly before dropping the phone and pushing up from the bed. "Let's go."

We trotted back to the yard and Jack jumped into the pool, right next to Spencer, and the giant wave he created almost knocked Spencer off his gator. Almost.

So I leaped from the side, grabbing my knees with both hands in perfect cannonball form, aiming for the same vicinity. Not only did Nick fall off his precious floatation device, the force of my wave sent it flying far enough away from him that

Jack could snag it and hop on.

I spat out some of the water that had entered my mouth before I realized it was a saltwater pool and not chlorine, and laughed when Spencer whined, "Hey! My gator."

Tyler was still in the hot tub nursing his beer, and Nick observed the chaos below from his perch at the top of the slide. "I'm coming down," he shouted before disappearing.

When he shot around the curve, this time he was flat on his stomach with a beer in his hand. He splashed into the water hard, the hand clutching his beer shooting straight up into the air as high as it could go so the bottle wouldn't go underwater. The sight of it reminded me that Jack and I had left our beers upstairs.

Gripping the edge of the pool, I pushed off with both hands, lifting myself out so I could go find the slide. I climbed the slight incline to the top and peered down, noticing a rock cave that the slide went through before plunging you into the deep end.

I sat down at the top of the slide, the water splashing against my back before I pushed off, racing toward the bottom. The cave was a lot bigger than I'd imagined, and longer. Cloaked by darkness for a second, I was momentarily blinded by the sunlight as I shot out and landed in the warm water.

"Awesome!" I yelled to no one in particular, and Jack laughed, now clutching the gator floatie with both hands as Spencer tried to flip him off and win it back.

"Not gonna happen for you, Spence. I'll never let this gator go!" Jack yelled as he pushed at Spencer's shoulders and splashed water with his feet.

"Jack's very attached to reptiles," I said as I swam up from behind, and Nick appeared, downing the rest of his beer before placing the empty poolside.

"Really?" Nick asked. "Reptiles?"

"No. My brother's a dumbass." Jack pulled the gator from between his legs and tossed it at Spencer's overjoyed face.

"Gator!" Spencer cheered and clutched the thing like it was his girlfriend.

"I think he's in love with inanimate objects." I pointed at Spencer, who sat petting the top of the blow-up gator's head like it was his favorite dog.

"I can hear you, ya know," Spencer said with a big grin. "Gator here doesn't talk back, doesn't argue with me. And we never fight, do we?" He went on and on, talking nonsense to the float while we all stared at him until he started cracking up.

"You're a sick fuck." Nick splashed him before getting out and wrapping a towel around his middle. "I'm starving. Tyler?"

Tyler hopped out of the hot tub. "I'll fire up the grill. Burgers and dogs okay with you?" he asked, and Jack and I nodded enthusiastically in unison.

I SPENT THE next five days with my brother and his new teammates. Most of my afternoons were spent alone while the guys were at the field, filling out paperwork and working out, but I didn't mind. It gave me time to work on my tan and float on the gator without having to share her with Spencer. He was very possessive.

I was fortunate enough to still be in town for Jack's first game as a professional baseball player, and I couldn't have been more proud. His new stadium was huge, way bigger than the one at Fullton State, and held a lot more screaming fans who already knew exactly who my brother was.

When the game ended, I'd never seen so many girls waiting for autographs before. The way girls acted at Fullton had been nothing compared to the way they were now. They flirted shamelessly with Jack, touching him and shoving their phone numbers into his pockets as we left the field one night. It was fucking insanity, but he seemed unfazed by it. His focus and heart were with only one girl.

By the time I left to fly back home, I'd not only grown attached to Jack's new house, but his new friends as well. I had never wanted to stay in one place so badly before. But Jack reminded me that he'd be on the road half the summer, and he'd be back home before I knew it.

So I begrudgingly agreed to go home. The knowledge that I'd see Melissa and Cassie again soon was the only part that made leaving remotely bearable; Gran and Gramps too. You never realized how much you missed someone until they weren't around on a daily basis, yelling at you about your language and the mess you left in the kitchen.

When Jack finally dropped me off at the airport, he left me with firm instructions once again to look after his girl and to finally try to pin down my own. I guess it was time to either shit or get off the pot.

He wished me luck as I walked into the terminal, heading home for the first time in my life without my brother.

Weird without Jack

BEING HOME WITHOUT Jack was weird as hell. It was one thing when he was gone for an away series of games; I always knew he'd be home soon. But him being upstate for months was a different beast altogether. And we weren't sure when exactly he'd be back for good. It all depended on how well the team did this summer, and how far they got into their post-season.

I missed him like crazy and found myself spending more time in his room than in my own. It helped just being in there sometimes, made him feel less far away.

I was in his room studying one just before dinner about a week after I'd flown home. The doorbell rang, and I heard either Gran or Gramps scrambling to get up to answer it.

"I'll get it," I shouted so they could stay seated. When I pulled open the door, a man stood there, holding a clipboard like a delivery guy, but he wasn't wearing a uniform.

"Are you Dean Carter?"

"Maybe," I said evasively, not sure what the hell was going on.

"I have a delivery for you. Sign here, please." He shoved

the clipboard toward me and handed me his pen as I looked on the ground for a package of some sort since he wasn't carrying one.

"What is it?" I asked as I signed where he'd indicated.

He waved a hand toward the gunmetal-gray Mustang parked at the curb, its windows tinted almost black.

Stunned, I stepped outside. "Um, I think this must be a mistake," I said, babbling like an idiot.

He frowned, impatient and not at all amused. "Do you know Jack Carter?"

"That's my brother," I said, still goggling at the brand-new car.

"Well, he must like you a lot. It's yours." He dropped a set of keys into my hand before handing me a copy of the paperwork I'd just signed.

I stood there with my jaw hanging open, unable to move or even believe what I was seeing. I knew damn well that Jack could afford this, but I didn't need a brand-new car. It was too much.

When I ran inside the house for my phone, Gramps shouted after me, wanting to know what was going on. Ignoring him for the moment, I dialed Jack's number and waited.

"What's up, little brother?" he asked, his tone filled with mischief.

"I think you know," I practically stuttered.

"What do you think? It's been your favorite car since you were thirteen."

"Jack, it's too much. Really. I don't need something like

that, I swear."

"I know you don't *need* it. But I *wanted* to get it for you. Just let me do something nice for you, okay? And by the way, a new Honda is coming for Gran and Gramps tomorrow. You've been warned. Gotta go," he said, and I stopped him before he hung up.

"Wait! Thank you. It's too much, but thank you. It's gorgeous."

"I know it is." He laughed before ending our call.

Well, shit. I had keys to a new Mustang burning a hole in my pocket and nowhere to go. My phone vibrated in my hand, and I looked down.

CASSIE: Are you back?

CASSIE: Come over.

CASSIE: I miss you.

CASSIE: I'm bored.

CASSIE: But that's not why I want you to come over.

Cassie had blown up my phone with five text messages in a row, and I laughed as I typed out my response.

DEAN: On my way.

I ran back into the living room and hugged Gramps.

"Do you see that?" I pointed out the living room window toward my car—*my car*—on the street.

Gramps squinted. "I see it."

"It's mine. Jack bought me a damn car!"

Gramps pushed out of his recliner and walked closer to the

window. He took a good look outside and turned to me with wide eyes. "Jack bought you that?" When I nodded, he turned and called out, "Ma! Get out here and see what Jack did!"

She came around the corner, her expression a mixture of concern and confusion. "What he did? What could he have done? Jack's not even here."

"That!" Gramps pointed at my Mustang.

"What about it? It looks like a bullet."

"It's mine," I said with a smile.

Gran's eyebrows shot up nearly to her hairline. "Yours? He bought you a car?"

"Apparently. And yours is on the way." I laughed, knowing that Gran didn't like big surprises. If I warned her now, it would at least give her a little time to adjust to the idea. "And don't try to talk him out of it. He's stubborn and pig-headed. He won't take it back."

"Well, I—" Gran stopped and shook her head, clearly at a loss for words.

"It's really nice, isn't it?" I draped my arm around her shoulders as I towered over her.

She peered out the window again. "It's more than just nice. You be safe driving that, you hear me?"

I nodded. "Cassie just texted me, so I'm going to head over there. You guys okay if I leave?"

"Of course. Go. Have fun." Gran swatted at my back. "Tell Cassie hello from me, please."

"Tell the kitten I miss her," Gramps called after me with a hearty laugh.

"I'm telling Jack you're in love with his woman!" I shouted as I ran out the front door.

Before I left, I walked around my car, inspecting it from every angle. It was gorgeous.

Jack was right; I'd loved Mustangs ever since I was a teenager, admiring their sleek lines and body style. The gunmetal color looked badass against the darkness of the tinted windows, and I shook my head, my mind still blown as I clicked the unlock button on the key fob.

When I opened the driver's side door, I was immediately struck with the new-car smell and the supple jet-black leather. The dashboard was black as well, with striking silver accents. It was exactly my style, and had Jack not picked it out for me, this was exactly what I would have chosen for myself. Once I could afford it, of course.

I started the engine, grinning at the sound of it, and then took off to head toward Cassie's. The gas pedal was a hell of a lot more sensitive than Gran's Honda or Jack's Bronco, and when I touched it, the car jerked forward with a surge of power. The brakes were touchy too. Whenever I tapped them even the slightest bit, I was slammed into the steering wheel. I must have looked like a kid with a learner's permit driving this thing.

Stopped at a red light, I turned up the volume on the radio and smiled as the pounding bass filled the car. Leave it to my brother to not only hook me up with a killer ride, but make sure the stereo was the best as well.

When I pulled into the apartment complex, I parked my

new baby far away from the other cars, wanting to avoid door dings or any other potential parking-lot issues. Excited, I sprinted to Cassie's door and knocked, but didn't wait to be let in. Ever since the night of the mugging, I'd stopped feeling like a temporary guest in Cassie's life and felt more like family.

"Sis!" I shouted from the front door, and Melissa's familiar squeal came from her bedroom.

"Dean, is that you? I'm naked! Don't come in here!" she shouted.

The thought of that instantly made my shorts tighten, and all thoughts of my new ride fled as my imagination went wild.

"Why'd you tell me you were naked if you didn't want me to come in there?" I called out, teasing her. Okay, I was only half teasing because if she let me, I'd run in that room and have my way with her in a heartbeat.

"Dean!" she shouted again from behind her closed door. "I swear to God!"

"You swear to God, what? Okay, I'm coming in. You don't have to beg," I shouted, taking two steps toward her room so my voice would sound closer, but stopped when Cassie slapped my shoulder, startling me from my game.

"Don't tease her," she said with a playful smile before giving me a big hug.

"Me? She's the tease in this relationship," I said against the top of her head.

Melissa poked her head out through her doorway. "I'm dressed now. You can stop tormenting me." She stuck out her tongue.

"I haven't even started yet," I said, channeling my brother's confidence.

"Who invited you anyway," she asked before coming out of her room in a tightfitting sundress.

"Don't listen to her, Dean. She knew you were coming over. What the hell's wrong with the two of you?" Cassie looked between us with a smirk.

"Oh, so you knew I was coming over and you got naked?" I couldn't stop, just had to torment her the same way she tortured me without even trying.

Melissa hooked her hands on her hips. "You're almost as annoying as your brother."

I gasped in mock horror before walking over to her and wrapping her in my arms. "No, I'm not," I said against her hair as I breathed in the scent of her fruity shampoo.

Her body melted against me, and for half a second I wished we were alone.

"But you have missed me, haven't you?" I asked, and she bristled, swatting at me to let her go.

"Maybe," she said noncommittally before walking into the kitchen and rifling through the cupboards.

"I have!" Cassie called out from the couch. "Seriously, come here and tell me about your trip with Jack. How's his house? Did you like his roommates? Was the field nice? How is he?"

"Jesus, Cassie, annoying much?" Melissa shook her head. "Ugh, ignore me. I'm starving. You two catch up."

"One question at a time," I said as I sat down next to Cassie. "I already forgot half the shit you asked."

She rolled her eyes. "How was your drive?"

I had to stop myself from scolding her the way my brother would. "It was good. Really good, actually. Uneventful. Northern California's kind of pretty, but in a different way from here."

She tucked her legs under her, apparently getting comfortable for an interrogation. "His roommates?"

"Super chill. You'll love them," I assured her. "They're really nice. I was worried they might be arrogant or really competitive, but they're not. He lucked out."

I explained to her that once you got to the minor leagues, your teammates were different from those you'd played with in school. You weren't around guys hoping for a shot to play professional baseball; you were surrounded by guys who were the best at it, and knew it.

Cassie smiled. "Oh, that's good. I'm so glad. He told me he likes them, but it's still nice to hear it from you. Jack said the house is great."

"Oh shit. It's legit. Cassie, you don't even know. Just wait 'til you see it," I said, unable to contain my excitement.

She poked her bottom lip out in a pout. "I hope I get to."

"Oh my God, already. Shut up." Melissa groaned from her spot on top of the counter. She was sitting up there, swinging her legs as she picked at the crackers and cheese on the plate she'd put together while we were talking. "Sorry, but she's been whining since he left. She seriously thinks she isn't going to see him this whole summer."

I turned to Cassie, an incredulous look on my face. "You think Jack would go the whole summer without seeing you? I'm surprised he's gone this long and survived."

Cassie shrugged. "No, it's just that he travels a lot and I'm busy with my internship. And I don't know when we're going to see each other." She sighed, putting on a lovesick face similar to the one I'd been seeing on Jack. "I just miss him. It's weird being here without him."

"You're telling me. You don't have to go home and live where he isn't anymore. It sucks."

She rested her hand on my knee. "I bet it's quiet. How are Gran and Gramps taking it?"

"I don't know. They seem all right. Gran's a little quieter than usual, but she keeps it inside. She's tough. Oh, they both said to tell you hello and they miss you. Although Gramps said he misses the kitten." I chuckled as she grinned. "You should stop by sometime. They'd love that. You too, Funsize." I looked back at Melissa, who stopped chewing to cock her head at me.

"What did you just call me?"

"You heard me."

"Why on earth would I go to your grandparents' house?" She frowned and shook her head at me like I was insane.

"So you can meet your future in-laws." *Shit.* That just came out, and it was too late to take it back.

Cassie burst out laughing, and Melissa hopped off the counter and stormed up to me.

"You think you can win me over with your nice-guy charm

and good looks, but I've got news for you, Dean Carter," she said quickly, as if she'd rehearsed it a million times before.

I cocked a brow as I waited for her to finish. "Yeah? Wait—you think I'm good-looking?" I grinned, and all my nervousness flew out the window.

"Oh, shut up. You know I think you're adorable. Have ever since I saw you in class."

"Then why won't you go out with me?" I asked, dead serious now, and she glanced at Cassie before looking back at me.

"First of all, you've never asked. And second, don't start asking now. It's too late." Without giving me a chance to respond, she whirled and stomped to her room, and slammed the door.

"What? How is it too late?" I called out before turning to Cassie. Women completely blew my mind sometimes.

Cassie shrugged one shoulder. "I have no idea. I'm sorry. She's always been weird when it comes to guys, but I don't know why she's like this with you." Tilting her head to the side, she looked closely at me as she asked, "Do you really like her or do you just think you do?"

I swallowed, wondering what the hell kind of question that was. "I really like her. I was interested in her before you and Jack ever met, so it's nothing weird like I feel I should date my brother's girlfriend's best friend or anything like that. I liked her first."

"I'll talk to her. See what I can do," she offered, and I thanked her.

I'd take any help I could get. If Melissa and I weren't a

good match, I'd at least like the chance to figure that out.

"So Jack seemed good?" she asked, changing the subject back to the one that bonded us. "He's been pitching really well."

"Yeah. He said his arm feels good, and he feels good. Even though the guys he's facing can and do hit him, it doesn't intimidate him, you know? He's so confident when he plays. You have to be tough like that in this game, or it'll destroy you."

Baseball was much more of a mental game than it was a physical one; Jack had taught me that much. Of course you needed strength and speed to run, hit, and throw, but it was so much more than that. And when you pitched, that was the toughest mental battle of all.

Your head had to be clear, focused, goal oriented. The second you let things get to you—fans in the stadium booing you, opposing teams talking shit, the batter glaring at you, shitty calls by the umpires, even your own insecurities—the moment any of those got inside your head, you were done for.

"I love knowing that he's excelling. Not that I had any doubts, but still." As if she'd just remembered, Cassie's eyes lit up as she said, "Jack mentioned that you were going to start interning with his agents."

"Yeah. I called them and basically said I'd be free labor as long as they taught me the ropes. It's been just the two of them for so long, I don't think they'd ever considered having an intern before. But apparently they can use the help, so I'm pretty excited."

I was actually more than excited for the chance to work with Marc and Ryan. I had no idea if it would be something I would enjoy and want to pursue in the future, but just having something I was interested in was encouraging. Especially being around goal-oriented people like Jack, Cassie, and Melissa, who already knew what they wanted to do and were pursuing it.

I was younger than they were and the expectation level for me was lower, but still. Jack had always known that he wanted to play ball, and I was certain Cassie always knew she wanted to be a photographer. I just wanted to find my dream too.

"How's your internship going?" I asked. "And how's the new camera?"

Cassie sighed. "The new camera is unbelievable. The model he got for me was way newer than the one I had, and it has the ability to shoot in ways that my other one didn't. I'm in love. With a camera. And my internship."

"It's that good?"

"It's pretty good," she said as Melissa walked back out of her bedroom and avoided looking at either of us.

Rather than stay there and make things any more awkward than I apparently already had, I decided to go back home.

"I'm gonna take off."

Cassie whined a little about my leaving as I pushed up from the couch. Reaching for her hand, I helped her up, and she gave me another hug.

"Come over anytime."

"You too," I said, reminded her that she was just as welcome at our house as I apparently was at hers. Well, at least *she* welcomed me.

"Shit. I forgot to tell you guys that Jack bought me a car!" I blurted, suddenly remembering.

"What?" Cassie's jaw dropped. "He bought you a car?"

"What kind?" Melissa asked from behind me. Apparently this was big enough news to stop ignoring me for.

"He didn't tell you?" I asked Cassie. "You seriously didn't know?" I had assumed that Jack kept very little from her, and it wouldn't have surprised me in the least if she'd been involved in some part of his plan.

"No! I had no idea." Her face lit up, as if Jack's gesture made her proud of him.

"Apparently he bought Gran and Gramps one too, but it won't be here until tomorrow."

Cassie's expression shifted, turning worried. "You don't think he'd do that for me, right? I'll kill him if he buys me something like that. He already bought me this camera, and I don't need a car."

I placed a hand on her shoulder to calm her down. "I'll make sure he knows."

"My car is here now. I convinced my parents to let me have it for the summer since I needed a way to get to my job every day."

Melissa waved her arms at us. "Hello! I asked what kind of car? Why are you both ignoring me?"

I turned to face her. "Why don't you come and see?"

Damn. This girl had suddenly made me channel all of my

brother's arrogance and confidence tonight.

Without another word, I walked out the front door into the night with the two girls trailing behind me, giggling and whispering.

"Jeez, where did you park? China?" Melissa asked as I walked past all of the normal visitor parking spots.

"I didn't want any door dings," I admitted, but wasn't embarrassed by the fact.

"Well, you won't have any because no one in their right mind would park this far—" She halted in her tracks, stopping mid-thought. "No way. Is that it? The Mustang?" Her voice was almost as excited as mine had been when I first saw it.

Darkness had fallen while we were talking inside. The car looked good under the streetlamps, but not as good as it did in the daylight. I wished that they could see it better.

"Wow, Dean. This is beautiful," Cassie said as she stepped closer to admire it.

"Open it!" Melissa exclaimed, clapping her hands and hopping up and down like an excited little pixie.

How could she blame me for wanting to take her into my arms all the time when everything she did was so damn cute?

I pulled out the key fob to unlock the doors, and Melissa hopped into the passenger seat.

"Now would be a good time to kidnap her," Cassie whispered to me with a laugh. "I'm going to go inside and leave you two alone." When I gave her a grateful smile, she grinned at me before she turned around and headed back to the apartment.

I stared after her for a moment, feeling like a dick for being thankful. Then I shook it off and hopped into the driver's seat.

"This car is hot, Dean. Hot like fire, hot!" Melissa said as she looked around and touched everything. She was so excited, I couldn't even get pissed that she was leaving fingerprints on all my new hardware.

"Yeah. It was love at first sight," I said, staring right at her as I said it.

When she saw my expression, she sighed, and her demeanor softened as she stared back. "Don't say that."

"Why not? Tell me, Melissa. Tell me why you and I are such a bad idea." I'd never pushed her before, but it was getting old being clueless. I was dying where we stood.

"I never said we were." She shrugged one shoulder and I leaned toward her, closing the space between us.

"Then why"—I brushed my thumb along her jawline and her eyes closed—"do you keep acting like it is?" I held her chin in my hand as her eyes reopened.

Melissa studied me for a moment, her eyes wide as they searched mine. Her face softened, her eyes turned hopeful, and I couldn't stop myself.

I closed the distance completely, taking her mouth gently with mine, not wanting to scare her away. A small moan escaped her and I opened my mouth, hoping she'd do the same. When she did, the kiss deepened, our tongues touching and teasing as we explored each other.

My breath quickened and my pulse raced when Melissa reached behind my neck to pull me closer, giving everything she had to the kiss, deepening it, reveling in it. God, how I wanted to grab her by the ass and pull her body on top of mine, but I didn't have the courage.

"Stop," she said, surprising me when she tried to pull out of my hold. "Just stop."

I froze, all of me releasing all of her. "Are you okay?"

"We have to stop." She shook her head as if suddenly regaining her wits, and said, "Shit."

"Did I hurt you?" I asked, not knowing what happened to make things change so quickly.

"No, of course not," she blurted before opening her door and hopping out of the car.

"Then what is it? What's wrong?"

Totally confused, I jumped out and raced after her. When I caught up, I grabbed her by the arm, spinning her to face me.

Melissa looked up at me and her eyes seemed to glisten in the dim light, but I couldn't be certain. Then she sucked in a quick breath and straightened her spine.

"Nothing. We . . ." She paused, stumbling over her words. "I just . . . We can't do this."

"I'm sorry," I lied, not a damn bit sorry that I'd finally kissed her. It just felt like it was what I was supposed to say. "I've wanted to do that for forever, and I thought—" Mentally, I scrambled, trying to figure out what to say to make this right. “Hell, Melissa, I don’t know what I thought.”

“We’ll just pretend it never happened, okay?” she said, her voice trembling. “Good night, Dean. I’m sorry.” Then she hurried away from me without another word.

Pretend it never happened? Fat fucking chance.

Dreams to Nightmares

I'D REPLAYED EVERY moment of that kiss for days, wondering what happened or where it went wrong. I was still no closer to an answer today than I was the day it happened. The only thing I could think of was that there was something holding Melissa back, but I'd be damned if I had a clue as to what it could be.

Summer was in full swing, and I'd started interning with Jack's agents a couple of weeks ago. I had no idea the amount of work and detail that went into being an agent, but I was fascinated by it all. The fact that the guys I worked for seemed to want the best for all their clients didn't escape me. I knew enough to know that there were agents out there solely focused on getting whatever lined their pockets the best, with no regard to what their client wanted or needed. Marc and Ryan didn't conduct their business that way, and I respected that.

They kept me running around, delivering contracts to players' houses, picking up office supplies, searching the Internet for new talent. I learned to create spreadsheets like I'd been doing it my whole life. Side note—I hadn't. I found myself thriving off the chaos, and the constant state of being busy gave my brain little time to think of anything but work. I loved it.

Cassie had been visiting Jack upstate this past weekend, and was on her way back home tonight. I'd done my best not to text either of them, knowing they didn't have enough alone time as it was. I'd been half tempted to call Melissa and take her out while she was at her apartment alone, but the other half of me was too scared to hear her tell me no.

If I was more like my brother, I'd force her to give me a chance, and would refuse to take no for an answer. But I wasn't like him when it came to matters of the heart. If girls rejected me, I walked away, believing it was what they wanted.

I figured that if Melissa wanted to see me, she had my number and knew how to use it. And so, in order to lessen the sting of her rejection, I simply avoided going over there or seeing her.

But the problem with that was she never seemed to leave my thoughts. I found myself hoping that our kiss in the car plagued her the same way it did me.

My phone blared, waking me up from a nap. Between school and work, I was exhausted, and had started taking random afternoon naps on the weekends the same way Gramps did.

Bleary-eyed, I looked down at my ringing phone and noticed Jack's name.

"Brother," I answered sleepily.

"You're not sleeping, are you?" he teased.

"Well, not anymore."

"Wake your ass up. I have something to tell you." He sounded excited, way too happy for Cassie having just left.

Intrigued, I rubbed at my eyes and perked up. "What?"

"I got called up to Double-A. I leave in two days."

"Shut up, man. Jack, that's awesome! Congratulations. It's only a matter of time before you go all the way."

"Don't jinx it, brother! I just had to tell you. I'm gonna hang up and call the house. Don't tell them. Let me."

"I won't. I'm proud of you," I said with a smile I wished he could see.

"Thanks. Talk soon," he said before ending our call.

I waited, listening for the sound of the house phone before hearing its shrill ring echo down the hallway. Gran's excited voice rang out, and I rolled out of bed to celebrate with them when they hung up.

JACK'S NEW LOCATION was in Alabama, playing for the Double-A Diamondbacks team. The next stop was Triple-A, and then it was on to the major leagues—or "the show," as the players called it. My brother was one step closer to the show, and I knew in my gut that it was only a matter of time before he'd make it there.

The best thing about him being drafted was that all the Double-A games were broadcast online, so I could watch them with Gramps. Tonight was no different, with the exception of the fact that I was on the edge of my seat. Jack had pitched six innings so far without giving up a single hit, a walk, or hitting a batter. No one had gotten on base.

I fired off a text to Cassie, making sure she was watching this too.

DEAN: He has a perfect game (but I'm not supposed to talk about it). Tell me you're watching.

CASSIE: I'm watching. What's a perfect game?

DEAN: When no one from the opposing team gets on base. Don't talk about it anymore. Just watch. And pray it lasts three more innings.

CASSIE: Okay! :)

Gramps and I sat glued to the damn computer, our faces inches from the screen as we held our breath with every pitch Jack threw across the plate.

Gran walked up every so often to ask for an update before scooting away again. She'd been spending an awful lot of time in that new car she hadn't wanted, making excuses to run to the store or pick up dry cleaning when we didn't dry clean anything. Gramps and I both laughed at her, knowing exactly what she was doing, but neither of us was crazy enough to call her out on it.

With each inning that passed, my nerves stretched even tighter. If I was this wound up sitting in my house just watching the game, how the hell did my brother stay so damn relaxed pitching it?

Gramps and I both knew the rules and superstitions about baseball, and we abided by them religiously. When a pitcher had a no-hitter going, on his way to a perfect game, you didn't talk about it. You didn't even mention it. I could only pray that my text message to Cassie hadn't counted. Even the rest of the team stayed as far away from Jack during their at-bats as they could, making him the most isolated player in the game. No one talked to him, not wanting to risk jinxing it.

In the bottom of the ninth inning, I held my breath as the last batter entered the batter's box. Jack was one out away from pitching a perfect game, something most pitchers never accomplished in their entire career.

The first pitch was a curve ball. Strike one.

Two more, big brother. You got this.

The next pitch was low and inside. Ball one.

Anxiety twisted my stomach as the next two pitches went by, one of them a foul ball that shot behind the dugout like a cannon.

Jack leaned down to read the sign the catcher gave him. He nodded, agreeing with the pitch choice. He released the ball and the batter swung as I held my breath, hoping like hell the batter would ground out if he made contact at all.

The ball slammed into the catcher's glove as the umpire screamed, "Strike three! You're out!" and the batter slammed his bat against the dirt.

"He did it! He pitched a perfect game!" I yelled at Gramps as if he hadn't just been watching the same thing I had.

We jumped up from our seats and hugged, shouting with excitement. From the look on his face, I knew Gramps was wishing we were there to celebrate with Jack in person as much as I was.

Gran walked in. "What's with all the yelling?"

"Jack pitched a perfect game, Ma," Gramps yelled before grabbing her and swinging around the floor, spinning and dancing.

I fired off a text to Jack that simply read, *Congratulations*, as one from Cassie came in saying how excited she was.

It was a good night to be a Carter fan.

MY CELL PHONE rang early the next morning and I grabbed it, silencing it before it woke up the entire house. I looked at the clock, noting how damn early it was before answering.

"Jack? Do you know what time it is here?"

"Dean. Ah shit, Dean."

I immediately sat up in bed, rubbing my eyes. He sounded weird, which couldn't be good.

"What's wrong? What's the matter?" My mind raced, wondering if he'd gotten hurt, or in a car accident. I couldn't have prepared myself for what was about to come.

"I fucked up, little brother. Shit, I fucked up so bad." He breathed into the phone, and I thought I heard him crying.

Chills raced down my body as worry and confusion ripped through me.

"What happened? What did you do? Jack, tell me what happened."

He sucked in a breath, the sound raspy in my ear. "I slept with some chick last night," he said, and my head started to spin. "I woke up this morning, and she was in my fucking bed." He sounded beyond disgusted.

"You what?" I shrieked. "Tell me you're kidding. Tell me you're fucking kidding, Jack."

I was instantly sick to my stomach. In one night, Jack had gone from having the greatest game of his career to completely obliterating his personal life. I knew it, and he damn well knew it too.

"I don't know what to do, Dean. I don't know what to fucking do." He sounded borderline hysterical, like he was going to lose it, and I didn't know what to tell him. What could I possibly say that would make what he'd done last night better?

"How can I fix this?" He sounded desperate, broken, and it fueled my sudden anger.

"Fix it?" I said with a sadistic laugh. "Yeah, right. Cassie will never forgive you for this."

"I know. You think I don't know that?" he shouted, but pulled himself together. "Sorry, man. I'm beside myself right now. I can't believe I let this happen." The sound of his footsteps in the background told me he must be pacing somewhere.

"How did you? How *did* this happen?"

I didn't want to believe the things Jack was saying. He loved Cassie more than he'd ever loved anyone, and somewhere deep inside I waited for him to yell *April Fool* into the phone, even though April had been months ago.

"The team went out to celebrate, and I got drunk. Really

fucking drunk. And this chick was relentless. I told her no a million times, but then I said yes once."

Oh Jesus. I could just picture the scene in my head—Jack out celebrating with his team after his big win, a groupie coming on to him, not leaving him alone. I'd seen it before.

But Jack had never had anything to lose before. And I honestly hadn't seen him allow that kind of thing around him since he'd started dating Cassie. To say I was surprised would be an understatement.

"Damn, Jack." I ran my hand through my hair, hating that he had done this. To himself, to Cassie, to me. I didn't want them to break up, and I didn't want to lose Cassie as a friend. "How could you do this?"

"I don't know, I don't know. I didn't want to. Fuck, I was beyond loaded last night. I don't think I've ever been so drunk before. I know it's no excuse, but I'll never drink again," he said, his voice anguished. "I swear it. I'll never touch another drop of alcohol. I'll never talk to another groupie."

Jack was bargaining—with God, with me, with whomever he hoped was listening. I'd never seen this side of my brother before, and it scared me.

I sat alone in my dark room, worried sick about all Jack could lose. The rational part of me knew the right thing to do was to tell Cassie, that she deserved to know, but the rest of me didn't want her to know. What purpose would it serve?

Was it worth the pain Cassie would go through if Jack was truly sorry? He'd never do it again; I was certain of that. Although, I would have bet money that he would have never done it in the first place.

"Are you going to tell Cassie?" I tossed the million-dollar question out there and waited for his response.

I thought I heard him sniff across the line and tried to imagine him crying, something I'd rarely ever seen in our entire lives.

"I don't know," he said in a low voice. "I called her this morning right when I woke up, and I wanted to tell her. I wanted to be honest with her, you know, do the right thing? But the second I heard her voice, I panicked. I couldn't do it. I'm so sorry, sorry for screwing up, but I don't want to lose her over this. I can't lose her."

He breathed deeply, and I could hear him pacing again. "I fucked up, Dean, I made a mistake. But I'll never fucking make it again. Ever. I swear. But if I tell her, she won't stay. She'll leave me. I know I deserve it, but it'll destroy me."

Jack was right. There was no way that if he confessed this sin to Cassie that she would forgive him and stick around.

He sighed, and the line was quiet for a moment before he asked, "What do you think?"

"I don't know. I'm really fucking pissed at you right now," I admitted. "But I don't know what the right thing to do is. If you tell Cassie, you're only going to hurt her and ruin the best relationship you've ever had. But if you don't, can you live with the lie? Or will it eat you up inside every time you look at her?"

"I don't know. I feel like the guilt from lying to her is my own fault. I'd suffer willingly if it meant she didn't have to know, and we could still be together. That girl is my world." He had whispered the last part, and I wondered if he was even talking to me anymore.

"You knew better," I told him. "I can't believe that you didn't know better."

My heart hurt for my brother, but at the same time I wanted to beat the shit out of him. For hurting Cassie, for risking his future. For letting me down.

I wanted to understand, tried to comprehend how he could let this happen. How his teammates could let this happen. Why didn't anyone try to stop him?

Jack's voice turned pleading as he said, "I made a mistake, just a stupid fucking mistake. Shit, I have to figure out what I'm going to do. Dean, you can't say anything to her, okay? You can't tell her, and you can't tell Melissa either. Promise me you won't say anything to anyone. You're my brother, and I don't have anyone else in the world that I trust the way I trust you."

"This is really messed up, Jack. I'm going to see her at school once it starts, and I'll have to lie to her. You know I'm a shitty liar."

It made me sick to know this horrible secret and have to keep it inside. Without a doubt, it would eat at me. My mind spun as I tried to calculate how long I could avoid Cassie without her wondering what was up. Probably not for very long.

"I'm really sorry for putting you in that position, little brother, but please. You can't tell her. Please just do this for me right now. Until I figure out what I'm going to do. Okay?"

I squeezed my eyes closed before rubbing my hand across my face. "You're my brother, Jack. I'm loyal to you, and I'd never betray you. But this really sucks."

"I know. I'm really sorry. Fuck."

"Just try and focus on why you're there, okay? Don't let this affect your pitching." Before he could argue with me, I said, "I know, I know. Easier said than done."

"No. It's good. I can take all my aggression out on the batter. Anger is a good motivator."

"Yeah, but heartbreak usually isn't."

Maybe Jack had the right idea before he'd met Cassie. Matters of the heart could be distracting, and avoiding relationships saved a lot of time and aggravation. Not to mention pain and heartbreak.

"I'll stay focused. Don't worry," he yelled, frustrated, and I heard glass breaking in the background. "Shit. I'd better go clean that up. Thanks for listening. I'm sorry I woke you up."

Yeah. I was sorry too.

From Bad to Worse

KNOWING THAT I was keeping this massive secret from everyone was eating me up inside. Gran called me *sour* the other morning when I snapped at her, and asked me what on earth had been eating at me lately. I couldn't tell her, so I lied and just said I was really tired.

I would never tell Gran or Cassie what Jack had done, but it was tearing me up inside to simply know about it. I almost wished that he'd never called me and confided in me, but everyone needed help carrying their burdens, and my brother was no exception. He called me because he had no one else to call. If our situations were reversed, I would have done the same thing.

Jack might be one of the strongest guys I knew, but when it came to Cassie, he had the softest heart. As much as his error in judgment pained me, I couldn't imagine what it must be doing to him. He called me every night, usually after he had just gotten off the phone with Cassie, consumed with guilt. He hated lying to her, but his fear of losing her outweighed everything else.

Our conversations were usually filled with him asking me

what I thought he should do, and me remaining silent on the other end of the line. I still had no clue, and I refused to be the one responsible for them breaking up. Hell, I hated the very idea.

There were moments where he broke down, overwhelmed with so much guilt that he would call me practically in tears, begging for a forgiveness that I had no ability to give him. He seemed to go back and forth; one moment he would convince himself everything was fine, and the next he was certain he and Cassie were doomed.

It sucked. And was exhausting.

A week had passed since "the incident," as I thought of it. Jack was still calling me daily, and was no closer to how he wanted to handle the situation than he had been the first night. I finally told him that if he wasn't going to tell Cassie, which I had finally realized that he wasn't, then he needed to try to get past it and move on before it ate him up inside and she figured out something was wrong.

That conversation appeared to reignite a little life within him, and each day that passed after it seemed to be easier. His calls became less frequent but when we did talk, the conversations had improved from him practically falling apart on the phone, to him simply asking how Cassie was and if I'd seen her lately.

I hadn't. Between the kiss with Melissa and this big secret of Jack's, I wasn't thrilled about seeing either of the girls. On weekdays it was easy to avoid them; I just claimed that I was too tired after working all day with Marc and Ryan. The weekends were a bit harder, but I'd still managed to blow them off without drawing any suspicion.

But school would be starting again soon, and any attempts to evade either of those two would be transparent. As hard as it was for me to dance around the truth, being around those girls was seriously going to test me.

Before classes started, Melissa finally sent me a text.

MELISSA: *I don't want things to be awkward between us.*

I responded right away, keeping my answer simple.

DEAN: *They won't be.*

But I didn't know. Maybe it would be weird when we finally saw each other, even though that was the last thing I wanted.

When Melissa didn't respond, I tried not to spend any more time thinking about her, but her stupid text had opened the floodgates in my mind that I'd tried so hard to close. Now all I could think about was her. And those lips. And the way she had moaned in my car when we kissed.

Damn it.

I needed to get this girl off my mind if she wasn't going to let me into her heart.

SCHOOL WAS BACK in session, and while the baseball team still had their groupies and fangirls pawing them and hanging on their every word, it was nothing in comparison to last year. No one could draw the kind of attention that my brother had. And all the girls who used to hound the crap out of me no longer had any use for me since Jack was off the market and also out of town.

The third day of classes, Cassie texted me to ask if I would have lunch with her and Melissa. I almost responded no, but I couldn't avoid them forever. They were girls, and girls were nothing if not amateur detectives in better clothes.

When I walked into the student union, I spotted Melissa before either of them saw me, and I wished for a moment that our kiss hadn't ended so suddenly. I couldn't help but wonder if that first kiss was destined to be our last, and I hated the thought.

I tossed my bag on top of the table, and the girls looked up at me with big smiles.

"I feel like I haven't seen you in a thousand years," Cassie said before scooting her chair over to give me a hug.

"I feel like I just saw you yesterday." Melissa stuck out her tongue before taking it back. "Just kidding. I've missed you."

Damn. She's missed me? What the hell did she mean by that?

"I've missed you guys too." It was the truth.

"What have you been doing? Are you still interning now that school started?" Cassie asked as she forked a bite of salad and brought it to her mouth.

"Pretty much just working and helping Gran in the garden," I said, but that was only partially true. If helping Gran meant lying in a hammock in the backyard, then sure, I helped. "But, yeah, I'm going to stay on with the guys. I really like it."

"That's awesome, Dean. I'm so happy for you." Cassie smiled as if she was proud of me, and it made me feel simultaneously good and awful.

"Isn't it weird being here without him?" Melissa asked. "Knowing that he isn't just at an away game and will be back tomorrow?" She waved a hand toward the tables filled with Jack's old friends and teammates.

"It's weird being anywhere without him," Cassie said softly, and I died a little inside.

Melissa pinned her gaze on me. "What about you?"

I shrugged. "I'm getting used to him being away, I guess. It might actually feel weird when he finally comes back home." I glanced at the other students going about their business in the student union, not wanting to make eye contact with either of the girls for too long for fear they could see right through me.

I hated keeping this secret. Wait, that wasn't true. Keeping Cassie from pain was something I was okay with doing; I just hated knowing what I knew. Jack needed to get his ass home and fix everything so I could stop stressing out about it.

Cassie sighed. "I can't wait for him to come home."

I nodded. There were only a few weeks left in his season. Hopefully they would fly by.

"I actually miss the little shit," Melissa said.

My heart sank. *If they only knew what I did, they wouldn't feel that way at all.*

I had to stop thinking about what my brother had done, but every time I looked at Cassie's face, I heard his voice in my head begging me to keep his secret. It was relentless.

Screw this.

"I gotta go buy some stuff before class. Sorry. I'll see you guys later." I shoved away from the table and hurried out of the student union before either of them could stop me.

Cassie sent me a text asking if I was okay before I'd even cleared the doors. I waited until my next class was over before responding that I was fine, and that I just needed to have some things before my next class and I'd forgotten.

Lucky for me, she seemed to buy my excuse.

MY CAR PURRED like the sleek beast it was as I pulled it alongside the curb in front of my house after classes a few days later. My phone rang right as I shut off the engine, and I checked the screen before answering. It was Jack.

"Bro, you're killing me," I said, ready to chew his ass about the problems I was having avoiding Cassie and Melissa until he got home.

"Dean." His voice had reverted to that desperate and horrible tone again.

Oh, hell no. Something wasn't right.

"What happened?"

"She's pregnant."

My head spun. And spun. And continued spinning until I

felt like I was going to throw up.

"Who is?" I asked warily, praying he didn't mean who I thought he meant.

"Chrystle. The chick I slept with. She's fucking pregnant, Dean, and she's keeping it."

My jaw dropped, and I clutched the phone tightly as I tried to process what he'd just said. Before I could wrap my brain around it, he went on, spitting out his news as fast as he could, as if that would make it easier to hear.

"I told her to get rid of it, and now I'm probably going to hell for even suggesting such a thing, but I'm being punished. Because I didn't tell Cassie what I did, and so this is my punishment, right?" He groaned and gritted out, "How is this happening?"

I was stunned. Not only had my brother slept with some other girl, but he didn't wear a condom? That was completely unlike him, and against everything he'd ever taught me about when it came to sex and girls. "No glove; no love" was his number one rule; the main thing he'd pounded into my head as soon as I hit high school.

"You tell me, Jack! How *is* this happening? You didn't wear protection? What the fuck were you thinking?"

"I guess not. I don't even remember fucking her, Dean."

I slammed my palm against the steering wheel, wishing like hell this was a lie. Again.

"I can't believe this," I admitted, absolutely hating that this was happening to Jack. Either he was monumentally stupid or just the unluckiest son of a bitch in the world.

"You and me both. I just—" He paused, and I heard the now-familiar sound of him pacing. "I tried so hard to move on from my mistake and find a way to live with the guilt, but I'm going to lose her anyway. After everything, I'm still going to lose her."

He meant Cassie, of course. It always came back to her.

"You have to tell her," I blurted.

Jack expelled a heavy breath. "No shit, I have to tell her. I can barely stomach the idea of hearing her voice once she knows. *Fuck.* I'm going to lose everything I ever wanted in my life the second I make that call. She's going to hate me and never forgive me. And I deserve nothing less."

"You still have to do it. Just tell her, and then come home. Send the chick money every month and be done with it."

I couldn't believe the words that had just spilled from my mouth, considering our childhood. I wasn't even sure where the words came from, exactly, but probably from a need to protect my brother if I could. He didn't even know this chick, and now she was pregnant? It didn't seem fair.

"I can't leave her," he said in a low voice.

"You can't leave who? This Chrystle girl? What the hell are you talking about?"

"Dad left us, and we grew up without a father. And then Mom left us, and we grew up without a mother. I won't repeat their mistakes, Dean. I know that Gran and Gramps have been the best, but they aren't our parents. And you know as well as I do how hard it's been to know that Mom and Dad willingly abandoned us. I can't—" He sucked in a breath. "No. I *won't* do that to my kid. I won't be like them."

I sat in my car, my eyes wide with shock at the ramifications of what he'd just said.

"Jack."

"I can't do it; it's not right. That kid would be as screwed up as we are, and it would be all my fault. It's not the kid's fault he's here—it's mine and Chrystle's. The least I can do is be a significant part of his life."

I shook my head, understanding his reasoning, but I didn't agree. Hell, I couldn't have disagreed more.

"I don't think that's true, Jack. You can still be a part of the kid's life, but you don't have to stay there to do it. Wait—" A singular thought hit me. "How do you even know it's yours?"

Jack sighed, and knowing him the way I did, I could just picture him yanking at his hair in frustration. "She had something from her doctor confirming how far along she is. And I asked all the guys if they've seen her out lately, and they hadn't seen her since the night she was with me. I don't know, Dean, she has all this paperwork that said the conception date was right around when we hooked up."

"Still doesn't mean it's yours. Just calm down and think this through. Don't do anything rash," I warned him, hoping to talk some sense into him. But Jack's head was a mess, and I didn't think there was any more room in there for me and my logical suggestions.

"I have to go. I have to call Cassie before I lose my fucking nerve." He exhaled into the phone. "I can't believe I have to do this, that I'm about to lose this girl. Can a man live without a heart, little brother? 'Cause we're about to find out."

The call ended before I had a chance to respond. My head spinning, I stayed seated in my car, wondering what the hell I should do. I considered texting Melissa or driving straight there, but maybe I would be the last person Cassie wanted to see after getting that phone call. It made me sick for her, and for Jack.

I couldn't go inside just yet, needing time to pull myself together. Gran and Gramps would eventually find out what Jack had done, but the news couldn't come from me; it wasn't mine to tell. So I just sat in the car with my thoughts spinning, taking deep breaths to slow my heart rate and calm the hell down.

I wasn't sure how much time had passed until my phone rang again, waking me up from my self-imposed daze. I assumed it was Jack, but I was wrong.

It was Melissa. *Damn.* This was one call I definitely didn't want to take.

My voice was small and tentative as I answered. "Hi?"

"Jesus Christ, Dean! Did you know? Did you?" she yelled, her voice extremely loud for someone so small.

"I just found out," I said, only referring to the pregnancy part, but I wasn't going to tell Melissa that.

"I can't believe this. How could your brother be so stupid?" she shrieked.

"I don't know, okay? He was drunk." I didn't mean to sound like I was defending him, but she apparently took it that way.

"That isn't an excuse! Being drunk doesn't make it okay; it just makes you an idiot."

"I know that. Nothing about this situation is okay, but why the hell are you yelling at me? I didn't do it!" I shouted back.

She sucked in a deep breath and let it out slowly. When she spoke again, her voice was calmer. "Cassie's devastated, Dean. I've never seen her like this."

My heart dropped. "What's she doing? Do you need me to come over?"

"No. I made her turn off her phone and go to bed."

"You made her go to bed?" I asked with a slight laugh, and not because I found it funny.

"Yes, I made her go to bed. The last thing she needs to do is keep puking her guts out. Her heart's broken. She's wrung out and needs sleep."

Oh hell. Knowing that Cassie was throwing up made me feel even worse. Of course she wasn't sick; it was simply the devastation that made her whole world turn upside down, including her guts. Literally.

"I feel awful," I admitted.

"Me too," she said softly. "How could he do this to her? I thought he really loved her."

"He does really love her. You have no idea how broken up he is over this. I've never in my life heard him as distraught as I did today. If he could turn back time, he would. He'd do anything if he could take it back."

"But he can't because he's ruined everything."

I sighed. "He knows. Trust me, he knows."

"This is exactly why you and I weren't a good idea."

What the hell? The one time I wasn't even thinking about me and this girl, she had to bring us up.

"What do you mean exactly?" I demanded, hating the defensive tone in my voice. "What the hell are you talking about?"

"Nothing. I gotta go," Melissa said, and disconnected the call.

I slid my phone in my pocket, wondering if I'd ever understand this girl.

And how on earth were we all going to get through this?

And Then Worse Again

JACK CALLED ME bright and early the next morning. He sounded like complete shit.

"I told her last night, little brother. I love her so fucking much. I can't believe I did this. How did I screw us up this bad?"

"I don't know," I said, not knowing what else to tell him.

"Did she call you? Have you talked to her?"

"She didn't call me. But Melissa did."

"I bet she was pissed."

"She was pissed, all right. Said Cassie was sick over it. Melissa made her go to bed."

Jack stayed silent for a long while before speaking again. "I know you have to go to school, but will you please call me tonight and tell me how she is when you see her? I fucking hate that you get to see her and I don't." The desperation in his voice was gut wrenching.

"I will."

"Thanks."

And he was gone.

I called Jack later that night to tell him that I hadn't seen

Cassie that day. It was the truth. Actually, I had seen her from the other side of campus, but I figured the last thing she needed was me drawing attention to her, so instead of shouting her name like I'd usually do, I left her alone.

He hounded me for days after that, asking how she was, how she looked, and if she'd mentioned him. And when I did finally run into her, I was stunned. She looked like a person who had lost everything—her face was pale, her eyes sad. It fucking hurt to look at her, and I was thankful Jack couldn't see her like this.

On the latest nightly call, Jack interrupted me as I was in my room, trying to study. He started out with the usual questions and I tried to avoid telling him specifics, pretending that I still hadn't seen her, but he called me out on my bullshit and insisted that I had to have seen her by now.

"You're not going to like it," I said, trying to warn him, hoping he'd back off.

"Tell me. How is she? How does she look? She's not responding to any of my texts."

"Wait. You're texting her?" I asked, surprised when I probably should have been anything but.

"I just want her to know how sorry I am, and how much I love her. And how fucking lost I am without her."

"Jesus, Jack. You can't do that to her." I flopped down on my bed, wanting to strangle my brother. How could he be so insensitive?

"Do what?"

"You think those kinds of texts are helping? No wonder

she looks like a damn zombie. She can't get past this if you don't let her. You can't keep saying things like that to her if you're not coming home to fix it."

"What do you want me to do?" he shouted. "You want me to just go away and pretend we never existed?"

"No. But I want you to stop being selfish and texting her because it makes *you* feel better. It's mean, Jack," I said, hoping he'd see my point of view. If he didn't plan on coming home to fight for her, then he needed to let her go.

"I just want her to know how sorry I am, and that I'd do anything if I could make this right," he said, his voice cracking.

"She knows. Deep down, she knows all of that already. You don't have to keep reminding her."

"You're right. I'll stop." His voice was hesitant, and I imagined his face all pinched with pain. "I'll stop."

"I'll call you if anything changes," I told him.

"Thanks. You haven't said anything to Gran, have you?" he asked, and I felt my back stiffen.

"No, but you've gotta tell her too. She knows something's up, but she's just stopped asking me at this point."

"I will," he said, but I wasn't reassured.

"Soon?" Hopefully I wouldn't have to keep this lie to myself for much longer.

"Soon."

"And Marc and Ryan too?" I asked, wanting to be sure all the bases were covered. All the people Jack trusted in his life needed to be involved in this. "But I'm sure they'll tell you the same thing I did. To freaking make sure it's actually yours before you do anything crazy like stay there forever."

"I know it's mine. She brought over all these charts with timelines and dates on them and shit. She has prescriptions and all this paperwork. It looks legit."

I breathed out in frustration. "I'm not saying that she isn't really pregnant, Jack. I'm just saying to make sure it's yours, is all."

"I already told you I'm staying here," he said, sounding agitated. "I want to be a part of my kid's life, Dean, and this is the only way."

I bit back the things I really wanted to say. I wanted to scream and curse at Jack, to smack him upside the head and try to beat some sense into him, but it was useless.

"You're stupid and stubborn. I'll just talk to you later. Call Gran soon, or else I'm going to tell her myself," I threatened before hanging up. It was an empty threat and he knew it, but it still felt good to say.

I sat motionless on my bed, processing everything Jack had said about Cassie. The fact that he'd been texting her blew my mind. For a moment I considered reaching out to Melissa, but wasn't sure what the hell to say. How could anything I did or said make a bit of difference? This was all new territory for me, and all I knew was how awful all of us felt because of it.

Frustrated, I tossed my phone on my bedside table and hoped like hell that Jack would call Gran and Gramps soon. I needed to be able to talk to someone else about this. Someone who wouldn't want to cut off Jack's balls and hang them from a rearview mirror; someone who would be more concerned with the decisions he was making for his future than for what he'd done to Cassie.

It was a brutal truth, but it was true all the same. When it came down to who I cared about more, my ball was in my brother's court.

WHEN I SAW Cassie at school the next day, I noticed that she seemed to be stuck in Heartbreak Central; her hair was a mess and her eyes were swollen and red. She didn't look better than the last time I'd seen her. In fact, she might actually have looked worse.

Worry for her prompted me to fire off a quick text to my brother.

DEAN: You're not still texting her, are you?

JACK: No. You told me not to. Why?

DEAN: No reason. She just looks really sad, and I wanted to make sure it wasn't because of anything you were saying or doing.

JACK: She looks sad?

DEAN: She always looks sad.

JACK: Fuck. Don't tell me any more. I can't take it. My heart literally can't take hearing that. It hurts so fucking bad. I hate what I've done.

I stared at his words for a moment. I had nothing to say in return that hadn't already been said, so I didn't say anything. As long as Gran and Gramps didn't know about Jack, I felt like I was walking on eggshells, waiting for the big explosion that was bound to happen.

SITTING AT THE computer at the sports agency the next afternoon, I was looking up clips about local ball players around the state when my cell phone vibrated. Normally I would ignore any calls I got while at work, but it was Jack.

"Can I answer my phone if it's Jack?" I asked Marc, who was busy going over some legal contracts.

"Of course. Tell that dickhead we said hello," he said with a laugh.

"I'm at work. What's up?" I said when I picked up.

"Ah. At Marc and Ryan's?"

"Yeah. Everything okay?"

"Well, I just wanted to let you know that I've asked Chrystle to marry me."

"You what?" I shouted as I shoved my chair out from under me and stood up. Marc looked up and squinted at me in confusion as I mouthed *Get over here!* to him, my eyes wide. "You are not marrying this girl!" I held the phone away from my ear a little so Marc could hear the conversation when he rushed to my side. "You don't even know if the damn baby is yours, Jack!"

"I know, but she said after it's born we can get a DNA test. She has no issues or problems with that. Hell, she keeps encouraging it. Tell me why she'd act like that if she didn't think the baby was mine?"

I ran a hand through my hair. "I don't know. I have no idea," I said. And I didn't.

"It's the right thing to do. You understand that, right? We came from a broken family, and then we had no family. I don't want my kid to grow up in a broken home. I want him to have everything we never did. I want him to have a mom and a dad who live together and are there for him."

Sick of hearing Jack's rationalizations, I shoved the phone at Marc and told him to talk some sense into his client.

"Hey, Jack, it's Marc. What's going on? I thought you had that hot little girlfriend here in town?" Marc's tone was light, but it was about to be anything but as Jack talked his ear off, filling him in.

I watched as Marc's expression shifted. First, his jaw dropped as he listened, and then he clenched his teeth as he paced the office with the phone to his ear.

A sick feeling of relief came over me then, which was totally selfish. Finally, I wasn't alone in this mess with Jack, and had someone else who could share the burden of worry.

"No, Jack. No," Marc insisted. "That's not a good idea. You don't even know if this baby is yours, and you definitely shouldn't marry her without proof. This kind of thing happens all the time. Girls try to trap professional athletes every day—"

He paused to listen. "I understand that, but—"

When Jack interrupted him again, he sucked in a deep breath. "I get what you're saying, but—"

This time, it sounded like it was Marc who did the interrupting. His expression was furious as he said, "Jack, this isn't a good idea. As your agent, I would strongly oppose you doing anything of that nature until after the baby is born and we have proof."

Shaking his head, Marc handed my cell back to me. "He won't listen," he said before stalking back into his office.

I put the phone back to my ear. "Jack?"

"I'm here. Don't do that shit again. This isn't anyone's decision but mine, and I've made up my mind. I've been thinking about this for some time now, and it's the only thing that makes sense. It's the best option."

"No. I don't see how you're coming to that conclusion at all." I wanted to rip every piece of hair from my head one strand at a time. I was convinced it would be less painful than trying to make sense of my brother's twisted logic.

"Little brother, listen to me," he said, and I stopped talking. "I was only calling because I wanted to ask you to be my best man. I need you." When I said nothing, just closed my eyes as I tried to stop the whirlwind spinning around me, he said, "Dean?"

I sighed. "Of course, man. Of course I will."

How could I not be there for Jack? He was my brother, and I'd do anything for him. Even if it meant going to a wedding I didn't agree with, and watching him ruin his life.

"Thanks. Means a lot. The wedding's soon."

"How soon?"

Great. Something else I could add to the list of things I couldn't believe were happening. It felt like I was living in an alternate universe these days, making me wish like hell I could find a wormhole.

Jack sighed. "I'll let you know."

"You've got to call Gran, Jack. Please. I can't keep lying to them."

"I know. I'm going to call her right now and tell her everything."

Finally. I breathed out a long sigh of relief for what felt like the first time in weeks.

"Good. Thank you for that. Are you going to tell Cassie?"

"Eventually," he said, his tone clipped.

"You're going to be the death of that poor girl." *And me*, I added silently as I imagined how much more crushed she would be after hearing this.

"Well, I'm already dead inside, so . . ."

I waited for him to finish his sentence, but he never did. We were silent for a moment, neither one of us saying anything until Jack finally said he'd better go call Gran. I couldn't end the call fast enough, I was so desperate for him to fill them in.

When I put down the phone, I looked up to see Marc leaning against his doorjamb, watching me with a worried look on his face.

"Marc, how do I stop him?"

He shook his head sadly. "I don't know, but if we can't, we have to at least get him to sign a pre-nup. We have to protect him when he isn't protecting himself."

"Agreed. Okay."

"Dean, go home. Your grandparents are going to need you

after that phone call. I'll try to figure some things out on my end."

"You sure?"

"Of course. Go."

"Thanks a lot." I shut down the computer and gathered my things before heading home, toward God only knew what.

I WALKED THROUGH the front door, anxious and filled with dread, not sure what scene I'd find inside.

As soon as the door slammed shut, Gran shouted, "Dean?"

Damn. She sounded upset, which she had every right to be.

"Yeah. I'll be right in." I trudged toward the kitchen like I was headed for my own execution, feeling as guilty as if I were the one who'd done something wrong.

Her face was pale as she looked up at me from the kitchen table where she sat with Gramps. "We just talked with your brother. How are you taking it all?"

That's her first question? "I'm a wreck, Gran. I don't want him to do any of this, but he won't listen."

She clucked her tongue. "He wouldn't listen to me either. He's very adamant about everything." She looked at Gramps, who was uncharacteristically quiet and serious.

"Jack wouldn't listen to Marc today either. He called me when I was at work and I put Marc on the phone, but he's so stubborn."

She nodded. "That he is. Always has been. No one makes decisions for Jack except Jack. I just wish we could get him to see this differently."

"You and me both."

"Is this why you've been acting so odd lately?"

When she tilted her head to the side, studying me, I felt horrible. I stepped over to give her a hug, and she kissed my cheek.

"I'm sorry, Gran, but Jack told me the girl was pregnant a while ago. And then he told Cassie. Since then, everything's gone to hell in a hand basket."

I winced a little, waiting for Gran's normal scolding about my language, but it didn't come. Which was a pretty good indication of how rattled she was.

"Oh no. Poor Cassie. How is she taking the news?"

"Not well. And she doesn't even know about the wedding yet, only the baby."

"Poor Kitten," Gramps said, finally speaking up.

Gran looked up at me with concern in her eyes. "I'm really sorry you've been dealing with all of this by yourself, Dean. And I wish there was a way to change his mind, but I think his mind is made up. Nothing I said stuck. And I tried. Believe me, I tried." She sighed, suddenly looking more tired than usual, and older too.

"Are you guys going to the wedding?"

Gramps let out a sound that sounded a little like disgust. "We can't travel all the way out there. You know we don't fly anymore. Your gran doesn't do well with flying."

We stayed up for an hour longer, talking over exactly what was said as my grandmother pried more information out of me about Cassie and how she was doing. Gran seemed concerned for her, for Jack, for me. It was her nature to nurture.

I told her that Jack had asked me to be his best man, and she nodded silently as if knowing that I had little choice in the matter. Going to the wedding was something I had to do.

When they finally told me they were heading to bed early, I yawned, realizing how tired I was as well, and emotionally spent.

"Are you okay, Gran?"

"I'm just sad. For all of us. We've all lost something tonight," she said sadly before patting my cheek and walking slowly away.

Welcome to Hell

I HADN'T KNOWN when it was coming, when Jack would tell Cassie about the wedding, but I was sick to my stomach with dread. I'd assumed he would tell her right after confessing everything to Gran, but I was wrong. Every day that passed after that was just another day that Cassie still didn't know. And now the wedding was only weeks away.

I felt like I should warn her somehow, but had no clue what to say or do. Part of me thought she honestly might be our only hope out of this hell. That if anyone could convince Jack not to do this, it would be her.

I'd tried to talk him out of it about twenty times since, but he was adamant, his mind made up. He had convinced himself that this was the only option so he wouldn't follow in our parents' footsteps. It was twisted logic that made no sense, but he didn't see it that way. And no matter what he said, I knew that he was still madly in love with Cassie, and the idea of him marrying someone who wasn't her had to be eating him alive.

Sitting in Jack's room, I was messing around with his mini basketball, shooting hoops like I used to do when he was still here. My cell phone rang just as I missed another shot—

Damn!—and Melissa's name appeared. I hesitated for only a second before answering.

"*Get the fuck over here*," she screamed into the phone before I even said hello.

My heart raced as a giant lump formed in my throat. Did this mean that Cassie knew?

"Uh," I said, trying to play dumb.

"Don't *uh* me, Dean. Get over here now. Jack just called. He's marrying that stupid girl? Cassie needs you." Before I could say anything, she gentled her voice. "Please come over," she asked nicely, but she had me at Cassie needing me.

"I'll be right there."

I ended the call and jumped up from the floor, having no idea if Cassie had had a good conversation with him or not. I assumed if she needed me, things probably weren't okay, but I didn't know for sure.

All my questions were answered the second Melissa let me into their apartment. Cassie's sobs could be heard from the front door, and it broke my heart to hear them.

"She's devastated," Melissa warned me before shoving me toward Cassie's bedroom.

Melissa and I walked into the room to find Cassie in the fetal position, her body wrapped up tight on itself as she sobbed, her face soaked with her tears. Every other breath or so, she'd move her face into her pillow and cry so loud and hard. I'd never seen anything like it, never seen someone in so much physical pain from an emotional wound.

I sat down gingerly at the foot of her bed and waited. My

brother was the one who had done this to her, and that knowledge made me feel somewhat responsible as well.

Not knowing what to do or say to comfort her—or even if I could—I reached out and touched Cassie's calf, but she quickly swatted my hand away.

"Say something, Dean," Melissa insisted, jabbing my shoulder with her finger.

Uncomfortable with all of this, I looked up at her pleadingly. "What do you want me to say?"

"Make her feel better. Tell her you talked to Jack. Something!" Melissa said, her eyes wild.

Cassie's head jerked up as she met my eyes for the first time. "You talked to Jack?" she said, her voice still racked with sobs.

"Yeah."

"And?"

"I don't know. He's completely irrational. I can't talk any sense into him at all," I admitted.

"What about his agents?" Cassie asked, her voice raspy from crying. "I mean, what good are they if they let him go through with this?"

Feeling useless, I shrugged. "They tried, trust me. I guess I should be thankful they got him to agree to a pre-nup."

Jack's agents and I had ambushed him on the phone one evening and told him we'd support this sham of a wedding if he had Chrystle sign a pre-nup. Predictably, Jack had argued with us, but I was prepared for that and brought out the big guns. I threatened not to come, that I wouldn't be there for the ceremony and stand up with him.

Thank God that worked. Jack hadn't listened to any other bit of advice, but he listened to that one.

"They did? That's good." Cassie looked up at me with the slightest bit of relief in her eyes as she wiped her nose with the back of her hand.

"They tried to get him to wait, told him to get confirmation that the baby was his, but you know Jack." I shrugged, figuring she knew as much as I did how stubborn and pigheaded he was.

Cassie sat up and pulled her pillow up behind her to lean against, her face puffy and her eyes red and swollen nearly shut from crying so hard and for so long. The sight gutted me.

"I'm sorry, sis. I tried to tell him this was wrong. I did everything I could to talk him out of it, but he won't listen. He's so stubborn, and he's convinced himself that what he's doing is right for the baby's sake. Gran even tried to talk to him," I admitted in a whisper.

"What? What'd she say?" Cassie asked, sounding hopeful.

I sucked in a long breath. "She told him that it doesn't take becoming someone's husband to become a good dad, that one has nothing to do with the other. She said that being a dad was a choice, and even though anyone could father a child, only a real man chooses to be a dad. She told him that being a husband was something that should be reserved for the person you truly want to call your wife."

A small smile appeared on Cassie's face. "Gran's good."

"What did he say to that?" Melissa asked, and I startled

with surprise. I'd almost forgotten she was even in the room.

"He wouldn't listen to her, either," I said, shaking my head as Cassie's smile disappeared. "He told her that his child wouldn't grow up in a broken home. That sometimes you have to be unselfish and compromise, even if it's not what you want, because it's not about you anymore."

"There's no getting through to him. How are your grandparents doing?" she asked, and my shoulders slumped forward.

"They're both really sad. They're worried for him. And they're worried about you."

She nodded but said nothing, just tugged at a shredded tissue that had been balled in her hand.

"He loves you, Cassie. He doesn't give a shit about this girl; he's just so fucked up from our parents that he can't see reason." I pleaded with my eyes for her to understand, wanting her to know just how messed up my brother truly was over this.

Melissa stepped closer, watching me as she said to me, "I feel like you wouldn't do this, though, and you both grew up in the same house."

She was right. I couldn't imagine doing this either, but I wasn't in Jack's position. Who knew how I'd react if this had happened to me?

"Yeah, you're probably right. But he's older and remembers things that I don't. He was the one who had to hold it together while our mom fell apart. He remembers the day our dad didn't come home. Honestly, Jack really lost it when Mom left. He was never the same after that, and he's been fighting his demons ever since."

Looking back at Cassie, I said, "I never thought he'd let anyone in. We would argue like crazy about how he always pushed everyone away until I realized there was no changing his mind. I don't think it's that he didn't want someone to love him—he just didn't want to risk loving them back. You know, in case they left him too."

I paused for a moment before adding, "Then you showed up and everything changed. You changed him."

Cassie's eyes welled with tears as she whispered, "He changed me too."

"I'll say," Melissa said. "She never let anyone in either. I knew the night she saw Jack that something was different." She turned to stare at Cassie as she spoke. "I could see it. Watching the two of you together, it was like watching fireworks light up the night sky. You burn brighter when you're together."

"But even fireworks burn out," Cassie said sadly, and my heart ached with the finality of her words.

WORD OF JACK'S wedding spread like wildfire. I had no idea how the press got wind of the news, but the school newspaper was having a field day with it, and then the local newspaper picked up the story. They all heralded Jack as our local superstar and celebrated his upcoming wedding to a Southern sweetie, a sentiment that I found puke-inducing.

Poor Cassie had to endure it all. She was humiliated, and

even if she never said those exact words to me, I knew she felt that way. I didn't want her to be alone, so I constantly texted Melissa to make sure they were together, or to ask if I needed to come over. Cassie was tough, but this was too much, even for a strong girl.

"Where is she?" I asked Melissa from our table as I scanned the student union, searching for Cassie.

"I don't know. I just sent her a text telling her that we were here, so you can calm down."

I scowled at Melissa just as her phone beeped, and she snatched it up to read the text.

"She's on her way."

"Good."

Concerned, I kept an eye out for Cassie, not wanting anyone to harass her or to be mean to her the way girls could sometimes be.

When she came through the doors, I spotted her right away, and noticed with dismay how people stopped what they were doing to watch her every move. They expected her to fall apart, break down in some way, which would give them something juicy to post on social media.

Damn vultures.

It took everything in me to not run up to Cassie and play bodyguard. She didn't need it, but I felt obligated when it came to her. I knew Jack would want me to protect her, especially since he couldn't anymore.

When her eyes met mine from across the room, she relaxed slightly, but by the time she reached our table, she was practically hyperventilating.

"You're okay. It's okay." Melissa reached across the table to grab Cassie's hand, and Cassie's eyes became glassy as she fought back tears.

I slid next to her and put my arm around her shoulders to comfort her. Pulling her against me, I told her in a low voice that it would all be okay as she worked on breathing normally.

A curvy blonde at the next table motioned toward us with a snide smile. "I guess if Jack dumped me, I'd date his brother too."

"Shut up, you stupid tramp," Melissa shouted, her face reddening. "All of you just shut the hell up and leave her alone!"

Brett and Cole had been sitting several tables away, but when they saw what was happening, they grabbed their trays and headed toward our table. A few girls tried to follow, but the guys told them to back off and announced loudly enough for everyone in the vicinity to hear that they weren't welcome.

Cole sat down on the other side of Cassie, his eyes holding a different kind of pain. "We're all really sorry about you and Jack, Cassie. If there's anything we can do, just let us know. You're still our family."

Brett dropped his tray opposite Cole with a clatter, and his unopened can of soda fell over and rolled around. "Girls are such bitches!" he said loudly before plopping down, causing the whole table to vibrate.

"Hey!" Melissa smacked his shoulder.

"Present company excluded, of course," he said sweetly

with a wink in her direction, and the hairs on the back of my neck stood up at the attention he was giving her.

Then Brett focused on Cassie. "Good to see you, Cass." He grinned and then bit off a monster-sized bite from his club sandwich, deliberately ignoring the bits of lettuce and tomato that fell out of his mouth as he tried to chew the ridiculous mouthful.

Brett's antics were so comical that Cassie started laughing. It was a sound we hadn't heard in forever, but once she started, she couldn't stop.

"There's the smile I love." I nudged her shoulder with mine.

"Are you still working at that magazine?" Cole asked, flicking an unopened bag of chips across the table to Brett.

"Yeah," she said with a wan smile. "They extended my internship another semester."

It pained me to realize that even I hadn't known that. With all the drama going on lately, I hadn't even asked about it.

"And they're sending her on an assignment!" Melissa squealed.

"They're what? You didn't tell me that." I frowned, frustrated at how out of the loop I was.

"She just found out, Dean. Don't get all pouty about it," Melissa said, and I chucked a grape at her head.

Cassie nudged me, bringing my attention back to her. "I think it's a test. They said they want to see what kind of emotions I can evoke in readers with my pictures."

"What kind of what?" Brett's face twisted in confusion.

Cole shook his head with mock dismay. "You're such an idiot."

"They said they wanted to see how I viewed the world." Cassie shrugged. "So they're giving me a chance to show them."

Cole turned toward her, seeming genuinely interested. "That's so cool. Do you think they'll hire you?"

"I don't know. I guess if they like what they see, but I still have a lot to learn. The photographers they have on staff are mind-blowingly talented. I only hope I'll be that good someday. Plus, their main offices are in New York. The only people they have in LA are the head of sales, a research-and-development exec, some freelancers, and me."

"Would you move to New York?" Brett asked.

Melissa seemed surprised, and Cassie met her gaze as she said, "Why not? You only live once, right?"

"Because it snows there, that's why not!" Melissa exclaimed, and pushed out her bottom lip in a pout.

Those damn lips of hers are going to be the death of me.

"New York seems pretty cool." Brett shrugged before finishing off his drink, and tossed the empty toward the trash can a few feet away. When it hit the edge and fell to the floor, we all burst into laughter and teased Brett about how much he sucked.

I was thankful it wasn't me. I always fucking missed.

Cassie seemed to be in a daze; her mind was definitely elsewhere. But I couldn't blame her. None of us could.

"Hello?" Melissa waved both arms like she was signaling a rescue chopper.

"I'm sorry, what did I miss?" Cassie asked, and everyone laughed again. Then she glanced at her phone. "I have to go. I have class in ten minutes, and it's on the other side of campus."

I made a quick decision, realizing I was quickly running out of time to come clean with Cassie. I hated hurting her any more than she already was, but I had to tell her the truth. She needed to know that I was not only going to Jack's wedding, but that I was going to be in it as well. And now was as good a time as any.

"I'll walk you." I stood up to join her, and everyone stared at me like I had just crossed some invisible boundary.

"You don't have to walk me to class, Dean. I'm fine," Cassie said as we left the student union.

"I know, but I wanted to talk to you."

"What's up?"

"I just wanted you to know that I'm going to the wedding. And he asked me to be his best man."

Cassie stopped abruptly and froze, and I thought she might drop the bag she was holding as her face twisted in pain. I reached out an arm to steady her, but she pulled away.

"Of course you are," she said, her eyes huge and pained as she looked up at me. "You're his brother."

Ashamed of myself, I lowered my gaze and kicked at the ground with the toe of my shoe. "I know, but I feel like I'm betraying you somehow. Standing up there with Jack, it's like saying that I agree with what he's doing. And I don't. I don't agree with it for one second, but he's my brother and I love him."

Cassie threw her arms around me, refusing to let go until I hugged her back. "I love you for caring about me, but of course you should be there for Jack."

"I just wish I could talk him out of it."

"Are Gran and Gramps going?"

"They're not. Gran claims she can't fly for that long, and Gramps refuses to go without her." I shrugged. "But honestly, I don't think they have the heart to watch him go through with it."

"Does Jack know they aren't coming?" she asked, and I knew it must hurt her to still care so much about him.

"He knows. I think he's relieved, actually. He feels like he let them down, you know? He's dealing with a lot of guilt right now."

Cassie pulled out her phone to glance at the time. "I'm gonna be late to class. I have to go. Thanks for telling me." She turned and started to walk away before tossing over her shoulder, "You're a good friend, Dean."

CASSIE MUST HAVE filled Melissa in because the next day at school, the pixie chucked a T-shirt into my lap.

"What's this?"

"Open it, dummy," she said with a wicked grin.

When I unfolded the plain white tee to reveal writing in black letters that read TEAM CASSIE, I smiled.

"Am I supposed to wear this around campus?"

"I thought you could wear it under your tux at the wedding," she said with a wink.

I let out a belly laugh, the first one in a long, long time. It was a huge relief that my interactions with Melissa had become comfortable again. Maybe it was because whatever was between us had taken a backseat to all the drama with Jack and Cassie.

I wasn't sure but underneath it all, I believed I still wanted to be with Melissa, or at least give us a shot. Jack had been right about one thing all those months ago—I didn't give up easily and tended to stay attached. I could see that now.

Grinning at Melissa, I said, "I am so doing that. I'm absolutely doing it. It'll be the only way I can give this wedding a big fuck-you without pissing anyone off."

"Thought you might like it." She gave me a big smile. "I have to go. Have fun in stupid Alabama with your stupider brother at the stupidest wedding in the whole entire world," she added with a scowl.

"Mature much?" I said, teasing her.

"Not really." She laughed before walking away.

Worst Wedding Ever

Cassie and Melissa had been oddly secretive since I'd confessed I was attending the wedding. A few days later when I joined them at lunch, they were talking in hushed whispers, and clammed up the second I sat down at the table. They were obviously up to something, but I was too chickenshit to ask.

For some reason, I still felt partially responsible when it came to Jack's screwup. Not that I played a role in it, of course, but simply because I was related to him. Guilt by association. Jack had hurt these girls, and I felt as if I'd hurt them as well.

The three of us refused to address the elephant in the room—Jack's wedding—and that was fine by me. The look on Cassie's face after I told her that I was going would be burned into my memory forever. Maybe they discussed the wedding when I wasn't around so they didn't put me in the middle? Hell, I honestly had no idea what went on in the female brain.

"When do you leave for Alabama?" Melissa asked as Cassie played with the fruit on her plate, pretending to be disinterested in my answer.

"In the morning." I dreaded the wedding, but was happy to see my brother. It had been too long, and so much had happened since the last time I'd seen Jack in person.

Cassie stopped forking her food and looked up at me, her eyes conveying an emotion that I wasn't equipped to read.

"I'm sorry," I said automatically, not knowing what else to say as she looked back down at her plate.

I wished like hell that I could take away her pain and change my brother's mind. One of the hardest things I was going to have to do was to stand up there and watch Jack exchange vows with someone I knew he didn't love, someone I hadn't even met yet. Thinking about it filled me with dread. It was challenging, to say the least, to stand idly by and watch someone you cared about make decisions you knew would screw up his life, even if you understood his reasons.

Which I did.

In theory.

I knew my brother and I understood his mindset, but that didn't mean I wanted him to go through with it. Seeing the future I once assumed he would have be replaced by this unexpected and unwelcome one sucked.

Maybe I could talk some sense into him when I got there. Maybe once I was there, in person, he'd listen to reason.

The idea of getting him to postpone the wedding filled me with a small sliver of hope, and I suddenly found myself looking forward to getting on the plane.

Alabama was hot. And sticky. Even though I'd taken the first flight out at the crack of dawn, with the time difference, Jack was already at the field when I landed. He wasn't pitching tonight, so I had no intention of going to the field to sit in this nasty humid heat.

Apparently Chrystle had offered to pick me up at the airport, but thankfully Jack talked her out of it and sent me a car instead. I walked outside, following the driver as sweat instantly beaded on my forehead. Southern California was hot, but this was something else entirely. This was heat wrapped in a moist towel. You couldn't escape it. The air felt heavy, like you could feel it as you breathed it in.

On the ride to Jack's house, I started to regret not asking if I could go the field instead. The idea of being alone with the girl he was about to marry made me uneasy. I'd spent so little time actually thinking about Chrystle at all, the thought of spending time with her alone gave me a sick feeling.

What if I hated her? Or worse, what if I liked her? The very idea that I might like this girl caused my stomach to roll. I would always be loyal to Jack, and I wanted him to be with someone who was nice and treated him well, but I also felt a sense of loyalty toward Cassie. And liking this girl who'd ripped their world apart almost seemed like a slap to Cassie's face.

I was torn, not sure which was the lesser of two evils—liking Chrystle or hating her.

When I stepped out of the car in front of Jack's house, a too-thin brunette came out onto the porch. I picked up my duffel and thanked the driver, wanting nothing more than to hop back into the car and head to the airport to fly home. She was strikingly pretty, and I cringed at the image in my head of my brother in the bar that night, trying to tell this girl no a hundred times, and then telling her yes once.

"Dean," she called out as she waved at me, smiling at me like we were old friends.

We weren't.

I forced a smile. "You must be Chrystle," I said, trying to be polite as I took in her perfectly toned body.

"We're both so happy you're here," she said, and I tried not to wince at her speaking for my brother already. "I've been simply dying to meet you. I'm so glad you're here."

Her voice was so different from what I was used to, slow and syrupy sweet like molasses with her Alabama accent, and I instantly questioned everything that came out of her mouth. I wasn't sure if I was just primed to dislike her, or maybe the mere sound of her overdone Southern drawl made me uneasy, but her voice seemed fake, every syllable stretched and drawn out.

"It's nice to meet you too," I lied.

I couldn't help it, but this girl was messing up everything. It seemed easy to blame her, at least in my mind, for every single thing that had gone wrong now that I was face-to-face with her. Maybe if she was the villain in this scenario, Jack wouldn't have to be.

"I made up the guest room for you. Jack stocked the fridge with beer, so help yourself." She smiled, her teeth overly white.

"Oh, and your tux is hanging in the closet. Jack picked it up earlier."

"Cool," was all I could manage to say in response to that topic.

"I'd offer to take your bag, but," she patted at her flat stomach, "I can't. You know, because of the baby."

"I wouldn't ask you to carry my bag anyway," I said with a huff. What kind of guy did she think I was?

She let out a giggle. "Of course not. How silly of me. If you want to follow me upstairs, I'll show you to your room." She started up the stairs, acting like a damn tour guide. "Isn't this place great? Your brother spoils me rotten," she cooed, and I knew she was lying. "It's just a rental because Jack says we could move at any time with his team."

"It's nice," I said, trying to be agreeable, but I didn't care about their stupid house.

Chrystle stopped in the hallway and said, "This is your room. You have your own bathroom too." She indicated an open doorway and I walked in, tossing my bag on top of the bed. "The TV is hooked up to cable, so you can watch whatever you want."

"Nice." I looked around at the huge room. "I think I'll take a shower. I feel kinda gross after that flight," I said, hoping for some peace and quiet.

She smiled again, her head tilting to the side. "Of course, sweetie. You do whatever you want. If you need anything, just holler." She stepped out and closed the door behind her.

Relieved that the dreaded introduction was over, I quickly

unpacked, wishing my brother was here already.

After my shower, I planned to hide out in my room until Jack got home, but my stomach rumbled. I hadn't eaten in hours and was starving, but to eat I'd have to go back out there and socialize. Remembering the beer she'd mentioned, I comforted myself with the fact that at least there was alcohol.

Chrystle refused to let me do anything myself. She served me, bringing me beer after beer and making way too much food for me. It would have been nice if I thought for one second it was genuine. It all felt like a show, and the truth was, I could get my own damn beer and make my own damn food.

She tried to be a good hostess and make small talk with me, but I kept pointing at my full mouth, pretending that I couldn't talk while I was eating.

A thought hit me, and I broke my self-imposed silence to ask, "Are you staying here tonight or are you sleeping somewhere else? You know, the night before the wedding and all." It was a strange question that surprised even me. I had no idea where that thought even came from.

"I'm staying here. Jack and I think that tradition is silly, and we want to wake up together on our wedding day."

Her voice had taken on a dreamy quality, and I wondered how much fantasy filled her damn head. There was no way Jack would say anything like that to her.

When she finally excused herself to go to the restroom—*thank God*—I bolted from the kitchen and locked myself in my room. A few minutes later, she knocked on my door.

"Dean, are you okay? Did you want to come out and

watch a movie or something?" she called through the door.

"No thanks. I think I'm going to take a nap. I'm beat," I called back. There was no way in hell I was moving from the bed.

"Oh, okay. Well . . ." She seemed to be at a loss, making me wonder if this girl wasn't used to hearing the word *no*, or not getting her way.

"Thanks again for the food," I called out to her, praying she would leave. "It was really good."

"Oh, don't think anything of it," she said through the door. "We're going to be family soon. You're going to be my brother too."

Chrystle's words had crossed an invisible line, making me angry. I wanted to smash through that door like the Incredible Hulk. The only girl I'd ever consider a sister was Cassie. I didn't want this chick as my sister. In fact, I didn't want any of this.

After she walked away, I actually did consider napping since there was nothing else to do, but my phone alerted me to a text.

MELISSA: How's Alabama?

I smiled.

DEAN: Hot. Sticky. Did I mention hot?

MELISSA: How's your dumb brother and that stupid girl?

DEAN: I haven't seen Jack yet. He's still at the field. I'm home alone with the chick now.

MELISSA: Shut up! What's she like? Do you like her?

DEAN: Fake. And NO.

MELISSA: LOL. Good. Well, I just wanted to make sure you got there. And I might miss you.

DEAN: I might miss you too.

MELISSA: :) See you when you get back. Don't forget to wear your shirt.

DEAN: I have it right here.

I pulled the TEAM CASSIE shirt from my bag, wondering how I was going to put it on without Jack seeing and getting pissed off. After deciding that I'd figure that out later, I tossed it onto the floor.

Whether I was truly tired, or maybe it was out of boredom, I wasn't sure, but I eventually did fall asleep.

The squeal of a car peeling out of the garage startled me awake at one point. But when I pulled open my door and yelled for Jack, there was no response. I shouted for Chrystle too, but the house was quiet.

So I went back to bed and closed my eyes, wondering when the hell my brother would get home.

"HEY, LITTLE BROTHER! Where are you?" Jack shouted from somewhere in the house, and he sounded happy.

Drowsy, I sat up and checked the time on my phone. It was late, and my room was dark.

I yawned as I stepped into the hallway to look for him, and called out, "What's up?" Following the sound of his voice, I found him downstairs in the entryway.

Chrystle stood by his side as he tried to stow his equipment in the closet. She kept touching him, trying to get attention or affection from him, but he ignored her, pulled away without even looking at her. When she put her hand on his arm, he pulled back and leaned away from her. If she put her hand on his waist, he wriggled out of her touch and stepped to the side. If she reached for his hand, he balled it into a fist, unable to be held.

I watched this, amused, wondering if Jack even realized what he was doing. His reactions looked almost second nature, as if he always pulled away from her touch without thinking twice.

"Can I talk to you out back?" he asked me, ignoring her.

Chrystle faked a yawn and batted her eyelashes at him. "You won't be long, will you, Jack?"

I realized in that moment that I really didn't like this girl. She hadn't done a damn thing to me, or given me a single reason to not like her, but that didn't matter. Maybe I was being irrational, not really giving her a chance, but I didn't care about logic. Deep down, I sensed that this girl was trouble, and I didn't like it one bit. And my brother was going to marry her.

"Go to bed without me, Chrystle. I'll be there soon," Jack said, his tone clipped and rude, and my brows went up. He'd never talk to Cassie that way.

He pushed open the back door and stepped outside as I followed close behind. He walked over to one of two lawn chairs on the patio and sat down, gesturing for me to take the other.

"So," I asked, "are you nervous about tomorrow?"

He glanced at me, his eyes hooded. "A little." Then he turned in his seat and angled his body toward me. "Listen. Did you know Cassie's here?"

I leaned back into my chair in shock, the weight of his words hitting me full force. "Excuse me? What do you mean, she's here?"

"She was waiting for me in the parking lot after my game tonight."

"Shit." I didn't know what else to say.

"You didn't know? I was certain you knew."

"I had no idea, Jack. I swear. I would have given you a heads-up or something if I knew." I shook my head before it hit me. "Which is why, of course, they didn't tell me."

"They who?"

"Melissa and Cassie. They were acting weird all week, but they didn't say why."

I thought back to the hushed whispers, the conversations that would stop whenever I came around. How long had they been plotting this?

Then I thought back to my flight from this morning and wondered if Cassie had been on the same one. No, I would have seen her. Melissa knew what time my flight was; she would have never allowed Cassie to be on the same one.

Jack caught my eye. "Does she ever talk about me?"

He hadn't asked me that since the day they ended things, and I had never offered, assuming the truth would be too big of a pill to swallow on top of everything else.

"Not when I'm around," I said truthfully, then steered the conversation back to tonight. "What did Cassie say?"

My head was spinning at the thought that Cassie was here in Alabama. I couldn't believe it. Was she planning on showing up at the wedding?

Jack shook his head in disbelief. "She asked me not to get married tomorrow."

"Wait—she flew all the way out here to ask you that?" I lowered my voice to a loud whisper. "She could've just called."

A little nervous, I cast a quick glance at the second-story window where Jack's bedroom light was on. I didn't trust Chrystle not to eavesdrop on our conversation, but when I was satisfied with the lack of shadows or movement in the window, I refocused on my brother.

Jack let out a low laugh. "I told her the same thing."

"That sucks," I said, shaking my head. "I know this is killing her."

His expression tightened, all humor gone. "I'm pretty sure it's killing both of us."

The realization hit me in that moment. Cassie must have thought the same thing I did before I left, that being here in person might be the only way to talk him out of making a huge mistake. I assumed that I would have a better shot getting him to call off the wedding once I was here versus a simple telephone call. Cassie must have had the same idea.

"Then why are you doing it?" I asked. "I mean, don't do it. Don't marry Chrystle."

If Jack was in as much pain as he said, then I couldn't understand how marrying this chick was going to make it better. I knew how he saw this situation, and I understood. I just didn't want him to do it, and honestly believed he would regret this decision for the rest of his life.

This would be a make-or-break decision for him—one of those defining moments you don't get back, you never get over, and you never truly come back from.

Jack gave me a disgusted look. "It's a little late for that, don't you think?"

He had a point. All the guests were already in town and the wedding was tomorrow.

Frustrated, I reached out and clutched his forearm. "Look, I get why you're doing it; I just wish you wouldn't. I know you still love Cassie."

He glared at me, and a muscle jumped in his jaw. "Of course I fucking love Cassie. But I cheated on her and got someone else pregnant. I'll spend the rest of my life loving the one person I can't have. That's my punishment for hurting her."

I blew out an exasperated breath as I shook my head. "What kind of fucked-up logic is that?"

"The only kind of logic I can live with. My pain is my punishment. I brought it on myself. I deserve to hurt since I hurt her. And I don't deserve to have her after what I did."

"Jack, you're seriously whacked," I whisper-shouted at him. "You know that, right? You could be with Cassie right now if you wanted to!"

His face was anguished as he said, "I can't," and I lost it.

Shoving up from my chair, I stood up and leaned into his face. "You're still hurting her. Every day you aren't with her, you're hurting her. And following through with this stupid wedding is probably going to fucking ruin her!"

I stormed back into the house and slammed the sliding glass door shut so hard it rattled.

Back in the guest room, I was practically jumping out of my skin. I paced next to my bed, unable to believe that Cassie was here and that Jack wasn't with her. No wonder he'd been late getting home tonight. But why hadn't seeing her been enough to change his mind? Hell, if Cassie couldn't convince him to call off the wedding, then no one could.

Knowing how much pain she must be in, I reached for my phone to text her. My fingers hovered over the screen as I rethought it, and I tossed the phone on the bed.

Nothing I could say to Cassie would fix the damage that was about to be done.

THE NEXT DAY, I sat in one of the private rooms in the church with Jack as we finished getting dressed. My TEAM CASSIE shirt was underneath my white tux shirt, and I glanced at the mirror once more to make sure you couldn't see the black lettering through the thin fabric. I had slipped it on while Jack wasn't looking, not wanting to piss him off. Satisfied it didn't show, I smiled. Wearing this without anyone else knowing was my own private rebellion.

"We could still bail," I said to Jack as he adjusted his tie, meaning every word.

He turned to me but wouldn't meet my eyes, and I'd never seen him look more miserable in his life. He looked like he was about to throw up.

"Jack?" I asked, trying to get him to acknowledge me. He raised an eyebrow, so I knew he was listening. "Seriously. Let's go. You don't have to do this. You don't have to marry her in order to be a good dad."

"Stop," he said, his voice pained. "Just stop."

"I'm just saying. You have a choice, damn it. You have options. I'm here. I support you bailing out, and I'll drive the damn getaway car."

He gave me a sad smile before frowning again. "We'd better go out there."

Jack couldn't have sounded less enthused, but I followed him anyway. Watching his slumped shoulders as he walked ahead of me, I wished that I was bold enough to throw him over my shoulder and run.

The church pews were filled with people I didn't know and hadn't met before. Apparently they were Jack's new teammates, and Chrystle's family and friends. I wanted to care—I really did—but I didn't. I didn't care about a single person here except for my brother and my unborn niece or nephew.

I probably needed to start factoring in that new family member as well. You couldn't exactly hate an innocent little baby.

As I stood at the front of the church next to my brother, he tugged at his tie as if it was choking the life out of him. He shifted on his feet as the guests stared at us, stupid smiles on their stupid faces.

Thinking that reminded me of Melissa, but I put her out of my mind. I needed to focus on Jack now.

Soft music played, and Chrystle's maid of honor walked down the aisle. We'd been introduced earlier, but I couldn't remember her name. Again, I didn't care.

The music changed, louder now, and the doors at the back of the church opened wide. Chrystle stood at the end of the aisle, wearing a white dress that left nothing to the imagination. Literally. I could see every curve, every muscle in her body.

I looked at Jack's face as he watched her walk toward him. He wasn't smiling like a groom should, and his eyes weren't filled with love. His expression was hard and resigned, like a prisoner about to do time.

"We can still leave," I whispered, and I swore I saw a glimmer of hope flash in his brown eyes. "Seriously, bro. We can go."

He barely shook his head, but it was enough that I saw it.

I looked back at Chrystle just in time to see her lay a hand on her stomach with a smile focused at Jack, and I thought, *This chick is good.* She knew damn well Jack didn't want this, and she knew what worked on him. Guilt. As long as she had his baby in her, she had him by the balls.

I stood by my brother's side, prepared to do whatever he needed me to. But when the preacher read the vows and Jack repeated them, sorrow swept over me.

Weddings were supposed to be happy. Today was supposed to be filled with love, joy, and the promise of two lives becoming one. But this wedding on this day felt like a death sentence, one I desperately wanted my brother not to serve.

"Ladies and gentlemen, may I present Mr. and Mrs. Jack Carter," the preacher announced with enthusiasm, and Jack's face drained of color.

"You okay?" I whispered.

"I gave up being okay the day I lost Cassie," he admitted in a low voice, and then his new bride yanked him down the aisle.

Starting a New Chapter

As I flew back to California after the wedding, I couldn't get the fact that Cassie had flown there to see him out of my head. I still hadn't talked to her, and I knew that Jack hadn't told me everything about their meeting. It killed me to think that she came out to stop Jack, and he had still gone through with the wedding, despite it all. As much as it sucked for me, I could only imagine how much it had to suck for Cassie.

I wished like hell I had a time machine for us all to jump into. But I didn't, and what was done, was done. I had to learn how to accept that. Or at least pretend to.

When I saw Cassie at school the next day, she looked defeated. I couldn't blame her. But when she read the front of my shirt, a smile tugged at her lips and she actually laughed. Realizing that I hadn't heard her laugh in what felt like forever, I pulled her into a hug.

"Nice shirt," she said, still smiling.

I glanced down at the black letters that spelled Team Cassie and shrugged. "I thought so."

"Where on earth did you get that?"

Melissa popped up behind us. "From me!"

"Yeah. From that one." I jerked my thumb in her direction.

Cassie looked between the two of us, and her smile dropped. "It's a really sweet gesture, you guys." She looked upset, and her eyes shone with unshed tears. "I'll see you later, okay?"

Shit. "I didn't think it would make her sad," I said to Melissa as she hurried away.

"It's not you. Everything makes her sad these days," she said with a frown.

"HEY, BRO, IT'S early," I said sleepily, answering the phone as I rubbed my eyes.

"Shit. I always forget the time difference. Sorry."

"No big deal. What's up?" I yawned, wondering why Jack was calling so early.

"Chrystle lost the baby yesterday."

Shocked, I sat straight up in bed. "Oh God, really? I'm so sorry. Are you okay?" I didn't know what to say. Would he be upset that she lost the baby, or would he be relieved?

"I will be," he said.

"So, what now?"

My head whirled with the ramifications. If there was no baby, then there was no need to keep Chrystle. It was a harsh truth, but true just the same.

"What do you mean?"

"I mean, you'll get a divorce, right?" I whisper-shouted, not wanting to wake up Gran and Gramps. "You're not going to stay with her now that there's no baby?"

What the hell was wrong with Jack? How could he not be on the same page as I was?

"I can't leave her right now, Dean. She's devastated. She can't stop crying."

"So what? She's a bitch. I'll fly out today and help you pack," I said, dead serious.

He laughed. "Even I'm not *that* heartless."

"Does Cassie know?"

"No."

"Are you going to tell her?"

"Not right now," he admitted.

"Why not? What is going on with you? Leave Chrystle and come make things right with Cassie!"

This should be the easiest decision in the world, and to me it was. What he needed to do was so obvious. Why in the world couldn't he see that?

"Not yet," he said.

"What are you waiting for?" When he didn't answer right away, I sucked in a sharp breath. "You're not in love with Chrystle, are you?" Just uttering the words made me want to throw up.

"Are you fucking crazy? I don't even know how to love anyone other than Cassie."

"Just making sure." I breathed out in relief.

"I'm gonna go. I just wanted to tell you. Can you tell Gran and Gramps, please, and let Gran know I'll call her soon?" His voice sharpened as he said, "Don't tell Cassie. She shouldn't hear it from you."

My heart sank. Another damn secret I had to keep from Cassie.

I sighed. "Fine. But you better tell her soon."

After he hung up, I sat there processing the information. More than anything, I wanted to call Melissa and tell her the news, but I couldn't trust her to keep something like that from Cassie. And I'd have to wait to tell Gran and Gramps later, when they were actually awake.

Until then, I tried to go back to sleep, determined that this was a good thing. Jack couldn't stay married to Chrystle now. I had to make him see that.

SOMEONE SHOUTED MY name as I was on my way to class, and I turned to see Cassie running to catch up to me.

"What's up?" I said, trying to act nonchalant, as if the past few months had been no big deal and I didn't have a huge freaking secret under my belt.

Cassie smiled, but it didn't reach her eyes. "I just wanted to tell you that I got a job offer in New York, and I'm taking it."

It was no secret that this was something she'd wanted to do, but I had a strong feeling that Jack's rejection helped fuel her desire to get away from here. And honestly, I couldn't blame her.

"Wow. New York, huh?"

"Yeah. It's a pretty incredible opportunity."

"When do you leave?" I asked, then realized that it was the middle of a semester. Would she leave school to do this?

She looked down at her feet. "In a few weeks."

"But school's not over."

"I know, but I have to give this a try. I have to see." She looked up at me, pleading with her big green eyes for my support. "You know?"

I nodded. "I get it. That's awesome, Cassie. Really. Congratulations." I reached for her and pulled her into my arms for a brotherly hug.

"Thanks, Dean. I just wanted to tell you myself, you know, before Melissa told you. But I gotta jet to class." She turned and rushed off in the opposite direction, leaving me standing there, amazed at how quickly things can change.

I called Jack when I got home from school, knowing he was most likely at the field already. When he didn't answer, I left him a message asking him to call me, no matter what time. As if he paid attention to the clock anyway.

"DEAN, I'M GETTING moved up!" Jack shouted when he finally called later that night.

"What? To the bigs?"

"Yes! I'm going to the show! I'm headed to Arizona!" He cheered into the phone, and I cheered with him.

"Jack, that's incredible! Congratulations!"

When the excitement died a little, he asked, "What did you need to tell me?"

His question reminded me why I'd called him in the first place. For a second, I contemplated not telling him at all, wondering if it even mattered anymore.

"Oh yeah. I just wanted you to know that Cassie got a job offer in New York, and she's taking it. I figured you'd want to know."

The line was quiet for a moment before he asked, "When is she moving?"

"A few weeks, she said."

Jack cursed under his breath, and it sounded like all the wind had been knocked from his sails. I had no idea what he was thinking or feeling, and before I could ask, he ended our call.

I tossed my phone aside, recalling my thought from earlier about how everything seemed to be changing so quickly. In no time at all, Jack's dreams had come calling, and now Cassie was moving across the country to follow hers.

As much as I embraced the change, I hated it at the same time. It scared me to think that Jack and Cassie were moving apart, instead of coming together where they belonged.

"HEY, LITTLE BROTHER, I don't have very long, but I wanted to call you real quick to catch up."

Jack talked quickly when he called these days. He'd been busier than ever since he got called up to the major league, and his free time had dwindled down to basically nothing. Not to mention the fact that he learned Chrystle had never been pregnant in the first place—she had faked her entire pregnancy to get Jack to marry her. He caught her in the lie and then kicked her out of their house. My brother's life was like a messed-up book you couldn't write.

"What's up?"

"You know we play at Dodger Stadium this weekend, right?"

I laughed and glanced up at his schedule taped to the wall above my bed, all of his games in the area circled in red.

"Really? Of course I know. The whole damn town knows."

"I already talked to Gran. She said that she and Gramps would love to go to any game that I pitched, but the thing is, I have no idea if I will or not yet. So I'm not sure what to do about that."

"I'll talk to her. What else?" I said, figuring that Gran and Gramps would be proud to be there regardless of what Jack did.

"I'm leaving tickets for you, Melissa, and Cassie at will call for Friday night's game. Try and get her to come, Dean. Please."

I sucked in a quick breath. "I'll try, but I'm not sure she will."

"I know. I know." He sounded defeated. "Just try anyway, please? I have to see her. I'm dying to see my girl. You gotta get her there."

"I'll see what I can do."

"Get back to me about Gran, okay?"

"What if they want to come on Saturday too?"

"Then I'll get them tickets. They just might be in a different section. Is that fucked up? That's fucked up, isn't it?" he said, suddenly stalling and unsure.

"We'll figure it out," I reassured him, not wanting him to worry about trivial things like that right now. He needed to focus on playing and playing well.

"See you Friday," he said before hanging up.

WHEN FRIDAY ROLLED around, we were almost certain that Jack would be pitching at some point during the game. Gran was actually feeling under the weather, and as much as it killed her not to go, she decided she'd better stay home and watch it on TV instead. Gramps refused to go without her, saying that they were a team and teammates stick together.

I fired off a quick text to Melissa before I left the house to ask her if Cassie was coming or not. She replied with a frowny face, and I told her to try harder. My phone rang immediately following that text.

"You kidding me? You think I'm not trying hard enough?" she yelled into the phone. This girl was always yelling at me.

"I'm just saying. Jack wants to see her. She has to come," I pleaded.

"I know all of that. But she won't, Dean. She thinks that if she sees Jack, she won't get on her plane tonight."

I squeezed my eyes closed for a moment, completely understanding that Cassie was fighting for herself. She needed to do this, and she knew exactly what was at stake.

"Okay. Well if she changes her mind before I get there, tell her we can leave early or something. I mean, doesn't she want to watch him play?"

Melissa sighed into the phone. "Of course she does. She just can't. I'll explain it all to you in the car. Hurry up and come get me."

She was so damned bossy.

When I pulled my car into the lot, Melissa was waiting for me outside wearing an oversized Diamondbacks shirt. I had planned to run upstairs to see Cassie and ask her myself, but realized when I saw Melissa that this was her way of protecting Cassie, knowing that I might be able to convince her to come.

She hopped into my car, buckled her seatbelt, and stared at me.

"What?" I asked, not knowing what she was looking at.

She smiled. "Nothing. Go."

"No," I said, surprised at my own stubbornness. Melissa was playing a game, and I wanted to play it back.

"What do you mean, no?" she asked as she folded her arms in front of her.

I narrowed my eyes at her. "I'm not going until you stop

being so bossy and start being nice to me."

"Nice, huh? What constitutes nice?" She raised her eyebrows at me in challenge, and I sat there dumbfounded for a second.

"A kiss. Kisses are nice," I said with a big smile.

Without a word, she leaned toward me and planted a kiss on my cheek, but lingered there for a second. "Can we go now?" she asked, her lips just inches from my face.

When I turned to look at her, our lips almost brushed, and I swore I saw her breath catch.

"Yeah. We can go now." *Two can play at that game.*

I turned away as if nothing had happened and stepped on the gas. "So, tell me what's going on with Cassie. Why wouldn't she come?"

"First of all, she's packing. You know she leaves late tonight."

"That's not why."

Melissa shook her head. "No, it's not. She said she can't see him. That seeing him would make her want to stay. And she needs to go."

I nodded. "I get that, really, I do. But Jack's not going to be happy."

"No shit. He's going to be pissed."

I shook my head. "No. I think he's going to be sad."

Stadium Seating

WE PICKED UP two of the tickets from the will-call booth and headed inside the stadium. I'd been here a hundred times before, but tonight felt different.

I'd always felt so detached when I watched the games here growing up, insignificant, merely an observer watching strangers play a game I had no part in. But tonight, with my brother actually playing on the field, I felt like an insider, part of an exclusive club.

Melissa skipped into our aisle first and sat down, leaving the extra seat open, and I plopped down to her left. Jack stepped out from the dugout, his expression curious. He looked up at me and Melissa before pointing at the open seat with a shrug, asking if Cassie was coming.

Melissa glanced at me before turning back to him, and when she shook her head, his smile dropped. He mouthed something, but neither of us could understand what the hell he was saying from that distance. Jack turned to look behind him and jerked his head before returning to the dugout.

A few minutes later, the Diamondback's batboy hopped the infield wall and walked up to us to hand Melissa a note.

She unfolded it before showing it to me.

Where is she?

"He told me that I had to wait for your response," the kid said, and shifted from foot to foot as he stood there.

Melissa reached for the pen in his hand and scribbled a response.

She couldn't come. She said it's too hard. Jack, she's leaving tonight for New York! She's moving there!

After folding the note in half, she handed it back to the batboy, and he hurried away.

"I'm switching seats," I said before hopping up and changing to the seat on her right, closest to the dugout so I could be nearer to my brother.

The note wouldn't make Jack happy, and I hated the fact that he was distracted by our presence. He'd always been so focused when it came to playing the game, but he couldn't possibly be focused tonight. And that sucked because he needed to pay attention to his job, not to who was or wasn't in the stands. He knew better than to lose his focus, and that was the worst part.

No, the worst part was that Cassie didn't come.

"You want anything from concessions?" I asked Melissa, but she shook her head.

I stood up and had barely been gone at all when I hurried back, feeling guilty for leaving her sitting there alone. Melissa could handle herself, but I hurried back to our seats anyway.

"Where's your food?" she asked, her brow furrowed.

"I already ate it," I admitted. I'd only bought a hot dog, so it didn't take long for me to inhale it.

"Pig," she said with a huff.

"I asked you if you wanted anything," I shot back, refusing to let her blame me for my lack of mind-reading abilities.

"Dean!"

I thought I heard my name but couldn't be sure, so I ignored it, staring at the field and occasionally glancing over at Melissa.

"Dean!"

I heard it again and turned to find Jack looking at me from the dugout. I looked back at him like he was crazy, wondering what the hell he thought he was doing.

"What time's her flight?" he shouted.

I glanced at Melissa, who was clearly as surprised as I was before I turned back to Jack. "She's leaving the apartment at ten thirty."

A crazed look came over his face, and I wondered for a moment what he was going to do.

"You don't think he'd leave, do you? Before the game even ends?" I asked Melissa, horrified.

She shrugged. "He's your dumb brother. You'd know better than I would."

"When it comes to Cassie, I don't know what he's capable of," I admitted as I leaned forward to peer inside the dugout for Jack, but couldn't see anything more than a line of legs in uniform pants.

For the rest of the game, I practically held my breath, praying that my brother wouldn't put his entire career in jeopardy just to go see Cassie. The moment the game ended, I caught a glimpse of Jack and breathed out a quick sigh of relief, thankful that he was still here.

His gaze met mine, and he jerked his head toward the rear of the stadium before disappearing.

"Shit, he's leaving," I told Melissa.

"We'd better hurry then!"

She jumped to her feet, reached for my hand, and tugged me out of the crowded stadium, shouldering her way past people who were moving too slowly. We couldn't move fast enough to catch Jack, and I knew getting out of the parking lot would be madness as well.

When we finally pulled into the parking lot of her apartment complex, there were no signs of Jack or Cassie, and I wondered if maybe he did get her to postpone her flight.

"You think they're upstairs?" I asked, my tone hopeful as we exited the car.

"I don't know. She was pretty adamant about getting on that flight."

"Yeah, but she hadn't seen him yet. Maybe seeing him changed her mind."

Melissa let out a huff. "The way seeing her changed his mind about the wedding? Fat chance."

I threw my hands up in surrender as we walked up the stairs. "Hey. You always get so pissy with me when it comes to that. I'm not Jack," I reminded her, and she laughed before letting out a soft gasp.

Following her gaze, I saw Jack standing alone in the parking lot, his jersey untucked, his baseball hat in his hand.

"Oh shit. Jack?"

Melissa's sympathy came through loud and clear, both in her eyes and in her tone. She might be on Cassie's side when it came down to it, but she had a soft spot for Jack and their relationship.

Jack turned toward our voices and looked at us blankly before recognition kicked in and he headed in our direction. He looked like hell, his posture defeated, and I sprinted down the steps to meet him.

"Come on, bro, let's get you inside." I wrapped an arm around his back and urged him up the staircase as Melissa unlocked the front door.

"Did you see her?" she asked once we were inside, and tossed all of her crap on top of the kitchen table with a clatter.

"I saw her." Jack's tone was cold as he tossed his hat on top of Melissa's things.

"Well, what the hell happened? What did she say?" she demanded as she hooked her hands on hips.

"She left." He shrugged, sounding completely dejected. "She's moving to New York."

"Well, of course she's moving to New York," Melissa said, as if his statement was the stupidest thing she'd ever heard.

I placed a hand on his shoulder and tried to explain it better. "Melissa just means that Cassie has to start living her life for herself. She has to make decisions that have nothing to do with you."

That got a reaction. Jack jerked his head up, his eyes burning holes through me. "I know that. You think I don't know that?"

"Do you? Do you really, or did you think she'd just leap into your arms and you'd live happily ever after?" He needed to live in the reality of what his actions had done to her, what they had caused her to do in return.

He smiled. "I thought there might be some leaping," he admitted, shrugging one shoulder.

Melissa's mouth twisted into a snarl. "That's bullshit, Jack. You expect her to give up her career because you asked her to?"

"I didn't ask her to give up her career. I just figured she'd at least talk to me. Postpone her flight. Give me a fucking chance."

"The way you gave her a chance before you married that skank?"

"Melissa," I said softly in warning, wanting her to ease up a little. Jack looked wrecked enough, and her harsh words weren't helping.

I placed my hand on her shoulder, and she relaxed slightly as she looked at me before focusing back on Jack.

His jaw was clenched; no doubt our words were swimming in his head as he tried to sort this all out. "You think it didn't fucking kill me to leave Cassie that night? All I wanted to do was stay with her, beg for her forgiveness and—"

"But you didn't," Melissa spat back, every ounce of frustration that she'd built up on Cassie's behalf spilling out. "You didn't stay with her. You left her crying in a parking lot alone while you left with that bitch!"

"I know what I did!" he immediately fired back, the veins in his neck throbbing. "You think I don't fucking know what I did? I have to live with it every second of every day. I fucked up, okay? We all know I fucked up!"

Jack slammed his palms on the kitchen table where Melissa had dumped her things, and we all watched as some loose change rattled and rolled onto the carpet below. He seemed to zone out, his eyes solely focused on the quarters and nickels on the floor.

"If you want to make it right, Jack, it's not enough to just know what you did. You have to know what it did to her." Melissa calmed down as she spoke, her voice no longer agitated. I knew she wanted him to see, to understand.

Jack swallowed hard and unclenched his jaw. "Tell me."

"Everyone knew what you'd done by the time Cassie got back from visiting you in Alabama. It was all over the newspapers that you were getting married and had a baby on the way. It was on Facebook. Did you know that the stupid school magazine she worked for had the balls to call and ask her for pictures of you? They said they only had old ones and wanted to know if she had any newer ones."

"You're kidding?" His eyes widened as he looked at her with shock.

"I wish."

His hands balled into fists. "I'll fucking kill them, the inconsiderate little—"

Melissa pointed an accusing finger at him, stopping him mid-rant. "It wasn't just the newspapers and social media. It was everywhere she went. School was the worst. Cassie couldn't even walk across campus without people making comments and snide remarks. She had the most personal and painful moments of her life on display for everyone to see and judge. And trust me, everyone had an opinion about your breakup."

Jack cringed. His hands reached into his hair and he tugged at it, the same way he always did when he was frustrated or uncomfortable. "I had no idea that was happening or I would've done something to stop it. I would've made sure no one ever said another mean word to her again."

"I'm not telling you this to make you feel bad, Jack. I'm telling you so you'll understand the repercussions your actions had on her. You made the mistake, but she had to pay for it." Melissa said the words calmly, but their edges were sharp.

He dropped his head fully into his hands and worried his hair, his fingers twisting the strands. When he looked back up, there were tears in his eyes.

"You broke her, Jack," Melissa said, delivering the final blow, and my brother looked like he'd never recover.

"I broke me too," he admitted, brushing away the lone tear that rolled down his face, and my own eyes stung at seeing him that emotional.

"Jack, look." Melissa sat down across from him and folded her arms on the table. "I love you, I really do. But you have to let her go do this."

He clutched at his chest as he swallowed hard. "I want her back. I need her. It's either Cassie for me or no one."

"I'm not the one you have to convince." She reached out her hand, her fingertips brushing over his knuckles before he pulled away.

He tore his gaze away from hers and met mine. "I know."

"She still loves you," I said, deciding it was time I jumped in here. When his eyes narrowed on me, I said, "What? You don't believe that? She does."

Melissa frowned at me. "It's not about whether or not Cassie loves him, Dean."

"It's a little bit about that, otherwise we wouldn't be having this conversation," I said with a chuckle.

Her expression softened and she bit back a smile. "Have you even been paying attention?"

"Dean's right," Jack said, interrupting the byplay between Melissa and me. "I wouldn't have a fighting chance if she didn't love me anymore."

"So, what are you gonna do?" Melissa folded her arms over her chest, watching him carefully.

Jack jumped to his feet. "First, I'm going to get that marriage annulled," he said with new-found determination. "Then I'm going to hop on a plane to New York and get my girl back."

Yes! I punched a fist in the air. If there'd been pom-poms on the table, I would have reached for them and done a victory dance.

But Melissa frowned at him, apparently not convinced.

"How?"

He exhaled quickly, seeming to deflate. "I don't know yet."

Uncertainty lingered in the air, making the silence that followed awkward. The pressure was palpable in the room. We were all aware that if Jack went after Cassie to try to win her back, he had to do it right or not at all. If he didn't think this through and screwed it up, he wouldn't get another chance.

Jack cleared his throat, breaking the silence. "Can I use the bathroom?"

"Of course."

"Can I use hers?" he asked, and I cast Melissa a sideways glance.

"Uh, yeah." She rolled her eyes, and I stopped myself from doing it too just to mess with him.

As he walked away, I remembered what state Cassie had left her room in. Jack would be devastated to see the things she left behind—memories of him, memories of them. The jar containing the quarters he'd given her still sat on a shelf. And while the majority of her pictures were gone, one of her and Jack still remained on her bedside table.

From the living room, we could clearly hear what sounded like a jar being put back down, and Melissa and I stared at each other as we both held our breath, waiting for Jack to return.

"How come some of her stuff's still here?" Jack asked Melissa when he reentered the living room.

She shrugged. "We figured it would be easier to leave it

here for now. We don't know how long she's staying there, and I'm not moving anytime soon. Besides, finding a fully furnished apartment in New York is easy."

"What do you mean, you don't know how long she's staying there?" He frowned and fidgeted, shifting his weight from foot to foot.

"She might hate living there. Or the job might not work out. She didn't know for sure, you know?"

Jack nodded his understanding before squeezing his eyes shut as if he was in pain.

Melissa glanced at me before asking him, "Are you okay?"

He opened his eyes and stared at us both before saying, "Just fighting ghosts."

Jack was coming undone, ready to lose it at any second. I was about to offer him an excuse to leave when he spoke up.

"I gotta get back to my hotel before they freak out and think I've gone AWOL." He reached for his baseball cap before walking to the front door.

"How'd you get here anyway?" I asked.

"I had a driver for the night. But I made him sit in the passenger seat while I drove his car here. Once I hopped out, I told him he could leave. I think he was relieved," Jack said before adding, "I also think he shit his pants."

I laughed. "So you need me to drop you off?"

"Unless you want me to take your car back to the hotel. But you'll have to pick it up first thing tomorrow so it doesn't get towed," he said, reminding me that his team was scheduled to head back to Arizona in the morning.

I glanced at Melissa before flashing my brother a smile. "Nope. I'll take you."

"Jack? Don't forget that I'm here too. You can call me anytime, and I'll help you if I can," Melissa said, her expression sympathetic.

"I'm gonna hold you to that." He tried to smile in return, but it was a pathetic attempt.

"Good. Because even though you're a stupid jerk-face, you're her stupid jerk-face, and you two belong together," she whispered before wrapping her arms around his waist and hugging him so hard, he made a face like he was dying.

"You're killing me, Funsize," he choked out, and she giggled.

When Melissa released him, I tossed an arm around her shoulders and squeezed as I looked down at her beautiful blue eyes. "I'll see you later, okay?"

"Okay," she said, looking up at me with an expression so soft and warm that it took my breath away.

I released her reluctantly, wondering if that look had always been there, or if it was only because of tonight. Or maybe I was just imagining things and there was no look at all.

Jack grabbed my keys from the table, tugged his Diamondbacks cap on his head, and waited for me to follow him out the door. We walked in silence toward the Mustang he'd bought for me, its tinted windows looking almost black in the darkness.

He tossed me the keys and waited at the passenger door to be let in. I clicked the key fob and two beeps filled the night air, and we both slid into the chilly leather seats.

The engine purred to life and I backed out of the parking space, my head racing with everything that had transpired this evening.

"What's up with you and Meli?" he asked out of nowhere.

Recognizing Jack's need to have the focus not be on him for two seconds, I grinned as I pulled out of the complex, refusing to look at him. "Nothing. Why?"

"Don't lie to me." He punched me playfully in the arm, causing me to yank the steering wheel, and the car swerved with a jerk.

"Hey! Don't do that!" Scared half to death, I shot him a mean glare before turning my attention back to the road.

"Tell me," he said, "what's up with you two? I saw the way she was looking at you."

I straightened up in the seat, thankful that I hadn't been imagining something in her eyes earlier. I'd needed my brother for the last few months to help me navigate whatever the hell was going on between me and Melissa, but he'd had his own shit to worry about. Now that I had Jack's undivided attention, I needed to take full advantage of that.

Glancing at him, I said, "What way? How was she looking at me?"

"You're kidding, right? You don't see the way she looks at you with her eyes all hot like she wants to eat you up? Are you really that clueless?"

I laughed so hard, I snorted. "She doesn't want me."

Jack shook his head with dismay. "How are we even related? Dude, she wants you. Trust me on this. I know women."

The roar of the engine as I accelerated onto the highway was the only sound in the car. I focused intently on the road ahead before glancing at my brother, who was still staring at me.

I released a long sigh. "I tried to kiss her once, okay? I mean, we did kiss once. I thought I'd read all the signs right, but she stopped me," I admitted, slightly embarrassed that I had to tell him about the failed make-out session.

"Did you ask her why?"

"No. I just apologized."

He laughed, and I wanted to punch him. "Jesus, Dean. I'd bet a thousand bucks that she wants you."

"Then why'd she stop the kiss?" I glanced at him again.

"That's a good question. You should ask her," he said. "Time to grow a pair, little brother. How are you going to feel if she starts dating someone else?"

I gripped the steering wheel so tightly that my knuckles turned white. "I'm not going to be happy."

"Exactly."

When I pulled into the hotel parking lot, Jack hopped out of the car before I'd even come to a complete stop. He walked around to my side of the car and I rolled down the window, thinking he had something to say. But he extended his hand through the open window, so I grabbed it and pulled him in for an awkward through-the-window hug. He pulled back after a few seconds, and we slapped each other on the shoulder before sharing a long look.

Jack could get on my last nerve like only brothers can do, but I'd missed him. And I hated like hell that he was leaving again so soon.

"It will all work out. You'll get her back," I said, hoping to leave Jack with something positive to look forward to. Plus, I wanted to believe that it could happen.

He shot me a quick smile. "I fucking better, or I don't know what I'll do."

"I'll help you."

Smiling, I grinned up at him. If there was something I could do to help get them back together, I'd do it without question. And he knew that.

Jack nodded one last time. "I'll need it." He took a step back toward the car and gave me one last pat good-bye. "I'll call you later."

"All right. Take care."

Fighting the Past

I'D FINALLY GOTTEN used to my brother being gone, but Cassie leaving for New York gave me a sense of abandonment all over again. My brain knew that I was being irrational, but my heart hurt because the people I loved most kept leaving me.

Although I knew it wasn't true—they weren't truly *gone*—inside I still felt dismissed, ditched in some way.

I sent a text to Cassie, and she responded almost immediately.

DEAN: Did you get to New York okay? How is it?

CASSIE: OMG, the city is unbelievable! It feels like magic.

CASSIE: You and Melis need to come visit me ASAP. :)

Her text made me smile, and also reassured me a little.

DEAN: I'd love that!

DEAN: I hate to ask, but how are you feeling after seeing Jack?

CASSIE: :(Walking away from him was really hard, but it was the right thing to do.

DEAN: Feel better! You know I love ya, sis. Chat soon.

After my morning classes, I texted Melissa to see if she still wanted to hang for lunch or not. Since it was just the two of us now, I wasn't entirely sure what we were supposed to do—carry on like nothing happened, as if the two people who were our glue weren't gone?

She responded that she did, called me a dummy, and I met her in our usual spot, elated.

"And then there were two," she said as I sat down across from her.

"Maybe it's us? Maybe we make people leave," I said, biting back a smile.

"Maybe it's you. People like me just fine." She gave me a big grin, and I wanted to disagree just to be argumentative, but resisted the temptation.

Instead I said, "I texted with Cassie this morning."

"Me too." She sighed. "My apartment is quiet, boring, and lonely with her gone."

My insides tightened. "I'll come over anytime you want. All you have to do is ask," I offered, hoping like hell she'd take me up on it.

"It's not the same," she said without meeting my gaze, and the blows to my ego continued.

"I know I'm not Cassie, but shit, aren't I better than nothing?" I asked, wanting even a crumb from this girl.

She frowned at me. "I don't want a boyfriend, Dean."

Well, that came out of freaking nowhere.

"I wasn't asking to be your boyfriend," I spat back, annoyed. "Seriously, what the hell is wrong with you? I just said I could come over if you were lonely and wanted company."

She shrugged. "I'm sorry. I just don't want you to get the wrong idea about us."

Although she'd said the words, I had a hard time believing them. Maybe it was the way she wouldn't look me in the eye when she said them.

Still annoyed, I told her, "I don't think there is an *us*, so you don't have anything to worry about."

Jack's advice came back to me, and I remembered him telling me to ask someone else out. I wasn't sure that I could do that when I wasn't really interested, but I figured I might be able to fake liking someone who wasn't Melissa just to see what she'd do. It was a stupid game, but I was willing to play it if it meant that she would have to admit to feeling something for me.

"Do you even like me? Because I think you do. I think there's something here between us," I said, laying my cards on the table.

"Of course I like you," she said with a dismissive snort, and I groaned in frustration.

"Then why do you keep pushing me away?"

"Because I can't do this with you, Dean. We're not a good idea."

"What? Not a good idea? We're the best idea there is."

She shook her head hard, as if trying to convince herself of something only she could understand. "No. Not after everything that Jack and Cassie have been through. I mean, we can't be together when they're not!"

"Melissa." I shook my head, trying to make sense of her nonsense. "I was interested in you before there even *was* a Jack and Cassie. So that's not fair."

She sucked in a small breath and whispered, "I liked you back then too. We just took too long, and they got together first."

Oh my God. I wanted to bang my head against the wall. This girl was driving me crazy.

"I don't understand what they have to do with us," I said stubbornly.

"Everything. They have everything to do with us."

I leaned back in my chair and crossed my arms over my chest. "I'm not giving up."

Melissa looked at me for a moment, her expression as soft as her voice when she finally whispered, "I don't want you to."

Somehow confused and elated at the same time, I yelled, "You make zero sense! None. Not an ounce."

She let out a frustrated laugh and shrugged one shoulder. "Welcome to my brain."

THE NEXT DAY I made sure that Melissa saw me walk into the student union with a pretty brunette and sit down with her for lunch. The truth was that Serena and I were study partners for one of our classes, but Melissa didn't need to know that. A moment later, I glanced back at the table Melissa occupied and noticed it empty. Curious, I wondered what that meant.

When the following day rolled around, I joined Melissa instead of ditching her.

"Where's your new girlfriend?" she asked, her tone snarky.

"Why do you care?"

"I don't." Her blue eyes narrowed as she faked a smile. "But is that what she is? Is she your girlfriend?" Her gaze darted around the room before meeting mine.

"No, but I was thinking of asking her out."

Melissa swallowed hard as she looked everywhere but at me. "Yeah, um." She gathered her things. "You should do that."

Reaching for her hand, I stopped her. "Unless there's some reason why you don't think I should."

Please be honest for once, I begged her with my eyes. *With me, with herself.*

"You can do whatever you want." She pulled out of my grip and stalked away.

Except give up on you, obviously.

JACK WAS COMING home today and I felt like a kid going to Disneyland, too excited to sleep. Gran was busy in the kitchen making food while Gramps pretended to relax in his recliner, but constantly looked out the front window for Jack's car. Everyone was excited.

When my brother finally walked through the door, I was holed up in my room, trying to distract myself with homework. Gran and Gramps's noisy excitement filtered throughout the house as the front door shut, and I headed into the living room where the conversation had already started without me. After catching up about his new workout routine and how the guys in the major leagues could not only hit Jack's pitches, but could hit them far, we headed into the kitchen for dinner.

Jack continued to fill us in on what we'd missed since talking to him last. The annulment paperwork had been officially filed in Alabama, so he was simply waiting for Chrystle to sign it, hoping it would happen in the next day or so. I worried that she wouldn't, but Jack seemed unconcerned, claiming that the two of them were over and she knew it, so why wouldn't she sign?

I choked back a laugh. "Have you met her? She's a total bitch."

"Dean! Language!" Gran's forehead furrowed as she shook a her fork in my direction.

"Sorry, Gran," I said, slumping a little lower in my chair.

Jack chuckled at Gran before turning back to me. "She signed a pre-nup before we were married, so she doesn't gain anything by not signing."

"Except control," I muttered.

"What the fuck are you talking about?" he snapped. Apparently I'd pissed him off, but I wasn't sure why.

Gramps cleared his throat. "How many times do we need to remind you both to watch your mouths?" He glanced at Gran, who gave him a nod of approval.

"Sorry, Gran," Jack said with a sigh.

"I just meant that she'd have control over you if she didn't sign the papers. She knows how badly you want out of this marriage, so it wouldn't surprise me if she pulled a bunch of sh—" I stopped myself, throwing a frown Gran's way, "*stuff* just to mess with you."

Gran nodded. "He's right, Jack. Chrystle's been so evil from the very start. What's to stop her from being difficult now?" she asked, her voice shaky.

"I don't know," Jack said with a shrug. "I guess I'm just hoping that she knows this is over, and there's no point in delaying the inevitable."

He was thoughtful for a moment, and I hoped he was considering something that I had assumed was obvious this whole time. Chrystle wasn't a nice person, so why would she be nice about ending their marriage? She was devious and malicious, and I had a strong feeling that she would make this difficult for him just to be a bitch.

When Gramps brought up Cassie, the conversation turned lighter.

"Gramps, if I didn't know better, I'd think you had a thing for my girl," Jack joked.

"Your girl?" Gramps leaned back in mock affront.

Jack dropped his fork to his plate as if saying *Game on.* "Uh-huh. My girl."

I laughed, wanting to play this game too. "Maybe I'll make her my girl. Keep her in the family."

If looks could kill, Jack would have murdered me. Apparently I'd gone too far. "And I'll disown you before I kick your—"

Gramps slammed a hand on the table. "Boys, that's enough."

I shoved a spoonful of rice into my mouth as I grinned at my brother, mumbling around it, "You're lucky she's like a sister to me."

"Yeah? I'd say you're the lucky one. 'Cause I'd kill you if you touched her, and you know it."

"I'm your only brother and this is how you treat me?" I laid a hand over my heart as if he'd hurt me deeply.

Gramps shook his head, holding back a smile. "You're trying to take the man's kitten, Dean."

When Gran laughed, Jack mentioned Melissa, changing the subject and putting the spotlight on me, which wasn't playing fair and he knew it. He continued to harass me, asking why we weren't dating yet.

Finally, I exploded.

"I don't know! She says she doesn't want a boyfriend, but I think she just doesn't want *me* as a boyfriend. Can we talk about something else now?" I begged.

"Who wouldn't want you as a boyfriend? That's ridiculous," our ever-loyal Gran said with a huff.

"Can we please talk about something else? Anything else," I pleaded, uncomfortable admitting to my entire family that this girl didn't want me.

Jack moved the conversation back to Cassie and the fact that he'd been basically stalking her online, following her work in New York.

That revelation ignited my temper, probably because I knew how hurt Cassie had been by Jack's silence since she moved. She would have never admitted it to me, not wanting to put me in the middle, but she told Melissa that she didn't understand why Jack hadn't reached out to her since his marriage was over. And, of course, Melissa told me.

Cassie assumed that he would have been fighting to get her back, and frankly, so had I. It pissed me off that Jack hadn't reached out to her once, and I couldn't figure out why. I knew he still loved her and wanted to be with her, so why wasn't he trying to make it right?

When he saw the look on my face, Jack glared at me and said, "After everything Cassie and I have been through, you think my following her work online is psycho?"

"It's a little weird, don't you think? You won't even talk to her in real life, but you'll follow her online?" I snapped back.

The chair scraped against the floor as Jack shot up, breathing hard.

"Jack, sit down!" Gran said sternly. "You two are acting like little boys."

He dropped into his chair, breathing deeply to regain control of his emotions.

After he'd calmed down, he said, "I can't talk to her until I'm not married anymore, okay? So until then, yeah, I'll follow everything she does online. If that magazine can give me a glimpse into how she's seeing the world, I'll take it. Because until I'm back in her life, that's the only Cassie I get. And if that makes me psycho, then I don't give a fuck. Sorry, Gran," he said quickly before she could yell at him.

"I'm going to ground you. I don't care how old you are," she said, but there wasn't much heat to it this time.

"He started it," he said, nodding his head toward me. "Let's talk about Melissa some more."

I lifted my palms in the air in defeat. "I'm sorry. Truce?"

Jack and I both calmed down, much to our grandparents' relief, and the rest of the meal was eaten in peace. Afterward, we forced them both to retire to their chairs in the living room while we cleaned up.

We stood at the sink, Jack washing while I dried. I hated drying. Washing was easier, but I knew better than to start a fight I wouldn't win. The younger sibling never won arguments like that.

"I told Melissa that I was thinking about asking this other girl out," I said, glancing at him while I dried the plate in my hand.

Jack smiled. "What did she say? What'd she do? If I was a betting man, and I am, I'd bet that Funsize didn't like that too much."

"I don't think she did, but she told me to ask her out. She told me I could do whatever I wanted." When I shook my head in frustration, Jack burst out into laughter.

"Of course she did. Would you expect her to say anything else?"

I stopped drying and leaned against the counter. "Yeah. I expect her to tell me not to do it."

His brow furrowed. "Not gonna happen, little brother. She'd never tell you to not date someone because then she'd have to own up to feeling something for you. And for whatever reason, she refuses to do that."

"Why? Why won't she just admit it?"

"I honestly have no fucking idea."

That was helpful. Not.

JACK BEING HOME was awesome, except for the fact that I still had school and had to work at the agency almost every day. We got the news that Chrystle refused to sign the paperwork, and while I wasn't surprised, Jack was flipping out.

In the meantime, I'd kept pushing him to talk to Cassie, to fill her in on what he was trying to do. Every time I brought it up, he flat-out refused and threatened my life if I gave her a heads-up in any way.

Jack was always putting me in these shitty positions when it came to her, and I was growing tired of it, tired of hurting Cassie when I knew it served no purpose. Jack never specifically said that I couldn't tell Melissa, though, and so this time I partially filled her in on what was going on, but made her promise to keep it to herself. She was a bit of a hard sell as she huffed and puffed, but eventually agreed that she would stay quiet . . . *for now.*

When an entire month had gone by and Chrystle still refused to sign the papers, I thought Jack might have a nervous breakdown or spontaneously combust. We talked constantly about how out of control he felt, and how by sitting in California doing nothing, he felt like he wasn't moving his life forward in any way. He compared it to being on pause, where nothing happened; you just lived in this stagnant existence, not moving in any direction.

So I shouldn't have been surprised when he brought this topic up during dinner one night.

"Hey, Dean. Question—how long is your winter break?" he asked, knowing that it was coming up soon.

I gave him an odd look. "We go back at the end of January, why? What's up?"

"You wanna fly out to Alabama and help me move my stuff back here?"

"Of course I'll go," I said without hesitation. "When?"

"After Christmas, we'll head out. I want to get out of that state as soon as possible," he said, his voice filled with disgust.

Gran reached out and squeezed his arm. "Did she sign the papers yet, dear?"

He shook his head, focused on his plate. "She's still fighting it. Says I can't prove there was fraud involved."

"So, wait." I wiped at my mouth with a napkin before placing it back in my lap. "Are you saying that there's nothing you can do to fight it?"

"I'm just saying that the burden of proof is on me. And how do I prove all that?"

"I'm worried, Jack. This is taking so long. The longer it takes, the more you have to lose," Gran pointed out, clearly talking about Cassie.

Jack sighed. "I know exactly what I have to lose."

"Then you gotta talk to her, man. You're wasting time, and Cassie thinks you don't care about her. She honestly thinks that you let her walk out of your life for good. She's confused. She's hurt. And you're just letting her feel that way when you could stop it."

Hopefully something I said would get through. He needed to reach out to her in some way, whether it was a text, an e-mail, or a voice mail at her office.

Jack shook his head. "I know you don't understand, but I can't tell Cassie that everything is going to be fine and that I want to be with her. Not when I can't be with her yet. Do you get that? Chrystle is a psycho who isn't letting me go, and Cassie would get sucked into it. She'd have to deal with Chrystle too. And I don't want her to ever have to think about that person again."

He gave me a pointed look. "You know how Chrystle is. Would you want Cassie to deal with that?"

When I shook my head, he said, "I don't want to put Cassie through that. I just want to reach out to her when I don't have a single piece of baggage holding me back from being with her forever." Studying my face, he groaned. "Does that make any sense at all, or do I sound completely insane?"

Unfortunately, I couldn't argue. "No. I get it. I totally get what you're saying. I just wonder if there's a balance there. Maybe I could tell Cassie not to give up on you? Something to give her hope."

"No," he said, his voice resolute. "As long as she's not dating anyone, I don't want you to say anything, Dean."

I swallowed. "Well, this guy from work keeps asking her out."

Jack's face hardened. "Has she said yes?"

"No."

"Then we still have time."

I bit my tongue, wondering how much of it he was willing to gamble with when it came to Cassie.

Getting Lucky

"SO DID YOU ever ask out Miss I'm-So-Pretty-It-Hurts-To-Look-At-Me yet?" Melissa asked me at lunch, nodding her head in the direction of Serena, who was sitting with a group of her sorority sisters on the other side of the student union.

I ducked my head to hide my smile. "Not yet. Why? Jealous?"

Melissa scowled. "Why haven't you? Asked her out, I mean."

"I thought you didn't care?" I asked before taking a bite of pizza.

"I don't. I was just wondering." She poked at her salad. "I just like to keep Cassie in the loop. She asks about your love life and stuff."

This time I did smile. "Ah. Cool. I can tell Cassie myself, you know."

We continued eating, and the silence stretched out uncomfortably between us.

A few minutes later, Melissa grabbed her tray and stood up. "I have to go. But I was wondering if you'd like to come over later?"

Although I was half-tempted to toy with her and tell her I was busy, I knew I'd better say yes before she changed her mind.

"Sure," I said with a noncommittal shrug.

"Okay. Text you later." She walked away, and I watched her as she went.

LATER THAT NIGHT, I showed up at Melissa's apartment with a cherry Slurpee in hand, trying to be charming. Apparently she had the same idea, because the smell of brownies hit me in the face when she opened the front door. We both laughed.

She reached for the Slurpee and took a quick sip. "Thank you so much for this."

I bent down to give her a hug and her lips were suddenly on mine. Shaking off the surprise, I gripped her by the ass and lifted her, and she wrapped her legs around my waist.

We're kissing. Holy shit!

Melissa's mouth was hot and wet and sweet, and I couldn't get enough. For a second, I wondered if I should walk us over to the couch or to her bedroom, but had no idea what to do, so I stayed put. As I stood in her entryway, holding her tightly by the ass, my hard-on stealing all of the blood from the rest of my body, I lost myself in that kiss, and hoped she was doing the same.

The damn buzzer from the oven sounded, pulling her attention—and mouth—away from me. She smirked as I set her back on her feet.

"I just wanted to do that," she started to explain, and I hoped like hell she wouldn't take it back. But then she said, "It doesn't mean anything, though, so don't read into it."

I rolled my eyes. Being with this girl was like being in a car wreck. Whiplash was guaranteed.

I followed her into the kitchen and watched as she pulled the brownies from the oven and switched it off. When she'd set them aside to cool, I reached for her arm and pulled her body firmly against me.

"You don't have to overthink everything all the time," I said as I wrapped my arms around her. "I'm fine if you just want to kiss me. I don't expect anything from you."

Without giving her a chance to respond, I pressed my lips against hers, and she leaned into me, the curves of her body molding against mine. She let me continue to kiss her, but I didn't push us any further, happy with what she chose to give me. And when I left her house that night, she kissed me goodbye, not the other way around.

I convinced myself that this was progress.

AFTER MY LAST final, I sent Melissa a text telling her to have a good winter break. She asked if I was still at school, and when I said yes, she told me to wait.

She walked up to me and gave me a hug. "I just wanted to

say 'bye." She smiled up at me and I actually considered kissing her in public, but figured she'd flip.

"Have a good break," I said, hating that it would be over a month before I'd see her again.

"Do you have any plans?"

I nodded. "I'm going to go to Alabama with Jack to pack up his house."

"When?"

"After Christmas."

"Has she signed the damn papers yet?"

"No."

She curled her lip up in a snarl. "I hate that girl so much."

"Join the club."

"Okay. Well." She looked up at me with those big blue eyes and wrapped her arms around my neck. I pulled her close as she whispered. "I guess I'll see you later." Her lips met my cheek, and then she let go and disappeared into a group of passing students.

Christmas in Alabama

I TRIED TO give Melissa space. Or maybe I simply wanted to give her a chance to miss me, so I let her take the lead when it came to our communications over the break. To my surprise, she either texted or called me every couple of days. I took it as progress.

"Who are you talking to?" Jack asked, punching me in the arm as he passed me on the couch.

"Melissa," I told him with a smirk, then spoke into the phone. "Melis, hold on a sec."

I covered my cell phone with my hand and lowered it toward my thigh so she couldn't eavesdrop. "She wants to come with us." When he looked at me like I was speaking French, I added, "To Alabama."

"Why?" he asked, clearly confused.

"She said she's bored at home without Cassie. And she wants to help. Personally, I think she just misses me." I laughed as if I were joking, but the truth was I was hopeful.

He paused for only a second, and when the confusion left his face, he said, "She can come."

"Really?" I was surprised, prepared to argue on her behalf.

"Yeah, I don't care," he said offhandedly.

"He said you could come," I said excitedly into the phone.

Melissa let out a huff. "Of course he said I could come. Why wouldn't he?"

"Just shut up and get over here," I demanded.

"I kind of like it when you're bossy," she said, and I thought I could hear the smile in her voice. "I'll come over tomorrow night."

WHEN WE LANDED in Alabama, Jack's house seemed different somehow. Maybe it was the lack of things—Chrystle's crap—that no longer cluttered every surface.

"This place is really nice," Melissa said, and Jack agreed before bringing in an empty suitcase from the garage.

After packing up the few items that Jack planned to bring back to California with him, we all sat in the kitchen, drinking beer.

"Can we go out tonight? Please? Somewhere fun?" Melissa begged, putting on the pout that always drove me crazy.

Jack smirked at her suggestion before glancing at me for approval. When I nodded, he said, "Sure. But there are only two bars in this town, and I was at one of them the night that ruined my life. I haven't set foot in it since, and never want to again. Bad juju. So that only leaves the other one."

"Yes!" Melissa jumped up and ran up the stairs. "I get to shower first!"

Once she was out of earshot, Jack turned to me. "What's the latest with you two?"

"She likes to kiss me," I said, smiling like a lovesick idiot. "A lot."

He gave me a disgusted look. "Are you in junior high? What the fuck does that even mean?"

"It just means that anytime that girl will let me kiss her, I'm going to take it. I like her, all right. I just don't think she really likes me."

He punched me in the arm. "Kiss her better then, jackass."

"I kiss her just fine, fuck you very much."

"Obviously not," he teased. "You want me to talk to her for you?"

I bristled. "Definitely not. The last thing I want is for you to talk to her."

"Just tryin' to help, little brother."

He took another sip of his beer before pouring the rest of the bottle down the sink. The shower turned off, and I glanced up the stairs.

"Go up there, already. What you should have done was hopped in the shower with her," he suggested with a laugh.

"You're such a dick," I shot back as I ran upstairs.

"But I'm right," he shouted, and I flipped him off over my shoulder.

LATER THAT NIGHT, the three of us sat around a tall bar table, drinking and laughing. Melissa pounded her fist against the tabletop before shouting over the loud country music, "Jack, I forgot to tell you that I sent Cassie the jar of quarters the other day!"

His eyes glazed over, and he looked lost for a moment. "Why?"

"She asked for it. And she made me promise to wrap it in a thousand layers of bubble wrap so it wouldn't break."

He raised his eyebrows, and a cocky grin appeared. He looked happy until he focused over my shoulder and his smile abruptly fell. A muscle tensed in his jaw, and I turned to see what he was staring at.

It was Chrystle. *Oh shit.*

"Oh, look who it is, Vanessa. My husband. And if it isn't his delicious brother too. Vanessa, you remember Dean, don't you? From the wedding?" She looked toward her friend, who shifted uncomfortably but didn't respond. "Hi, Dean. How you doing, sweetie?"

I stared at Chrystle, wishing like hell she'd disappear into a puff of smoke, when I noticed Melissa's hands balled into fists.

"Jesus, Jack, I guess it's true what they say about beer goggles," Melissa sniped, giving Chrystle the once-over with pure disgust in her eyes.

Chrystle's jaw dropped slightly and her eyes widened as I fought back a laugh. "What did you say?"

"I said you're as ugly on the outside as you are on the inside," Melissa spat out, clearly not intimidated by anything or anyone.

"And just who the hell are you?" Chrystle pulled her shoulders back and tried to sound tough, but failed.

I noticed Vanessa fighting to hide a grin, and wondered what that was all about. Vanessa had been her maid of honor.

"None of your fucking business," Melissa shot back before taking a sip from her glass.

"But it is my business. See, you're sitting with my husband and my brother-in-law," Chrystle said as she ran her fingertips down my arm.

I tensed before swatting her hand away. Damn, I felt violated.

"Oh, great." Melissa rolled her eyes. "You touched her, Dean. She's probably pregnant now."

When Melissa's meaning sank in, Jack burst out into knee-slapping laughter and I joined in.

"Why don't you take your ugly skank ass away from our table so we can enjoy the rest of our night?" Melissa turned to look at my brother. "Seriously, Jack. How drunk were you to fuck that?"

I shook my head in amazement at Melissa's lady balls, knowing that she was trying to be extra vicious to give Chrystle a dose of her own medicine, and I loved every second. That bitch deserved nothing less.

Chrystle's face turned an unattractive shade of red and she scurried away from our table, almost tripping on an out-of-place chair. Vanessa shot us a look that almost looked embarrassed before she trailed behind her.

"Holy shit, Funsize. That was awesome." Jack reached out

to high-five Melissa from across the table.

"The easiest way to get under any girl's skin is to call her ugly," she said matter-of-factly. "Especially when she's not."

I nodded and smirked at her. "Good to know."

"Don't get any ideas, buster. You pull that shit with me and I'll never speak to you again," Melissa said with an extra dose of sass.

"Yes, ma'am," I said in my best Southern accent.

As the three of us walked toward the bar's exit a little later, Chrystle stepped in front of Jack and grabbed his arm.

He jerked his arm from her grasp as he said loudly, "Don't fucking touch me, you crazy bitch."

"I just want to talk to you, Jack." She batted her eyelashes and tilted her head in a fake attempt to appear sweet.

Jack glared at her. "How about we talk after you sign the papers?"

Her mouth pursed in frustration. "I'm not signing those. You can't prove anything, and you know it."

"Keep telling yourself that," he said.

Chrystle smirked and folded her arms over her chest. "You're lying."

"Just remember how many friends you have before I subpoena them all and make them testify against you. If you get them to lie on the stand, I'll make sure they go to jail."

She dropped her arms and her eyes grew huge. "You wouldn't dare!"

"The fuck I wouldn't." He leaned in close to her face, making sure she understood just how serious he was, and how willing to do whatever it took to get her to go away.

"It won't work anyway. I've covered all my bases, so to speak." She grinned wickedly, and I wondered what made someone turn so vicious.

"Just sign the fucking papers, Chrystle."

"No."

"Why the hell not?"

"Because I refuse to make it easy for you to get rid of me." She smirked again before looking at Melissa and me.

"Is this a fucking game to you?" Jack asked through clenched teeth, and I knew he was starting to lose it.

"I want to stay married, so I won't sign anything if I can avoid it."

I placed my hand on his shoulder to hold him back and remind him to keep his cool. "Avoid it?" I repeated to her. "You think you can avoid this?"

"Actually, yes, I do." Her voice was dripping with confidence, and I couldn't wait to see this bitch fall.

Jack threw his hands up in the air. "You're just a bad person."

"So are you!" she fired back.

"No. I'm an asshole. There's a difference."

Melissa stepped forward, her hands fisted, and I grabbed her shoulders to hold her back. My feisty little pixie looked ready to get herself into trouble, and the last thing I needed was to have to bail her out of jail tonight. She tried to wriggle away, but I tightened my grip.

"I'll do whatever I have to do to be rid of you," Jack said in a low, menacing voice in Chrystle's face. "You hear me? Whatever I have to do."

"Are you threatening me?" she asked, her voice deliberately raised to draw more attention to the scene she was creating.

"If I were threatening you, you'd know it. Sign the damn papers."

Jack turned away and punched the door open as I followed behind, dragging Melissa out by her arms.

Once in the car and on the road, we all seemed to finally exhale. I rolled down my window partway and allowed the air to blow over me, needing a little cooling off.

"I can't believe we saw her tonight," Melissa said from the backseat. "She's wretched, Jack. In every way."

"She's worse than I remember," I said, nodding.

Jack glanced at us. "Do you guys get it now, why I can't go see Cassie until she's gone? I have to be rid of that woman completely before I knock on Cassie's door."

Being here now, seeing and hearing Chrystle the way we just had, it did make more sense to me. Jack wasn't avoiding Cassie for no reason; he honestly believed he was protecting her. And after what happened tonight, I didn't blame him one bit.

We walked into the nearly empty house and I reached for Melissa's hand. "You okay? I thought you were going to kill Chrystle back there."

"I wanted to. Once she started saying that shit to Jack, it's good you held me back," she snapped, her sass coming back in full force with the memory of earlier, and Jack and I both laughed.

"Honestly, I think I would have paid good money to see you hit her," Jack said with a smile.

Melissa jerked her thumb toward the door. "We could always go back."

I grabbed her and lifted her off the ground. "We're not going anywhere, you feisty little thing."

She tilted her head back to kiss me and without thinking, I kissed her back, no thought of where we were, or that Jack was standing right there.

"Jesus, it's about time," he blurted, and the moment stopped. Melissa abruptly pulled out of my arms.

"Shut up, Jack," she said before heading upstairs.

"Thanks a lot," I said, socking him in the arm.

"I didn't know she'd stop!" He threw his hands up in surrender. "Sorry."

I groaned in frustration before trudging upstairs to my own bed.

Alone.

THE NEXT MORNING, we all woke up to the sound of the doorbell ringing incessantly. I heard Jack head downstairs to answer it, so I rolled back over and buried my head in my pillow until he started yelling. At that I jumped out of bed and ran downstairs, convinced that Chrystle was here trying to pull something.

I reached him just as he closed the door, holding some paperwork in his hand. At the sight of it, I was actually happy for a moment, thinking that Chrystle had signed the annulment.

He glanced up at me after scanning the papers, completely annoyed, by the looks of it. "We've been served."

"We've been *what*?"

"Chrystle filed a restraining order against all three of us, saying we threatened her life and she feared for her safety."

Dumbfounded, I stared at him as the words sank in. "All *three* of us?" I asked, emphasizing the number.

"Yeah. Melissa too."

"Better not tell her that, or she might give Chrystle something to fear."

"Tell me what?" Melissa appeared at the top of the stairs wearing next to nothing.

"Nothing, Funsize. Go back to bed," Jack told her, and I smacked his arm, enjoying the view.

"You're not the boss of me, Jack. But I'm not ready to get up yet, so see ya later," she said before trudging back to her room.

Chrystle's allegations were so ridiculous that Jack and I couldn't even bother to be concerned about them. Besides, we knew we'd be gone in a day, and Chrystle would never see us again anyway.

Every time I thought I couldn't dislike this chick more, she gave me another reason.

You're Taking Too Long

WE GOT BACK to California with a couple of weeks still left in our winter break. Melissa left for home again instead of staying alone in her apartment. She'd told me on more than one occasion that she actually liked her parents, and she enjoyed spending time with them. That was something I'd never be able to relate to.

When we first got back, I figured it would only be a matter of time before Chrystle would sign the papers for Jack and he could get the show on the road, but the days turned into weeks, and there was still no word.

Melissa had called him one night, apparently fresh off a phone call with Cassie, screaming and yelling at him. I couldn't hear what she said, but I could hear her shouting over the phone from where I sat on the other side of the room.

Jack tried to calm her down, but she wasn't having any of it. When he hung up, he looked at me, shaking his head.

"What the hell was that?" I asked.

"She's pissed. Oh Lord, is she ever pissed at me."

"I gathered that much. Why?"

He sat down next to me and slumped back into the couch

cushions. "She said that I need to tell Cassie what's going on. She said that for all she knows, Chrystle won't ever sign the papers, and I'm making Cassie suffer for it." He cringed when he said the last part.

"Why don't you just tell Cassie you're on your way? You're working on getting to her, to just hang tight or something. Anything is better than the nothing she's had. It's been months, Jack," I reminded him, as if he needed the reminder.

"I can't do that, little brother. I can't tell her that when I have no idea how long this is going to take. Then what? She's just supposed to be in limbo, waiting for me while I sit here and do exactly what I'm trying to do right now? I feel so powerless, and it frustrates the hell out of me and pisses me off. I don't want Cassie to feel like that, and if I go to her right now, that's all she'll end up feeling. And it will be my fault."

I didn't know what else to say. Jack was stubborn. His mind was made up, and there was no changing it. Lord knew I'd been down that path before.

"What else did Melissa say?"

"That I had until I left for spring training to talk to Cassie, or she was going to tell her everything."

"She's brutal," I said.

"Then she told me all about this guy who keeps asking Cassie out. And she said that she was going to encourage her to go out with him and forget all about me," he said, his tone bitter and pained.

"Do you really think she'd do that?"

I wasn't entirely sure that Melissa had it in her to do something like that, knowing everything that she knew. But then again, when it came down to it, her loyalty lay with Cassie the same way that mine lay with Jack.

Jack gave me a grim look. "Yeah. I do."

THE SEMESTER STARTED, and I was slammed already with classes that were more challenging and required more of my time. Because of the heavy class load, my hours at Marc and Ryan's agency had dwindled.

"I have to report for spring training in a week," Jack said as he poked his head into my bedroom.

I frowned at him. "I know that."

"So let's go get dinner. Just me and you." He smiled, and I couldn't get dressed fast enough.

We drove to our favorite restaurant where we used to eat all the time as kids with Gran and Gramps. It was basically a diner that hadn't been updated for as long as I could remember. The red vinyl booths were still red, and still torn in small sections that pinched your skin if you sat down wrong.

I think Gran brought us because of the menu diversity—the four of us could be craving something different for dinner and we could get it here. There was no arguing when we came to the diner.

Jack and I placed our orders, and when I asked for a double serving of their famous mashed potatoes, he started laughing.

"Remember that month when you refused to eat anything except these mashed potatoes? And Gran would get them for you and you'd eat them until you got sick?"

I nodded. "Of course I remember." They were my favorite, and I would gorge myself on them and then have a stomachache later that night every single time. "And you begged for a chocolate shake with extra whipped cream every time we came here. Gran always gave in."

He grinned. "I knew she would. That's why I begged."

When the waitress placed a chocolate shake in front of him, Jack dipped his straw into the whipped cream and balanced a giant dollop on it before shoving it in his mouth. I always wondered how he managed to do that without dropping it, but he never did.

He took another jab at the white stuff with his straw before putting it in his mouth again. "Seriously. Best whipped cream ever. Nothing ever tastes like this."

The waitress came back with my mashed potatoes, and my mouth watered as I inhaled the steam rising from them, buttery-smelling and delicious.

"The rest of your food will be up shortly," she said with a curt nod.

Jack watched her walk away. "She hates us."

"Probably just you," I said with a grin before sticking my fork into the potato mountain. Blowing on the forkful for a few seconds, I moved it to my mouth and moaned. "So good."

Once I'd worked the mountain down by half, I asked, "Are you excited for baseball to start?"

"Definitely. I need to get my mind in order. All this time off is too much time to think. I like being busy."

"What are you going to do about Cassie?" I asked, not wanting to ignore the elephant in the room any longer. "And you know, what Melissa said?"

"Chrystle still hasn't signed the papers. Marc mentioned the other day that we should think about withdrawing the annulment papers and filing for divorce instead."

"So will you tell Cassie that?"

He shook his head as he sipped on his straw. "No. Chrystle could still avoid signing those too."

"Melissa's going to tell her." I eyed him over the table, knowing that Melissa wasn't kidding about her drop-dead date for him. When she made a promise, she stuck to it, and this one was no different.

"I know."

"Maybe that will end up working in your favor," I said, and he shot me a glare. "I'm just saying. It might not be the worst thing in the world if Cassie knows what the hell's been going on for the last four months."

Jack looked away and shrugged. "I guess we'll see."

"SHE SIGNED THEM! Holy shit, brother, she signed the papers!"

I held the phone away from my ear as Jack shouted his news. His voice was excited, making me realize just how long it had been since I'd heard him sound genuinely happy.

"That's awesome! Why? Why now?" Wondering what could have changed to make that chick finally give in, I asked with a shudder, "Did you have to give her all your money?"

He laughed. "No. Her best friends called me. Said they had some serious dirt on her, and that they'd testify against her if necessary. She caught wind of that and signed, hoping to save face."

I was stunned. "Well, who cares how it happened, I'm just so glad it finally did!" I jumped up, dancing around in my room in celebration. After all, nobody could see me. "So you're calling Cassie as soon as we hang up?"

He groaned. "Not quite yet. I need a little more time."

My dance moves halted. "What the hell for now? Jack—why?"

"You don't know everything, little brother. I just need a little more time."

"I don't understand you at all. Do you even want to be with her anymore?" I pushed the one button that I hoped would get a reaction out of him.

"Shut up, Dean. You know my whole world is about that girl. Don't ever question how I feel about her."

I glanced at his schedule, noting that he had a game in New York coming up. Maybe he was planning on waiting until he could see her in person.

"You'll be in New York soon, you know."

"Trust me. I'm aware. It's not like she'll be at my game."

"Well, she would be if you told her to come see you."

"I gotta go. I just wanted you to know she signed the papers."

THE NEXT TIME I had lunch with Melissa, she looked agitated, like she was holding something back from me. We hadn't been seeing each other as much as usual lately. She'd had to switch a class around, which meant our schedules didn't sync up during lunch every day like they used to.

"What is it?" I asked, watching her fidget across the table.

"You know I gave your stupid brother the deadline, right? I'm sure he told you." She eyed me, stabbing her fruit with her fork.

"Yeah, I knew about it."

"Well, you also know that he still hasn't talked to her. And so I was going to tell her, you know?" She glared at me as I swallowed a bite of my sandwich. "I wanted to tell her what was going on so that she'd stop being so sad all the time. But when I talked to her—"

She paused, waiting for me to look up at her. "She sounded . . . happy. She sounded really happy, Dean. Like she was finally settling in there and moving on with her life without your brother. And I couldn't do it. I couldn't tell her because I knew it would devastate her."

I froze with my sandwich midway between my tray and my mouth, processing the conflicting emotions her news stirred up. Half of me was thrilled for Cassie, happy that she wasn't miserable anymore. But the other half was devastated, knowing what this could mean for Jack.

"So you didn't tell her anything at all?"

"I couldn't. And the worst part was—" She took a bite of her own sandwich, chewing and swallowing quickly before she said, "I sort of understood what Jack has been saying this whole time. How he was waiting to get it all in order before he went to her. It finally made sense to me."

"Chrystle signed the papers," I said quickly, holding my breath as I waited for Melissa's reaction.

She slammed her fist on top of the table. "She *what*? When? How long ago?"

"It just happened." I shushed her, trying to calm her down when I noticed the number of people staring in our direction.

Her breathing quickened as her fury mounted. Before I knew it, her eyes were shooting daggers at me.

"And he didn't call her the second it happened? The second he knew he was free? Okay, I take back everything nice I just said about your stupid brother. I don't understand him at all, and I hate him again," she practically growled.

Melissa shot to her feet and snatched up her tray. "I'm calling him later, I hope you know, and giving him a piece of my mind!"

I SENT JACK a text to warn him that Melissa was going to call him, and she wasn't happy. I also demanded he call me right after and tell me everything. He did.

"That was fun," he said instead of hello, and I laughed nervously.

"I bet. She was a real peach today after I told her that Chrystle had signed the papers."

"Yeah, she asked me what I was waiting for, and I tried to tell her that I needed to see if a few things would fall into place first. But she wouldn't listen and flipped out." He sucked in a deep breath. "She ended the call by telling me to leave Cassie the hell alone and to stay out of her life forever."

I chuckled. "For such a little thing, she sure is vicious."

"Good thing I'm not afraid of her," he said with a laugh.

"So you aren't going to *leave her alone and stay away from her forever*?" I asked, mimicking Melissa's voice.

He laughed loudly. "I could never do that. Ever. I need her too bad. You know it. I know it. Hell, the whole world knows it."

Annoyed, I said, "You sure as shit have a funny way of showing it."

"Patience, little brother. And faith. Can you have both of those in me right now, please?"

Honestly, I wasn't sure I had it in me. I wanted to believe Jack, but his track record in the last year had sucked.

Happily Ever After

I UNDERSTOOD MELISSA'S frustration and anger; I'd felt it as well. But when I woke up this morning to my phone pinging with a jillion text notifications, I finally understood everything.

Jack had been traded to the New York Mets.

My brother had switched teams in order to be closer to Cassie, and I'd had no idea. He'd kept it from me, kept it from everyone. *That* must have been what he was waiting on finding out about all those weeks ago.

My phone pinged again.

MELISSA: *Did you know? Did you know he was getting traded?*

DEAN: *I had no idea. He didn't tell me a thing.*

MELISSA: *Sneaky little shit.*

I laughed before typing out my own text to my brother.

DEAN: *Dude, you got traded to the Mets and didn't tell me? How the hell did you get them to let you do it? Good luck with your girl. Call me after you see her. And you'd better get her back.*

After what felt like an agonizing amount of time, he finally responded.

> *J*ACK*: She's in my arms right now, little brother. All is right in the world. Sorry I didn't tell you about the trade, but I had no idea if it would go through or not. Have to go finish making up for lost time.*

And he did. After having a bunch of sentimental gifts delivered to Cassie's apartment, he showed up in a Mets jersey with a dozen red roses at her front door. I had to give it to him; Jack was the best when it came to grand gestures.

And just so we're clear, I'm determined to get my girl as well; it just might take me a little longer. It's a good thing I'm patient and think she's worth the wait . . . and all the trouble.

Epilogue

Sami

SO APPARENTLY THAT'S how my parents met, but it took them *forever* to finally get together. At least that's what Uncle Jack always says before Aunt Cassie smacks him in the arm. He says my mom ran more hot and cold than a faucet, and it took my dad losing his temper at an airport in New York one night for her to finally realize what she had to lose.

Aunt Cassie always chimes in at this point in the story to remind him that Gran played a big part in their getting together too. I guess Gran was the one who got my mom to admit to being scared—terrified, actually. Mom was afraid that if things didn't work out between her and Dad, she would lose her best friend because of it.

Anytime someone tells this story, I'm the only one who nods along, completely understanding what they're saying. My twin sister, Sadie, and my cousin Jacey always look around like it's the craziest idea ever.

But I get it. I understand.

Friends come first. *Sisters before misters.*

You see, Mom and Aunt Cassie have been best friends since they were in high school. And once Aunt Cassie and Uncle Jack got together, it made my mom pull away from my dad, even though she liked him. She was terrified that if things went sour between her and my dad, that it would make everything awkward, and Aunt Cassie would feel like she had to choose a side.

Mom assumed she'd lose. And she didn't want to risk it, so she tried to stay away from my dad, but apparently that didn't work. Because he's adorable and totally in love with her, and they're almost as nauseating as Uncle Jack and Aunt Cassie.

It's cute, though, in a creepy, old-person kind of way. And I'll be the first to admit that I hope to fall in love like that someday.

Sadie and Jacey always tease me for being a hopeless romantic. But honestly, with parents like mine, how can I not be?

Thank you for purchasing this book.

If you enjoyed it, please consider writing a spoiler-free review on the site from which you purchased it. Reviews help self-published authors like me spread the word about their work, as well as help potential readers make a decision as to whether they'd like to purchase this story.

Thank you.

Please join my mailing list to get updates on new and upcoming releases, deals, bonus content, personal appearances, and other fun news!

http://tinyurl.com/pf6al6u

Acknowledgments

Thank you to my team—Pam Berehulke, the best editor in the free world, and Michelle Warren, the best cover designer in all the land! The two of you always help me complete my vision, whether it's with words or with designs. It's an honor to work with you both. Never leave me. <3

To my girls Jillian Dodd and Tara Sivec, who always have to read the roughest of rough drafts and never fail to give me honest feedback. I value you both as artists and as friends. Thank you for always having my back.

Krista Arnold, who listened and then encouraged me when this little idea bloomed into a full-fledged book. You probably have her to blame for this story even existing, so direct any and all complaints her way. LOL

My girls in The Perfect Game Changer group and my All Stars always make even the darkest days brighter. I don't know what I did to deserve readers like you, but I am forever grateful. Thank you for all your love and support, and for being so good to each other.

Yo, AMP Energy Drinks. This one's for you! Because, really? A care package filled with Sugar-Free Blueberry and White Grape drinks for my #WritersFuel?! Hell, yes! You're awesome. Thanks for the support and the delicious beverages.

And to my son, Blake, who is the light of my life. You make me laugh harder than anyone else. You always get super excited for whatever I'm working on, wanting to hear all about it, and always—I mean *always*—offer your opinion. I love you the most.

About the Author

Jenn Sterling is a Southern California native who loves writing stories from the heart. Every story she tells has pieces of her truth in it, as well as her life experience. She has a bachelor's degree in Radio/TV/Film and worked in the entertainment industry the majority of her life until she became a writer—which she claims is the best thing that's ever happened to her.

Jenn loves hearing from her readers and can be found online at:

Blog & Website:

www.j-sterling.com

Twitter:

www.twitter.com/RealJSterling

Facebook:

www.facebook.com/TheRealJSterling

Instagram:

@ RealJSterling

Also by J. Sterling

In Dreams

Chance Encounters

10 Years Later – A Second Chance Romance

THE GAME SERIES

The Perfect Game – Book One

The Game Changer – Book Two

The Sweetest Game – Book Three

THE CELEBRITY SERIES

Seeing Stars – Madison & Walker

Breaking Stars – Paige & Tatum

Losing Stars – Quinn & Ryson (Coming Soon)

HEARTLESS, A SERIAL

Episode 1

Episode 2

Episode 3

HEARTLESS, THE BOX SET

Episodes 1–3

Printed in the USA
CPSIA information can be obtained
at www.ICGtesting.com
LVHW092320110124
768819LV00008B/245